the house on the dunes

the house on the dunes

NANCY SWEETLAND

Divine
Garden
Press

Published by Divine Garden Press
P.O. Box 371
Soperton, GA 30457
www.divinegardenpress.com

ISBN-13: 978-0692250341
ISBN-10: 0692250344
Library of Congress Control Number: 2014944934

Cover & Interior Design by Divine Literary Services
www.divinelit.com
Cover Photograph: ©Soupstock

To my mother, Helen Mortensen, who allowed me to know only part of her story. I wished for more.

1

OLIVIA, 1984

"*E*meralds? My mother owned emeralds?" Olivia Hobart, dressed in her best suit for the reading of her mother's will, leaned forward in Tyson's law office, her mouth agape.

Her husband, Bert, blurted, "And a house on Lake Michigan? Well, wasn't she the surprising old lady!"

Olivia frowned. "Please, Bert."

Fidgeting between them, her plump bottom overflowing the seat of a straight-backed chair, Pamela, 27 but with the mind of a 5-year-old, swung sneakered feet and pulled at her blond ponytails. "Emeralds good, Mama?" she asked.

Olivia patted Pamela's knee and turned to the lawyer. "Mr. Tyson, is this some kind of joke?"

Albert Tyson smiled and shook his head. "No, no joke. I wasn't aware your mother owned a house other than the one on the farm, either, or emeralds. But I didn't draw up this will. The senior partner who died before I came into the firm drew it more than thirty years ago."

"Thirty years!" Bert stood up. "How could she have something for that long and her family not know? Is the will still legal?"

"Oh, yes," Tyson said. "It's been reviewed regularly. I didn't read the legal description of the farm to you, but it's all correct, as well as the information about the house on Lake Michigan. Unfortunately there is no information on the emeralds, and I have no idea where they are. Perhaps you'll find them at the house. But there's a final note referring to the Lake Michigan property." He adjusted his glasses and read, "My story is there for Olivia to find."

"Huh." Bert hitched up his pants and looked at his wife. "It's only forty miles from here. We've got some time before we fly back to Portland, Livvy. Let's go take a look at this mystery house your sweet, old mother kept hidden for thirty years." He snorted. "I'll bet it's a dump."

A half-hour later, they traveled toward Lake Michigan on a road soft in spots with early May mudholes. Bert carefully steered his latest Buick around them. "Wouldn't you know I just had this buggy washed," he complained.

Olivia felt his sideways look, but lost in thought, didn't comment. *Missing emeralds? A house on the dunes? How could my mother have kept such an important part of her life completely hidden? She was a simple Wisconsin farm wife, wasn't she?*

"Might as well talk to myself," he mumbled.

Pamela bounced on the rear seat. "Too bad to get dirty, Daddy," she said.

"Well, at least *some*body cares how we look."

Olivia pointed to six-foot stone pillars flanking a gravel entrance. "There, Bert. Slow down."

They followed a winding lane between neatly trimmed trees and skidded to a stop when Bert stomped on the brake pedal in surprise, killing the engine.

Olivia just stared at a house high on the bluff overlooking the water.

It certainly wasn't a dump.

The two-story, sparkling white Dutch Colonial dominated the landscape. Deep green shutters flanked crisscrossed windows. A screen porch facing the water appeared to run the full length of both floors. A well-kept garage with what looked like an apartment above it stood back toward the wooded area surrounding the clearing.

"It looks lived in," Olivia said, frowning.

"Yeah." Pamela craned her neck out her lowered window. "Somebody here?"

"This place is worth a small fortune," Bert said. "If this is yours, Livvy, we're in clover!"

Olivia raised her eyebrows. "We?"

"Well . . ." Bert let the word drop.

They got out. Olivia shivered from the raw breeze off the water.

The side door of the house opened with a well-oiled swish, and a tall, thin, slightly stooped man who looked nearly 80-years-old moved slowly into the sun. His pale eyes narrowed as he scrutinized Bert, Pamela, and finally Olivia. He leaned on a gnarled walking stick, stepped with care off the cement step, and peered into her face, nodding. "You're Cathy's girl, then."

Cathy? As far as Olivia knew, her mother had been called Catherine all her life. "You mean Catherine Sommers?"

He nodded, his Adam's apple bobbing up at the same rate his chin came down. "Figgered you'd be comin,' now she's gone on."

"Wait a minute. Who are you?" Bert moved in on them. "How did you know Catherine Sommers was dead?"

The old man stepped back a pace and frowned at Bert. "My God, man, didn't your ma ever tell you not to break in on a conversation?" he asked, then turned back to Olivia. "I was talkin' to Cathy's girl here. What's the name again?"

"Olivia," she said.

He nodded again. "Right. Course. Should'a remembered, but you were such a little bit of a thing, few times I saw you." He looked back at Bert. "She could'na been more than 2-years-old, then they stopped bringin' her. Well. This your own?" He peered at Pamela.

"Yes. My daughter, Pamela," Olivia said, putting an arm around Pam, whose face was expressionless.

The man studied her for a moment then asked Bert, "Yours, too?"

Bert sucked in his breath and said, "Of course."

Olivia asked, "What's your name, please? Do you live here?"

The old man chuckled. "You don't remember old Tim. Timothy Ryan. Course you wouldn't."

"How about explaining yourself?" Bert said. "This is the right place, then?"

"Oh, you got the right place by sure." Tim Ryan chuckled, turned slowly, and beckoned them to follow him inside.

2

CATHERINE, 1917

*L*ow whispers wafted into 11-year-old Catherine Sommer's half-sleep. She sat up to concentrate on the voices outside her bedroom door.

"How's Catherine taking it?"

"Shhh, not so loud. You mean, will she be able to help Seth and Irene, being the only one left?"

"Oh, she will. Catherine always does the right thing, you know." There was a pause. "She's not like Aurelia was."

Catherine flopped back and pulled her covers up around her ears. *I'm not like Aurelia was, for sure.* Aurelia, the darling dark, curly-haired favorite who always got away with everything by somehow placing the blame on Catherine. Aurelia, who died this morning at age 12, leaving Catherine to try to fill Aurelia's special, first-born place in the hearts of their aging parents.

Catherine knew she ought to be sorry Aurelia was dead.

Of course, she was sorry, but somehow tears for Aurelia wouldn't come; the tears that flowed were for Catherine herself.

There were times through the years when Catherine's tears, flowing in the privacy of her bedroom, actually were for Aurelia, or rather, were because Aurelia was dead, particularly when Catherine's parents insisted she stay at home instead of going away to college.

"But I want to teach," Catherine said, pleading for understanding. At 18, she was tall and slender. Her sandy-blond hair, now darkened to the rich color of ripening corn silk and braided in a dignified coronet, emphasized her wide forehead, slightly arched brows, and deep blue eyes.

"Fine. So teach when we're gone," Seth Rothe said, patting her slim shoulder. "It's good you should keep busy. But you can learn right here at normal school." He smiled. "You can even come home for lunch."

So Catherine, who always did everything right, attended normal school (abnormally, she thought) and even came home for lunch. She made no friends to speak of and existed in her cocooned world with Seth and Irene Rothe.

Though she was certified to teach, her days after normal school were threaded with old-maidish needlework and afternoon teas with her mother's friends, who expressed vocally how Irene was so lucky to have a daughter who hadn't "run off" like some of theirs had.

Catherine poured tea, listened, and sewed until she was 30-years-old, stockpiled linens and embroidered underthings in a cedar chest handmade by her father. But she secretly rejoiced when Irene, well into middle age when Aurelia and Catherine were born, died peacefully at 75, and Seth, who found no reason to live now Irene had gone ahead, joined her less than a month later.

Dozens of hothouse flowers surrounded the mahogany casket. Seth's favorite hymns, "Rock of Ages" and "Holy, Holy, Holy," floated serenely through the carnation-scented air.

Dad's funeral is wonderful, even better than Mother's. Catherine knelt at the open casket, but she wasn't praying. Her thoughts were of handsome Joel O'Brien. Though she had known him for only a few weeks, he had claimed her heart.

Joel, with his quizzical smile and his I'll-take-you-away-from-all-this and show-you-the-world promises.

"Really! Look at her!" Emma Stock whispered to another of Irene Roth's friends just within Catherine's hearing. "You would almost swear Catherine is smiling! Would you believe it? And after all Seth and Irene did for her."

In less than two weeks, the Milwaukee house was sold, and Catherine eloped with Joel, who really had meant it when he said he would take her away. He also took away her money from the sale of the house even though he assured her he didn't need it. Being a brush salesman was so lucrative.

"Well, all right, I'll put it in trust for you then, Catherine," Joel said, running his fingers through his thick, wavy brown hair as if he didn't really want anything to do with money. "Here. Keep this much for yourself." He handed her fifty dollars.

"I won't need it, Joel," Catherine said, smiling. "You'll take care of me."

One summer night four months later, lying naked in a rented room in Kansas, Catherine ran one warm, moonlit finger down the soft curly hair on Joel's chest. "It's happened, Joel. I'm so happy! But I didn't want to tell you until I was sure."

"Sure of what?" He sat up. "What's happened?"

"We're going to have a baby, Joel! Isn't it grand?"

"Grand!" Joel yelped, threw back the sheet, and leaped out of bed. Standing in the moonlight, stripped of his salesman's self-assurance, he croaked, "Grand?"

"Aren't you glad?" Catherine asked, hugging her bare knees. "Weren't you hoping, too? Oh, Joel! It's going to be so wonderful!"

The next morning when she awoke, Joel was gone.

Catherine tried to forgive him, telling herself he was just too young, too free, to take responsibility for a family. She was sure he would come back, repentant, loving, and willing to begin again. So she stayed on in the lonely rented room amidst the clucking of landlady Heycraft's inquisitive friends, took in sewing and altering, and waited for her baby.

Joel didn't come back.

Months later, through an exhausted haze, Catherine stared up at a kindly, white-haired doctor.

"I couldn't do anything for them," he said in a tired, choked voice. "They were just too small, too early."

Catherine only nodded, damp strands from her loosed coronet straggling across the pillow.

"I'm so sorry," he said, touching her limp hand. "I'll send the undertaker. I'm sorry. Sorry."

She closed her eyes against the sorrow in his.

Three days later, Catherine stood in a small, flat cemetery. The raw, harsh Kansas wind whipped her long grey skirt as she watched shovelfuls of dirt splatter on one pine box too small to hold two lives.

"You shouldn't be out here," Mrs. Heycraft said. "Come." She put a gentle hand on Catherine's arm. "It's too soon."

"No," Catherine said. "It's too late."

The next day she burned the poems she had written for Joel, gave away the tiny, hand-sewn garments, and took the train back to Wisconsin.

SEPTEMBER, 1937

Catherine looked up from the paper she was correcting, a frown creasing her wide forehead. "Amery," she said quietly, so as not to disturb the other students in the one-room school at Middle Creek.

The too-slight, white-haired boy in the front row jumped. "Teacher?" His voice quivered.

If only he weren't so timid. "Come here, Amery."

He stared wide-eyed at her.

"It's all right, Amery, really. Come here, please."

A snicker from the back of the room turned Amery's pale head. He hesitated.

"Be quiet, Dale," Catherine said to the big-bodied 16-year-old who grinned and ostensibly buried his face in his book where Catherine suspected he had hidden something of more interest than geography, possibly one of his detailed drawings of what he thought was female anatomy. She sighed, trying not to show her repulsion of Dale's dirty person and his equally dirty mind. He should have been out of grammar school years ago, but in this farming community children often only came to learn when they weren't needed for field or livestock work.

Amery sidled next to her desk and clung to the edge of it with a small, trembling hand.

"Don't be afraid." In the three weeks school had been in session, she had assessed most of the children's abilities and many of their personalities, but Amery Houle was a puzzle. She was certain he was highly intelligent, and though small for a second-grader, seemed physically sound. Yet something wasn't right.

She held his reading paper. "Amery, I know you know these answers. I know you can write well, too, but this paper is not well done. Yesterday's was the same. What is the trouble?"

His gaze dropped to the floor; his small shoulders slumped.

"Can you tell me?"

His knuckles whitened on the edge of her desk.

"Amery. Your reports from last year are excellent. You didn't have any trouble then."

He shook his head, eyes downcast.

"Look at me, Amery." Catherine took his small chin in her hand to study his pinched face and caught her breath as his pale eyes squinted. "Why, you can't see very well, can you?"

His small lips clamped together. Tears welled up and he ducked his head. "No, teacher," he said so softly she hardly heard him.

"Well." She took a deep breath. "It's nothing to be ashamed of, Amery. At least, we know the problem with your schoolwork."

His whole small body tensed and tears spilled out. "Don't tell my mother! I'll do better, honest. I'll stay after. Please, Miss Rothe."

"Not tell your mother? Why, Amery, why not?"

"Just don't tell her. Please." He sniffed.

"But I must." Catherine covered his small hand with her own. "I know she'd want to help. Perhaps glasses will make all the difference."

Another snicker from the back of the room. "Crybaby Amery," Dale scoffed, just loudly enough to be heard.

"That's quite enough, Dale," Catherine snapped. "Busy yourself with your work. Amery, I'm going to give you a note for your parents. I want to talk with them about your eyes."

"No! My mother's sick. Real sick. You can't talk to her." His expression pleaded.

Catherine paused. "Oh. I see."

Amery kept his gaze on the floor. "But maybe you could talk to my father. Maybe he'd come."

"Of course he will. Sit down, then. It's almost time to go home. I'll write the note right now."

The next morning, an answer from Oliver Houle stated in clear, small script that he would come as soon as he could after school let out for the day.

Catherine studied his handwriting as she waited in the quiet schoolroom amid the mixed smells of sawdust floor cleaner and the crisp aster-and-goldenrod September air wafting in through the open windows. She tried to imagine Amery's father, pictured him an older man, perhaps even as old as Levi Sommers, who was kind enough to come whenever the play yard needed mowing. She also pictured Oliver Houle as heavy-set and overalled, with dirty fingernails. In her short experience at Middle Creek, it seemed most of the fathers fell into such a category. She could only hope Amery's problem was correctable, and his father would be receptive to getting help.

She finished the next day's plan and was wet-wiping the long blackboard behind her desk when a clear voice startled her.

"Excuse me."

Catherine whirled, her eyes wide, her heart pounding. The damp rag landed with a moist plop beside carefully polished riding boots.

"Oh, I am sorry," he said. "I thought you'd heard me come in." He picked up the cloth and finished wiping the last section of blackboard himself.

Flushing, Catherine accepted the rag. "You startled me, is all. I don't usually fly off like that."

He brushed back his pale hair, so like Amery's, with the palm of his hand and smiled. "I'm sure you don't."

Oliver Houle was tall, slender, and only a few years older than Catherine herself. His fingernails, she noticed, were scrupulously clean. He wore immaculate riding britches and coat, not farmer's work clothes. Realizing her appraisal was quite forward, Catherine blushed and dropped her gaze to the pile of papers on her desk. "I'm so pleased to meet you, Mr. Houle. Please sit down. About

Amery . . .”

She felt him study her for a moment. “Of course,” he said. “About Amery.”

The next morning, a small voice broke into her thoughts as she readied the day’s lessons. “Teacher?”

She looked up. “Yes, Amery?”

Amery stood quietly beside her desk for a moment and then thrust out a fist-squashed handful of yellow and gold chrysanthemums.

Catherine took them and loosened the tough, browning stems. “Why, Amery! How nice! And what pretty colors! I must thank your mother.”

Amery shook his tow-white head. “No. My father.” He looked down at his scuffed shoes. “He said you’d like them.”

Catherine’s felt her mouth turn up at the corners. Oliver Houle had sent them? “Oh, I do, Amery,” she said. “Tell him I like them very much.”

Later in the afternoon, Catherine looked up from her paper-strewn desk to see Levi Sommers hesitating in the schoolroom door, his worn straw hat in one hand. Behind him the flaring colors of early October merged in the hazy air.

“Mr. Sommers! It’s so nice to see you again.” Catherine smiled, rose, and held out her hand. Something solid about Levi Sommers made Catherine feel safe. Perhaps his sturdiness brought her father to mind. "Do come in and talk for a minute."

Levi crossed the planked floor, walking lightly in spite of heavy work shoes. His bibbed overalls were worn, but clean. His work shirt, open at the throat, was rolled to his elbows. "Just for a little if you aren't caught up," he said. "I want to mow the play yard this afternoon, if you'd like."

"Oh, wonderful. The grass is almost up to little Billy Redmond's knees." Catherine pushed aside a pile of papers and smiled as she leaned her chin on her hands. "Please, sit down."

Levi lowered himself next to her desk on the straight-backed chair which mischievous children had learned was definitely not a place of honor. He ran his fingers through thick salt-and-pepper hair.

"I sat in front of you at services yesterday," Catherine said. "Your deep voice adds so much to the beautiful hymns."

She watched his grey eyes light with pleasure. He smiled, his teeth white in his weather-burnt face. "I do love to sing," he said. "Hymns, especially. They're so . . . permanent, I guess. We sing the same ones today we did when I was a boy." He leaned back, observing the papers decorating the walls. "You've made this schoolroom nice, Miss Rothe. Homey."

"Thank you. The children like having their papers and artwork hung up. Besides," she smiled, "it hides the cracks in the walls."

Levi nodded, smiling, too. "Old building. I went to school here myself, way back. I believe the walls were cracked even then." He shifted his weight and leaned forward.

"Miss Rothe—"

She held up a hand. "Oh, please, it's Catherine. We are going to be friends, aren't we?"

He hesitated. "Catherine, then." He turned his hat in his hands, then blurted, "Would you come to the church social Saturday night?"

"Why, I was planning to."

"With me, I mean." His eyes held hers as she felt surprise color her face. She hadn't thought of Levi Sommers as a man, more like a friend of the school district, so to speak. Someone she could call on if she needed anything. She knew he had never married. Amy Walker, landlady at the farm where Catherine roomed, said he'd never been interested in the women around Middle Creek.

"With–with you?" she repeated, feeling her face blush. *How embarrassing to sound so flustered.* "I mean—"

He broke in, smiling. "Oh, I know I'm older and all. Probably you're surprised I would ask." He lifted his chin. "And so will be all the ladies of the church, I'll grant. But I'd be privileged," he faltered and then added, his face reddening, "you wouldn't have to worry—"

She was sure she wouldn't. She'd planned to go anyway, alone, ever since she'd heard about the social. And it had been a long time since she'd been squired to a doing. "Well, yes, I would love to go with you, Mr. Sommers."

His fingers loosened perceptibly on the brim of his hat, and she realized he had feared she would refuse.

"It's Levi."

Smiling, she nodded. "Levi."

In the warm-for-October evening, Middle Creek's small country church bustled with activity. Covered dish in hand, Catherine felt stares as she walked with Levi across the fenced churchyard toward the door. Her escort seemed oblivious to the open curiosity, though she was certain he realized his attentions to the schoolmarm wouldn't go unnoticed in this small, close-knit community.

Catherine pushed out her chin and straightened her shoulders. So what if Levi Sommers was supposedly uninterested in women? She wasn't trying to seduce him. Besides, it must be boring to be the only bachelor around. Over the years, there must have been a good deal of matchmaking worked on Levi by mothers who would have loved to see their daughters married to the successful, respected farmer whose sizeable dairy herd was second only to the Houles'.

Her thoughts kept coming back to Amery's handsome father. Would the Houles be at the social? She wanted to meet Amery's "real sick" mother.

"Hello, Mrs. Winkel. How are you, Mrs. Dodge?" Catherine swept up to the long table in the church hall and deposited her dish of buttered, parslied potatoes as though she'd been attending socials here for years. "Everything looks so good! And how is your rheumatism, Mrs. Alper?" The women smiled and answered in kind, except for the Widow Shimmek, who muttered just loudly enough to be heard, "Well! No fool like an old fool," before smiling brightly in Catherine's direction. "How nice you could come, Dear."

Catherine looked beyond the laden table and felt her face unexpectedly warm as her eyes met Oliver Houle's. He stood with one hand resting on the back of a wheelchair and then leaned down to speak to the seated woman who looked much older than Catherine had pictured. Bonnie Houle was pale and thin, with dark hair pulled severely back into a tight bun. Her expression evidenced disinterest in her surroundings. *She looks as though her sole purpose here is to make others uncomfortable.* Give her a chance, Catherine told herself, and put a hand on Levi's sleeve. "Please excuse me for a minute. I want to meet Amery's mother."

"Of course, Catherine." Levi seemed a different man this

evening from the roughly-dressed farmer Catherine was accustomed to seeing at the school. Part of it was his carefully pressed Sunday suit, but more was the youthful gaiety shining from his eyes and ready smile. She was glad she'd dressed in her prettiest.

Catherine purposefully wended her way toward the wheelchair and put out her hand. "Mrs. Houle?"

The woman smiled faintly and raised her brows, but she didn't reach out.

Before Catherine could become uncomfortable, Oliver clasped her hand. "This is Miss Rothe, Bonnie." He enunciated clearly, as though his wife's physical incapacity also affected her hearing. "Amery's teacher."

"Oh, yes." Bonnie Houle spoke without inflection. "Thank you for your concern, but I'm afraid it's no use worrying about Amery's sight."

Catherine gasped, her eyes widening. "No use?" She looked quickly up at Oliver. "Mr. Houle, what does she mean? You were going to have his eyes tested."

"We did." He glanced around the crowded, noisy room. "There's a condition—oh, Bonnie, this was not the time to bring it up!" He swallowed and glanced around the crowded, noisy room. "I'll come to see you, Miss Rothe. I can't talk about it here."

"Of course." Empathy in Catherine's eyes met torment in his. "I am sorry. Please come." She looked down at the woman in the wheelchair. "I had hoped to meet you under better circumstances, Mrs. Houle."

Bonnie Houle lowered her head. "There never will be any better circumstances for me." She shut her eyes and caught her lower lip in her teeth. "But of course it's not your burden, is it, Miss Rothe?"

Catherine stared at her and then up at Oliver. He mouthed, "I'm sorry," silently, then said, "I'll come by on Monday, at the school . . . if it's convenient?"

"Oh, yes, please. There must be something we can do."

"We?" put in Bonnie Houle, her eyes narrowed as she looked up at Catherine. "Aren't you overstepping your position, Miss Rothe?"

"Bonnie, please!" Oliver Houle's anguish pleaded Catherine's forgiveness. "I'm sorry. I'll explain on Monday."

"Please do." With a curt nod toward Bonnie, Catherine turned away, simmering. *How rude! And selfish! To feel I'm 'overstepping' because I care about Amery's eyesight. What inexcusable manners! No wonder Amery said I shouldn't talk to his mother.*

Catherine took a deep breath, squared her shoulders, and walked toward Levi. Bonnie Houle wasn't going to spoil Catherine's evening, and she certainly wasn't going to let the woman spoil Levi's. She smiled toward him as she wove her way back across the church hall, pleased to see his expression soften as though he had just discovered something precious.

On Monday, Catherine watched the children trail away through October's crisp air. This day seemed endless, and more than once she had caught herself surreptitiously watching Amery squint over his work. Surely somewhere there was help for him. Her gaze followed his slight figure as it trudged, alone, over the hill toward home. To be so small and not to see well and to have a mother who didn't seem to care. Catherine sighed, resting her forehead against the cool window glass. The Houles' dairy farm was large, possibly one of the largest in the state. If money was needed, surely the Houles had more than enough.

"Need any help, Teacher?" An insolent voice broke into her

thoughts.

She whirled, her eyes wide. "Dale!" Her hand flew to her throat as she caught her breath. "You startled me. I thought you left with the other children." She tried to keep her voice steady. He was so large, and he stood so close she could see every strand of his oily unwashed hair and smell his equally unwashed body.

Dale Horner snorted. "Other children? Why d'you treat me like them? I ain't no child, and you better believe it."

Catherine moved to put her desk between them and stacked some papers to keep her hands steady. What could she use to fend him off? The biggest weapon at hand was a twelve-inch ruler. "Treat you like what, Dale?" She tried to keep her voice steady. "After all, you *are* one of my pupils."

His glinting eyes narrowed. "Yeah, but I could be a lot more to you, if you'd let." He advanced, his thumbs arrogantly hooked on his overall pockets. "If you get what I mean."

Catherine's chin came up. "I don't care what you mean, Dale. Please leave this room." She knew her voice sounded far braver than she felt as she looked up at his pocked, stubbled chin. Was this boy really only 16? He could easily pass for older with his swagger, his muscled body strong from field work, and his farm-fostered knowledge of the facts of life.

One corner of his mouth turned up in a smirk. "Please leave? Is that what you really want, Miss Rothe? I don't think so. I think we could be good friends, if you get what I mean." He stepped toward her.

"You've been reading too many books, Dale, and not the kind to help you in school. I want you to leave. Now." His body smelled like a rutting animal.

He began to round the desk. "I won't."

"I think you will." Oliver Houle's voice was hard as steel. He took two steps from the door and gathered Dale's wrinkled shirt front in a white-knuckled fist. "Get out. Now."

Catherine's body flooded with relief. Thank God Oliver Houle had come at this moment.

Dale shrank visibly but forced a show of bravado. "Amery's daddy, so? Come to see the teacher? Maybe she'll be friendlier with *you*."

Oliver Houle jerked the shirt once and pushed the boy toward the door. "I said go! And if I so much as think you've bothered Miss Rothe again, your father will hear from me. Get it?"

Scowling, Dale settled his shirt. "Yeah, I get it." He straightened his shoulders and sauntered toward the door. "See you tomorrow, Miss Rothe." The heavy oak slammed behind him.

Catherine swallowed and sank into her chair. "Thank you."

Oliver touched her arm. "Are you all right? Has this happened before?"

"Yes, I'm all right. No, it hasn't happened before. Dale likes to frighten people, is all. I don't think he would have harmed me." She hugged herself.

Oliver's eyes darkened. "Oh, wouldn't he? I'm not so sure." He took a deep breath. "I don't think you'll have to worry about him anymore. His father is a good farmer, but meaner than anyone I've ever met. He beats his children as well as his animals, and one word from me about this would be all it would take, and Dale knows it." He shook his head. "Are you all right? God, I'm sorry this happened."

"He's my pupil. I should be able to handle him. I'm just glad you came when you did."

"He's bigger than most grown men."

"He surely is." Catherine straightened her shoulders. "Anyway, thank you. Now, let's forget Dale. What about Amery? Please, tell me what you've found out." She gestured him toward the straight backed chair. "I couldn't believe your wife's attitude . . ." She stopped, amazed as she watched Oliver Houle.

Though there had been no doubt of who was in control with big Dale Horner, at the mention of his wife, Oliver Houle's broad shoulders slumped. He made a gesture of futility, both palms up. "There isn't much to tell. At least not yet. The doctor we've seen diagnoses 'a degenerative condition.'"

"But surely he's not the only doctor. You are going to take him somewhere else, to another, a specialist?"

Oliver nodded. "Of course. Milwaukee. To one of the best eye men in the country, they say, but they don't offer much hope. Oh, God." Oliver got up and thrust both hands deep into his pockets, turning so Catherine couldn't see his face. "Forgive me, but damn!"

"What if we had caught it earlier?" Remembering Bonnie's remark about "overstepping," Catherine added, "Or shouldn't I even ask? Would it have made a difference?"

"Perhaps. Who knows? We wouldn't have caught it now if not for you. Amery would never have said a word, you know. He would have just gone blind as a bat without ever asking for help." He paced across the area in front of her desk, turned, and paced it again.

"But why wouldn't his mother have noticed?" Frowning, Catherine studied Oliver's face. "He must have been bumping into things, spilling his milk—"

"He may have. I'm not with him a lot. He's not much use at the farm, slight as he is and so young. You'd understand if you knew Bonnie better. She's," he shrugged, "well, you saw her at the social on her *good* behavior. She seems to feel between Amery and me we've caused her all the grief in the world." He stopped pacing; his eyes met Catherine's. "Well, I may have caused her some, but not Amery. She's very good at making us feel guilty."

"For what?"

"Everything. You name it." He sighed and rubbed the back of his neck. "Her condition. The fact we live on a farm in Middle

Creek, instead of in Milwaukee or Chicago, where she could see the opera, go to plays again, where she could entertain. Oh, Bonnie loved to entertain. She could give you a list a yard long." His voice dropped off, and they were silent.

Echoes of the children's voices had disappeared from the cooling air. The darkening schoolroom seemed charged with something unfamiliar. Somehow, something had changed. She shook off the feeling and rose. "Then how is Bonnie taking this about Amery?"

Oliver made a derisive sound. "The way she takes everything. As though it's one more cross for her to bear. She isn't thinking of Amery at all, of what's happening to him, or what will happen. She's so damn wrapped up in herself." He took a deep breath and faced Catherine. "Sorry. I don't see her clearly, and I'm probably unfair. She's been sick a long time. Almost six years."

"I shouldn't have asked." Catherine reached out to touch his sleeve, thought better of it, and clasped her hands together. "It's none of my business, but is there anything I can do? Anything at all?"

"Do?" He stared at her so intently Catherine lowered her eyes. "You're doing it." He took a few steps toward the door, stopped as though making a decision, and pulled a small piece of paper from his pocket. "Here," he said abruptly. "Amery said you liked the chrysanthemums. I'm glad." He paused, holding the paper as though he meant to put it back. "And he said you liked poetry."

"Oh, I do! I used to write. A long time ago." Catherine smiled. "You've written something? May I read it?" She held out her hand.

"This isn't Keats, but maybe you'll understand."

Imagine. A farmer writing poetry. But Oliver Houle was no ordinary farmer. She studied his face. *What about him draws me so strongly? His air of unhappiness? The sense of futility when he speaks of his wife? Or the tenderness, the caring, he shows toward Amery? The same concern she would want her own children's father to have shown. Certainly there is no comparison to Joel O'Brien, unless by opposites.* At the thought of Joel, familiar resentment welled up; she pushed it away. Would she ever stop remembering, stop being bitter?

Oliver Houle placed the paper on her palm. "Promise you won't laugh?"

"You know I won't." The small, crisp paper seemed to vibrate in her hand.

"Don't read it until I've left." He stopped at the door. "Thank you . . . Catherine." With a courtly bow, he was gone.

Catherine fingered the paper. Amery knew she liked to read poetry, so Oliver Houle had written some. She was sure Bonnie wouldn't think kindly of it if she knew.

The carefully scripted words burned into Catherine's mind:

From a child's hand you take my gift.
A bud unsunned may never grow
But seed once planted, has a right to bloom
And other dying growths must make room.

Catherine shook her head and slipped the small poem into her pocket before locking up and walking down the dusty gravel road toward her small room at Walker's farm. "My gift" must mean the chrysanthemums, but the "bud unsunned?" What seed had a right to bloom?

Someday, perhaps, if the opportunity presented itself, she would ask Oliver Houle to explain it.

Or, perhaps it would explain itself.

Or, she thought, savoring the possibility, perhaps it already had.

3

OLIVIA, 1984

Olivia followed Tim Ryan into the house with Bert so close behind he stepped on the heel of her shoe.

"Well, heavens, Bert," she said, stooping down to slip into her sling-back pump. "Back off a little."

"Sorry," he mumbled.

Her gaze assessed the large, airy kitchen. The clay tile floor was scrupulously clean. A modern stove and refrigerator stood against one wall, a floor-to-ceiling fieldstone fireplace took up another. Two companionable-looking wooden rockers faced the hearth, as though, she thought, many long conversations had passed between them.

A large archway led into a light, many-windowed dining room with another stone fireplace against one wall. White French doors led to a screened porch almost overhanging the bluff. Through the glass, Olivia noticed two distant sailboats gently bobbing in the spring breeze. The mist was lifting, and reflections shimmered off the deep blue-grey of Lake Michigan. Tim Ryan thrust open the French doors; sea gulls' haunting mews wafted in on the damp air. The four of them walked through to stand on the wide plank floor of the lower porch, breathing in the enormity of this sea-fresh world, so different from the closed, landlocked area of Middle Creek.

Olivia shook her head, emotions surging through her body.

This house enveloped her with open arms, as though she had come home to a familiar, loved, and loving place which had long been waiting for her.

And it's mine. Mine alone. I've never owned anything in my name.

"Nice chairs, Mama," Pamela said, plopping her heavy body down on a sea-green cushioned wicker chair. Olivia came back to the present. *I'm never alone. I can't remember being alone.*

Tim opened another set of French doors from the porch, and they passed into a spacious open living room holding comfortable overstuffed chairs. A low round table of polished maple held a cut-glass decanter and two wine glasses on a crystal tray. Sun-sparkled rainbows thrown from the bottle dotted the off-white walls of the long, many-windowed room running the full length of the house to an open staircase leading up from the far side. A heavy double door led to the well-trimmed lawn separating the house from the two-story garage.

"Look, Mama, the front's at the back in this house!" Pamela giggled.

"Nice, ain't it?" Tim asked, nodding. "Open, summertime, the breeze goes all through."

"Beautiful," breathed Bert. "A house like this on the market today—why, you could ask your price, Livvy."

Tim jerked around, narrowing his pale eyes at Bert as he almost poked him in the stomach with the end of his gnarled cane. "You ain't thinking of selling!" he accused. He whirled back to face Olivia. "You ain't!" he said fiercely.

Dazed, as she thought Alice might have felt after landing at the bottom of the rabbit hole, Olivia shook her head. "I'm not thinking at all, Mr. Ryan. Surely not of selling. I didn't even know about this house until a couple of hours ago."

"Well, then, it's just him." Tim cocked his head toward Bert. "And it ain't his," he added, chortling and slapping his leg.

Bert looked injured. "I was just remarking."

Olivia muttered, "Better remark to yourself, Bert."

Pamela chugged ahead of them, pulling her extra forty pounds toward the open stair. "Let's look up here." She puffed. "C'mon."

They followed her lumbering steps up to a square central hall opening on the north side to a small back bedroom and a storage room taking up fully one-half the area and on the south to the biggest, brightest, most welcoming bedroom Olivia had ever seen.

She caught her breath at the sheen on the wide-planked, pegged oak floor. Double floor-to-ceiling windows, diagonally crisscrossed, filled the south wall. A tiny, blue, gold, and green stained-glass window, six-sided like a porthole, was placed high in the middle between them. The walls were a pale blue, the filmy drapes a soft sea-green, the comforter and small overstuffed chair a deeper shade of the same green. Another set of French doors opened onto the second-story porch, a replica of the lower, except here the wicker furniture was painted deep blue, and the cushions were brilliant flowered blue and green.

"What an odd little window!" Olivia exclaimed, reaching up to touch the colored glass. Through it the sun turned her face golden, then green and blue as she moved closer. "It doesn't open." She ran her finger around the edge. "It doesn't seem to fit with the rest of the house at all."

Tim Ryan chuckled. "Oh, it fits all right. It's the thing caught Miss Cathy's eye right at the start. She loved that window."

"She did?" Olivia tried to picture her mother loving a window. Evidently there were a lot of things about her mother Olivia didn't know, had never known, and perhaps would never know.

"Yep. It's why they bought the house."

"For a *window?*" Bert asked, his eyebrows raised.

"What he said. The Mister." Tim studied Bert for a minute

before he said, "People buy houses for lots of reasons."

Later, Bert accelerated through the stone pillars as they turned onto the main road. "Old Tim's really something. Acts like he owns the place."

"Well, I suppose he feels he does," Olivia said. "He said my mother hadn't been there often these past few years. There's a story behind him, you can bet. Where do you suppose she found him in the first place? He must have been young, back then."

Pamela hummed tunelessly in the back seat.

"Looks to me," Bert said, sucking his front teeth, "like there's more than one story. What about your old mother? All this secret stuff. I thought her life was an open book. You know, ordinary, like the rest of us."

Olivia sighed. *I thought so, too.* "I guess nobody's ordinary."

"Ah, don't argue words. You know what I mean." Bert carefully dodged a puddled pothole reflecting soft blue sky. "Well, now we can head for home. Thank God. Get back to regular living. Eat right."

Olivia turned to stare at him. "Go home?"

"Home. Oregon. Remember? Where we live?"

"Are you being sarcastic?"

"Well," Bert said, frowning. "You didn't think we would stay here, did you?"

Olivia didn't answer.

"Well, you didn't," Bert stated. "Thing to do is get hold of a good realtor and let him handle the sale."

"The sale of what?"

"Of what?" Bert repeated. "Of what do you think? The house, of course."

"I'm ready to go home," put in Pamela from the back seat. "I like home."

Bert chuckled. "See? Even old Pam knows it's time." He glanced meaningfully at Olivia, then back to the road.

Olivia said nothing. *Leave? When I've just come?* Then she almost laughed aloud at herself for feeling so strongly about the house.

"Livvy?" Bert said. "Answer me."

"All right." Olivia shrugged, a small smile playing at the corner of her mouth. Her earlier feeling of excitement, change, flowed through her, along with a new strength. "I'll answer you. I'm not going. Not right now."

"What?" Bert involuntarily stomped on the brake. The back of the car slid sideways on the soft gravel and the engine sputtered to a stop. "What? Livvy, for God's sake, this is no time to play games."

"Don't swear," Olivia said. "It sets a bad example. Who's playing games? I simply said I'm not going back home right now. Is that playing games?"

"It might be," Bert muttered. "I hope to God it is."

"It's not. You go on ahead, if you're in such a hurry," Olivia said. "I won't stop you, not for one minute. Pam and I will stay here at Dunes House." The name rolled off her tongue as though she'd been saying it all her life.

"Stay here?" Pamela echoed. "Oh, no, Mama, I want to go home."

"Me go ahead!" Bert's face flushed. He started the car again and steered with fervor around another pothole. "My God, Livvy, you're my *wife*. I need you at home. And what will people say?"

"Say?" They'll probably say, 'Where's Olivia?' and you can tell them—oh, tell them I've left you forever. Ran away with a traveling salesman. I don't care what you tell them. It's nobody's business anyway."

"They'll think something's wrong no matter what I say. Have you lost your perspective? You've never gone away before."

"I'm not going away," Livvy said. "You are. Let them think what they want. Tell them I inherited a fortune in real estate and jewels and I'm staying to work things out. You can eat in restaurants, you know, Bert. I don't have to be there just to cook and wash your underwear, now do I?"

"You always were," Pamela said, hooking her chin over the back of the seat, a worried frown on her broad face. "Always."

"Then maybe it's time I wasn't."

"This isn't you talking, Livvy. You're upset. Too much excitement."

Olivia laughed. "Maybe excitement, but you can bet not too much."

There was silence for a short time before Pamela offered, "Daddy, I can cook."

Bert snorted. "Sure you can."

"Of course, she can. Of sorts." Olivia wrapped her mind around what it would be like to be away from Pamela, and for Pamela to be away from her. *"You keep her too sheltered, Olivia,"* *Livvy's friends said more than once, and in varied ways. "She's a big girl.* *She's capable of working somewhere, maybe not supporting herself but at least* *earning some of her keep, you know. And learning a little bit about self-* *worth."* Olivia hadn't pursued those conversations. Didn't she owe it to Pamela to take care of her? *"And what about when you die?" they* *went on. "Then who'll baby her? She'll end up in an institution, and it will* *be your fault. She's not nearly as dumb as you make her out to be. You just* *need to feel guilty. You think it's your fault she's retarded."*

All the arguments played through Olivia's head. Perhaps it was time to let Pamela do a few things on her own. Keeping house for Bert, even though it wouldn't amount to much, might be a start. And Olivia wouldn't be away forever, just long enough to learn a few things about her mother's life.

They were back to the blacktopped highway now. Bert, agitated, almost pulled out in front of a fast-coming semi, thought better of it, and waited.

"Or, you know, we could just move here and live at Dunes House," Olivia said. "All of us. It is beautiful, isn't it? So clean and fresh there above the water. So welcoming."

"Not to me. I don't want to live here," Bert sputtered. "Out here in the middle of nowhere. I'm an industrial real estate man, in case you don't remember. Good at it, too. You see any industry around those sand hills? I'd have to drive to God knows where, probably Milwaukee, to get any business. No, thanks. You'll have to sell the place as soon as you can." He reached over and slapped her thigh. "Hey, Livvy, I know just the piece of property to invest in, too. Right downtown Portland. Make some real money!"

"And I suppose sell the farm, too, though it's been rented by the same family for the last fifteen years, and they're doing very well." Olivia spoke slowly, rubbing her leg where Bert had slapped it.

"No, no, don't be a dunce, Livvy. The farm's making money. No need to sell that."

Olivia sighed. "Bert," she said in a tone of voice she had never used to him before, "shut up."

The next night, Olivia lay wide-eyed in her beautiful blue bedroom at Dunes House, listening to the soft slap-lap of water on the Lake Michigan shore just below the bluff. A three-quarters moon reflected a rippling path dancing across the water. She'd sat on the upper porch for a couple of hours earlier, just watching the changing light.

For the first time in her married life, which had been, come to think of it, her whole adult life, Olivia was really alone for more than a couple of hours. She had come back every summer to visit her mother for a week, but always Pamela had been with her. It seemed there had always been Pamela and almost always Bert.

Where did I find the nerve to send Pam back with Bert, after all these watchful years?

Olivia shook her head, amazed at the change she'd felt just coming into this house, as though she were a different person. She was at home, complete here on this wind-swept bluff over shimmering water.

Her mind flipped back to a scene she hadn't thought about in years.

They had parked on a country road not far from the Sommers' farm. "Bert, I don't know how I can tell my parents," she'd said, near tears. A slender 16, Olivia was usually self-confident, but right now her self-confidence was pretty low. "Especially my father."

Young Bert Hobart ran a hand through his neatly slicked-back hair and leaned his elbow on the window of his used-but-in-good-condition Ford sedan. His self-satisfied expression (one he wears to this day, thought Olivia, breaking into the memory) hadn't been visible in the dark.

He shrugged. "So we'll elope. We won't tell them anything. By the time they find out, it will be too late."

"But Bert, they'll still find out."

He snorted, smacking the steering wheel with the flat of his palm. "Not much chance of them not. It's pretty hard to hide a baby, Livvy." Bert was quiet for a minute. "All right then, we won't elope. We'll just hurry up and get married. I'm done with school. We'll move out to Portland. I told you I was going into real estate there with my uncle Joe anyhow. You know I am. Your parents know it, too."

"But my father, Bert—"

He turned to face her. "You can't be daddy's girl forever, Livvy. He'll get along without you. Fathers do. He's got your mother, doesn't he?"

Olivia remembered clearly the crickets' farewell-to-summer

song creaking in through the car's open windows while neither of them spoke. Then her hand had crept into his. "Bert, I'm scared. Are you scared?"

Moments elapsed before Bert's voice, low and not as blustery as usual, reached her through the summer night. "Yeah. Yeah, Livvy, I'm scared."

Olivia brought her thoughts back to the present, startled with the realization her life had been completely sucked away by others. Always. When she hadn't been doing something for Pamela or Bert, she'd spent her energies on quote, good causes, unquote. "Keep it up, Livvy, it's good for my business," Bert was fond of saying. "Get out there and get your name—*our* name— known for doing good."

She hadn't even taken a lot of time for reading, which she really enjoyed, except for the book club selections the church group listed for discussion. She'd always wanted to write but there had never seemed to be enough time to start, or enough interesting things to write about. But she had, through correspondence (because Bert didn't want his colleagues to know his wife hadn't graduated from high school) finished her high-school degree. It was a matter of pride. She had done it, even though she'd done it Bert's way.

Olivia smiled into the darkness, thinking of the pout on Bert's florid face as he had thrown his and Pam's suitcases into the car for their trip home. Was it only this morning?

"I wouldn't have believed you'd desert us, Livvy. I mean it's not like you. You always did what was good for me—for us, I mean," he corrected, his face flushing. "What in God's name are you going to do here?"

She'd shrugged. "I'm not sure yet. Talk with some people, find out some things. Try to unravel her story, as my Mother said in her will. Look for some answers—I don't know. Find out who I am, maybe, by finding out who she really was."

"Who you are? You're Mrs. Bert Hobart. Answers to what? Look where? So your old mother owned a house you never heard of. So what?"

Olivia sighed. "I'd think you could understand, Bert, but try anyhow. Who was she, really? Surely not the person I thought. Why was this house a secret? Didn't my father know about it? Surely he must have. I remember her going away sometimes when I was small. I never knew where . . . she never told me. To 'renew,' she said. If my father didn't know, then why not?"

"Get in the car, Pam." Bert slammed the last suitcase into the trunk. "So you got a house. You've got to decide what to do with it, is all. It won't be hard to sell, in spite of old Tim Ryan, if you can find somebody with enough money to afford a property like this. I don't see any need at all for you to stay here, not even for a day."

"No," Olivia said. "I know you don't. But I'm going to."

Her stomach churned as she waved to Pamela's worried face while the car spurted away, gravel flying. Of course, he didn't want her to stay. Bert had never wanted her to do anything which didn't further his ambitions or his comfort.

Hugging herself, she'd lifted her chin and returned to the house, smiling at the beautiful solidness of its architecture, its setting, its promise.

Lying in bed now, she smiled again. Well, she had done it. Sent him off. She really had, after all these years of being predictable Mrs. Bert Hobart. And she had turned Pamela loose. Not a lot, but a little. She hoped she hadn't made a mistake. Perhaps she should have insisted Pam stay here at Dunes House.

The world—my world, anyway—is full of should haves. I wonder how many should haves my mother thought about, or did and perhaps regretted. Olivia snuggled comfortably into her soft pillow in her beautiful blue-green bedroom and fell asleep.

The next morning, Olivia settled herself on the lower porch, a cup of Tim Ryan's thick, boiled coffee liberally laced with cream steaming on the small wicker table beside her chair. Morning sun streamed across the floor, palely warming the early May air. She gazed out over the water. It seemed an age since Bert and Pamela had driven away.

In Olivia's lap lay a packet of old letters tied with package string. Reading them seemed an invasion of privacy, sort of like going through another's underwear drawer. She fingered the cord, her feelings mixed in spite of Catherine Sommers' written wish to share her story with Olivia. "Tell me about my mother, Tim," Olivia had said over toast and jam. "How you knew her. What she was like when she was here."

Tim swallowed, his Adam's apple bobbing tightly under the stretched parchment of his throat. He pierced her with his pale gaze, deliberating, before he said, "You might look through the storeroom, Miss Livvy. There's a trunk up there she kept some things. She wouldn't mind, seeing's she left them. Might not be much there."

"But what was she *like?*"

The old man stared past Olivia, out beyond the shimmering slate-grey lake which changed color minute by minute throughout the day. For a moment, he seemed lost in reflection before he said, "What was Miss Cathy like?" His expression softened. "She was like sunshine." He rose. "Miss Livvy, if she'd wanted me to talk, she'd have left me word."

Now Olivia sat with her hands folded over the envelopes, asking herself what she really did want to know. "Sunshine," Tim Ryan had called her mother, who had been so quiet, so serene, such a "Catherine" type of person. Not "Cathy," bubbly, perhaps, warm and bright like sunshine. What a charming touch of loyalty when he said Miss Cathy hadn't left him word to talk.

Probing into her mother's past left Olivia more than a little uncomfortable. The packet in her lap seemed almost ominous. She asked herself if she really wanted to open a Pandora's box. *I own this house. I own the farm bringing in a most comfortable living, and I don't need to be financially dependent on anyone ever again, whether I learn Catherine Sommers' true story or not.*

For a few seconds, Olivia considered never being dependent on Bert again or tied to his dull, pompous, real-estate-is-all-there-is life. She'd daydreamed often of becoming somebody on her own. Perhaps researching for serious writing which might bring someone a new understanding of their life. But the daydreams had never been more than dreams, never could be, because Pamela had always—would always—need care. Olivia and Bert had been made aware of that fact on the night of Pamela's birth.

Olivia remembered lying back on the stiff hospital pillow, exhausted, delighting in her new role of mother. Now the nurse would lay their new daughter in her arms.

Bert, disheveled, came into the room. "Well, *you* look pleased," he said. "As for me, I'm tired. It's been a long night." He sank down on the ugly orange plastic chair near the empty bed across the small room.

"Oh, Bert, I can't wait to see her!" Olivia said, leaning forward on one elbow. "Can you?"

"I could have waited a few years."

Olivia caught her breath. Her hazel eyes flashed. "Bert Hobart! Don't you ever say such a thing, not as long as you live, you hear? We have a child. She didn't ask to be born and she's never—NEVER!—going to know we weren't ready for her. I'll leave you if you ever say—"

The door opened, and a rustling nurse came in carrying a

small, tightly-wrapped bundle. She wasn't smiling, nor was the silver-haired doctor who followed. At their expressions, Livvy clenched her hands into fists, and Bert rose uncertainly from his chair.

Now Livvy shook her head, bringing herself back to this day, to Dunes House. Of course, she couldn't consider just herself. She had no right. Of course, she would have to go back to Portland. But not yet. Not just yet.

The envelope on top of the packet was not addressed. Olivia opened it, expecting a note. Instead, there was a single slip of paper with a few carefully penned lines. There was no date.

"Why, it's a poem!" Olivia exclaimed aloud, and read:

"From a child's hand you take my gift.

A bud unsunned may never grow

But seed once planted has a right to bloom

And other dying growths must make room."

Olivia raised her eyebrows and muttered, "Not great poetry. Doesn't make much sense, either." She held the limp paper in her hand, looking out over the water. She'd never known Levi Sommers to write poetry.

But then, she thought, considering the events of the past week, maybe she had never really known her father either.

Olivia went on through the envelopes and loose papers; there were children's drawings, probably from Catherine's students during her year of teaching before she married Levi Sommers.

Olivia studied a printed note:

Thank you for the present. I like it very much.

I will be home pretty soon.

Amery Houle

Home from where? The Houles had lived not far from Sommers' farm where Olivia grew up. She remembered Amery as a quiet, colorless boy whose eyesight had grown progressively worse in spite of numerous operations until he was nearly blind when Olivia left home. *Amery must have been eight or nine years older than me. My mother must have been his teacher. I wonder what his memories of her might be and where he is now.* The last she had heard, he was teaching out East. Olivia didn't remember what.

She turned over another paper. Her eyes widened as she read, "Someday I will give you emeralds."

She stared at the small gift enclosure card. Heavy parchment with an elegant, gold-embossed wreath on the front, it was small but expensive, even in those days. It was not signed. Olivia got up and went into the kitchen, holding the note in one hand as she poured herself another cup of thick coffee from the blue-enameled pot. What might have been enclosed with the card?

Coffee in hand, she stood at the kitchen window and studied the garage with its second-story apartment where Tim lived. He probably knew everything Olivia wished to know about her mother, and he wouldn't talk; he didn't feel he had the right. What marvelous loyalty, she thought, knowing—and, she realized, regretting—there wasn't anyone in the world who felt that kind of loyalty to her.

She walked slowly back through the airy living room to the porch, still carrying the little card. There was nothing to note what the gift might have been, but "Christmas, 1937" was penciled on the back. Before Olivia had been born. The card could have been from anybody.

"Someday I will give you emeralds." Evidently someone had. Once more Olivia studied the writing. It had all the same characteristics as the penmanship on the poem about flowers.

But it's not my father's writing! Surprised, Olivia examined it more closely.

"Letter for you, Miss Livvy," Tim Ryan's crackly voice broke into Olivia's thoughts. Startled, Livvy put down the packet of papers, suddenly realizing the sun had gone under and ominous clouds were building up over the lake.

"A letter?" she repeated. Bert and Pamela couldn't possibly have written yet. And if Bert had, Olivia was sure she wouldn't want to read it. He would still be mad at her or would have moved into his pouting stage; she didn't need to experience either one. After a week or so, she'd go into town and call. She was glad no telephone had been installed at Dunes House.

"Thank you." Olivia reached out for the almost weightless envelope simply addressed to Olivia Hobart. Hand delivered? There was no stamp.

"Found it in the mailbox, down at the road," Tim offered. He stood expectantly, and Olivia realized, of course, he was curious.

She stuffed the envelope into the pocket of her heavy sweater. "I'll read it later."

Tim's face fell, and Olivia was almost sorry she hadn't opened it in front of him, but it really wasn't any of his business. "Would you mind leaving my cup in the kitchen on your way out?" she asked.

Tim picked up the cup but didn't leave. "First letter's come here for a long while," he said. "Miss Cathy used to write me when they were comin' so I could spiff up the place." He looked absently out over the water. "It was always happy when she was here. Wisht she'd've come more often."

Olivia looked up at him. "Don't you have any family, Tim? Nobody writes you?"

"Got one nephew somewheres, don't rightly know where now. He ain't much of a writer." Tim turned to go, leaning on his gnarled cane. "Need any help with anythin', Miss Livvy, just you tug on the pull by the kitchen door. Rings a bell out in my place over the garage, you know."

Olivia didn't know, and thanked him. Smiling, she watched the old man step carefully through the French doors into the house. He really had been curious about the letter, though too polite to say so. She probably should have opened it while he was waiting. What did she have to hide?

Tim turned beyond the door and took a step back into the room. "I know how to keep my mouth shut, y'know. Did it for years. Don't have to worry." He nodded, his Adam's apple bobbing. Olivia realized with a start of surprise he must think the letter was something Bert shouldn't know about. The old man was inviting her confidence, and she was touched.

"I believe you do, Tim Ryan," she said, smiling.

Tim leaned on his burled cane, studied her for a moment, then looked past her out over the lake and said, "Storm brewin,' Miss Livvy. You afraid of storms?" Without waiting for an answer he added, "Get some dandies here on the lake. Come up real quick. Waves fifteen-twenty feet high, sometimes." He paused, as though waiting for her to say something. When she didn't, he sniffed and said, "Well, you call me you need anythin,' hear?" Tim let himself out through the kitchen door; she heard it close with a smart click.

A loud rumble of thunder rolled through the screen and trembled along Olivia's body as she lifted the flap on the envelope. She shivered and pulled the front of her sweater closed, thinking what it might be like to have no family at all, no one to even know whether you were alive or dead. What if old Tim should have a heart attack or something? She had no idea whom to contact. She would have to inquire to find out where the "somewheres" nephew was.

There was only one page in the envelope, a small one, and printed on it in block letters with a red marking pen was:

"DANGER! GET OUT!"

Olivia's mouth opened in astonishment. "Danger. Get out," she read aloud, voicing the words to make herself believe what she held in her hand.

She sank back in the wicker chair just as an enormous finger of lightning jagged down to the water not far from shore. The sizzling crack of thunder was almost simultaneous.

"Storm brewing," Tim had said. It surely was. She fingered the note. Perhaps one was brewing in her life as well as in the weather?

She examined the plain, ordinary white envelope. There was no postmark, no return address. It must have been hand delivered, but who even knew she was here?

Except Tim. Would Tim want her out?

She didn't think so, and the envelope was addressed with a bold hand, not an old man's writing. She shut her eyes and listened to the sudden hiss of hard rain hitting the porch screens. A soft mist sifted through onto her legs, but she didn't pay it any attention.

Someone wanted her out of Dunes House. But why? "DANGER! GET OUT!" was melodramatic at best, like something out of a Victorian novel, she thought. Lady inherits beautiful estate. Lady stays there alone—not quite alone, giving old Tim his due—to unravel mysterious life of mother. Lady is threatened.

Well, maybe not threatened, she thought. Maybe advised is a better word. Lady is advised to get out.

Should she show the warning to Tim? Perhaps it was some kind of joke. Surely, he would know something about it, how it got here, who brought it. She looked at the paper again. If it was a joke, it was a poor one. She crumpled it, threw it into the wastebasket near the chair, and went inside to change her now-damp shoes, closing the French doors behind her against the deafening storm.

Olivia's mind caught the sound before her sleep-drugged body did. She moved restlessly and turned into her pillow to regain the pleasant state of unconsciousness she had finally achieved after tossing and turning for so long. The piece of paper with its large printing of "DANGER! GET OUT!" continually thrust its image into her mind.

She hadn't shown the note to Tim; perhaps she should have. She'd tossed it into the wastebasket instead. After lying awake most of the night, she determined to show him the note in the morning.

Now the sound came again, a gentle tapping floating into her consciousness. Reluctantly, Olivia opened her eyes. The French doors to the upstairs screen porch allowed a light breeze to move the curtains gently over the windows. She sat up, woozy from lack of sleep. It must be almost morning; there was an opaque grey quality about the dark.

There *was* a sound; it hadn't been her imagination. The tapping began again, not exactly frightening, more of an annoyance, but it didn't *fit*. Skin prickled on her upper arms, and an involuntary tightening of her jaw muscles made her ears tingle. Probably just an animal, a mouse or chipmunk chewing on something, Olivia told herself, straining to catch the noise again.

No. It was a human sound, as though someone were loosening something carefully and trying to be quiet doing it.

She lifted her covers and swung her bare feet down onto a soft, plush rug. In one swift movement, she was padding quietly through the porch doors. There was just enough light from the coming dawn to illuminate the blue and green cushions on the chairs. She stopped and listened.

The tapping began again. Olivia shivered and, holding her breath, moved to the screen. She looked down at the small stretch of land that bordered the house and dropped off fifty feet to the sand beach below. The storm had spent itself and there was nothing unusual to be seen. Near the water the wet roof of the boathouse gleamed.

The tapping stopped before Olivia could locate its direction.

Hugging herself and shivering—whether it was chill dampness or her nerves, Olivia wasn't sure—she stood motionless waiting for the sound to come again. It didn't. Only the soft lapping of water on sand reached her ears; it was too early even for sea gulls. She returned to bed.

"Tim, may I speak with you a minute?"

Tim stopped raking fallen twigs, leaned on the rake handle and squinted at Olivia. "Surely, Miss Livvy." He was chewing on the end of a dry twig that he pulled out of his mouth and tossed onto the pile in front of him. "What's it?"

"Last night—" Olivia started and then stopped. The whole thing seemed silly in this morning's clear, storm-washed sunlight.

Tim waited patiently, his pale eyes taking in every inch of Olivia. "You're taller'n her," he commented. "Otherwise, you're a spittin' image."

"Of my mother? People used to say so." She took a deep breath. "Tim, last night I heard a funny noise. Did you?"

His pale eyes sparked and narrowed. "What kinda noise?"

"Creepy. Like a tapping, sort of. In the middle of the night, on toward morning. Like somebody was trying to open something, maybe. Did you hear it?" She watched for his reaction. *Perhaps he'd not only heard it, perhaps he'd made it.*

Tim picked up another twig and ran it around the gum edge of his upper teeth before he answered, "Can't say I did." He looked out over the lake before continuing, "This is an old place, though. Sometimes after storms, nature just has to rearrange things, let them settle back in. Suppose you heard a couple of trees shiftin' their branches?" He asked the question as though he expected her to know.

"I don't think so. It stopped before I could find out where it was coming from."

Tim considered, his spare body leaning on the rake handle. "Used to hear stories about this place. Ghosts and all that, but I never saw signs of anythin' unusual. More likely just those old trees there by the porches organizin' theirselves. Storms like last night disarrange a lot of things on the shore along here. Wind gets a real sweep at the land, y'know." He began to rake again, and Olivia stood watching. He obviously wasn't going to say any more. His explanation didn't sound very plausible to Olivia, but she didn't have a better one.

"Did you empty the wastebasket on the porch this morning, Tim?" she asked as she turned to go back into the house.

"Haven't been in the house at all, Miss Livvy, 'cept to make coffee in the kitchen early. Why?"

The note and its envelope had been gone when Olivia looked for them this morning. "I just wondered," she said.
Perhaps she had stuffed them into her sweater pocket? No, she was sure she hadn't.

Tim had to be lying, but why?

4

CATHERINE, 1937
December 23

*A*t last, muffled laughing shout echoed through still, snowy air as warmly bundled children disappeared beyond curtains of swirling flakes. Sighing, Catherine shut the school's heavy oak door firmly. It hadn't been an easy day. Dale Horner had been at his worst, taunting the younger children, particularly little Amery Houle, and making sure Catherine was well aware of it. Well, Catherine thought, next week Dale will have to pick another target. As soon as Christmas was over, Oliver (Why did her breath catch at the thought of him?) would take Amery to Milwaukee for his operation.

"Why wait so long?" she had asked.

"To give the specialist time to be sure of his new procedure," Oliver answered.

Catherine surveyed the schoolroom, decorated with carefully colored Christmas scenes for the evening's program. There wasn't a space without something red and green hung on or over it. She smiled. Even the window shade pulls sported red paper bells.

Both the side blackboards presented pictures done in colored chalk, one with a Santa Claus climbing down a somewhat tilted chimney, the other a manger scene crowded with every animal the children could imagine. The room held more than the trappings of festivity; the atmosphere of electric anticipation the children had left behind waited to be picked up on their return.

A tall, feathery pine, hand-cut by Levi Sommers off his back forty, stood stalwartly on the corner of the somewhat shaky plank stage supported by sawhorses. The tree was hung with fragile, faded ornaments which had been kept in the basement since the district's beginnings, along with a well-squashed rope of silver tinsel and one new ornament handmade by each child. It will be prettier when the room darkens, thought Catherine, though she knew the children saw it as beautiful beyond words even in harsh daylight.

The stage was covered with an ancient figured rug Levi's grandfather had donated years ago. At its unrolling, Catherine was nearly overwhelmed by pungent mothballs popping noisily across the wooden floor.

"Catch them for next year!" called one of the older boys. "Then we don't have to put in so many new ones!" There had been a laughing scramble for the balls as Levi chuckled and spread the rug over warped planks.

"It's the same every year, Catherine," Levi said, turning her name on his tongue as though he loved saying it, thought Catherine. "I do so enjoy being part of this," he added. "It's almost as if some of the little ones were mine."

He should have had children to cherish, Catherine thought now, remembering the wistfulness in his voice. She straightened the old blue velvet drapes Levi had threaded on a clothes pole above the stage front. Everything was as perfect as she could make it. Now if only the children remembered their lines.

She sank down at her desk, which had been moved to the back of the room, thinking of Levi's remark. She felt that way about the children too, especially the younger ones. Catherine picked up her red pencil to correct the last spelling papers, deliberately pushing away memories of the windswept Kansas cemetery and tiny twins who would never see a Christmas.

A knock on the door startled her, and she realized it was nearly dark. How long had she been sitting there? "Who is it?" she called.

"Oliver Houle."

"Oh!" Her hands flew to her hair, straightened her bodice. She caught her breath, swallowed, and called out, "Come in."

"I would if I could. The door's locked. And I'm suffocating in snow out here."

Catherine hurried through the cloakroom, opened the heavy door, and gasped, "Oh, my goodness!"

Oliver's shoulders and head were blanketed with cottony snow.

"You're nearly covered!" She laughed. "I didn't realize it was snowing so hard. Please, do come in." She resisted the temptation to brush the flakes off his damp hair.

Oliver stamped snow from his boots. "I thought you might still be here, and I wondered—aren't you going to eat any supper? Let me give you a lift to Walker's."

"Oh, thank you, but I brought something. I know the children will come back early, and I need to get the coffee cups from the basement for the social after the program." Catherine clasped her hands behind her back. "But it's nice of you to offer."

What am I thinking, wanting so badly to touch him? A married man, father of my student. A schoolgirl crush by a lonely teacher. At least, he doesn't know about it.

Oliver smiled. "It was just an excuse anyway. I have something for you." He held out a small, red-ribboned box.

"A present! Why, Amery could have brought it tonight."

He shook his head. "It's not from Amery."

"But—" Flustered, Catherine accepted the small package, her eyes searching his. "I can't—I shouldn't!"

"I know. But you will, won't you? It isn't very much, not what I would like—" He dropped his gaze, straightened his shoulders, and said formally, "Please. Take it in the spirit it's given. You've done so much for Amery. And for me."

Catherine, her face hot, clasped the small box to her breast, repeated, "The spirit it's given?"

Oliver's touch on her hand sent electricity through her body.

"I believe you understand." He nodded when she didn't move away. "I know you do. You must."

From the open door, she watched snow swirl around his departing form, her lower lip caught in her teeth. The small box in her hand brought a warmth she thought she'd put aside forever when Joel O'Brien disappeared from her life.

She stamped her foot and closed the door sharply. How stupid to care first for a man who cheated you and now for another who could never be more than a friend. And how stupid *not* to care for Levi Sommers, who she knew each day was moving closer to openly declaring his love. Why was life so complicated?

Her hands shook as she untied the ribbon to find a simple brooch, a circle of gold, and a card with small, neat script: "Circles are unending." There was a space and then:

"Someday I will give you emeralds."

Lessons would start again on Monday. Catherine had spent the better part of Christmas vacation planning classes and rearranging the room for more informal seating to ward off mid-winter doldrums. Being busy helped keep her mind off Amery's operation and, not so successfully, off Oliver Houle. How she had missed seeing him since the night of the Christmas program.

As she packed away Christmas ornaments a cheerful "Hello!" startled her. She looked up, her face flushing with gladness, her heart pounding at the sight of his tall figure.

"Oliver!" She hurried toward him, one hand unconsciously touching the small circle of gold at her neck. "I'm so glad you're back. How's Amery?"

Oliver strode toward her, his pleasure obvious. "We don't know the outcome yet. I brought Amery home, but he's to keep quiet and stay in bed with his eyes bandaged for three weeks. He's a brave little trouper. He says he feels fine."

"The operation was a success, though, wasn't it? I mean the doctor was optimistic?"

"As much as he could be." Oliver's warming gaze traveled her face, her neck, and stopped at the gold pin. "Thank you for wearing my gift," he said, taking her hands in his. "I hoped you would."

Had he thought I wouldn't? "I love it," she said, "and I treasure it."

His hands were warm, compelling hers to stay within his hold. "I wonder," Oliver said, "if you would come by and talk with him?"

"Oh, yes. I had planned to as soon as I knew he was home. In fact, I'll keep him up with his lessons."

"I know it's an imposition, but his days will be so long."

"Nonsense," Catherine said. "I want to come."

At the sound of cleared throat, Catherine realized her hands were still in Oliver's. She pulled them away, her color rising. "Levi! I didn't hear the door."

Levi studied her face for a moment, then moved to Oliver. "How's the boy?"

"Good as could be expected, Levi. I was just asking Miss Rothe if she would come to see him."

"And, of course, she will. Catherine, I came to see if we

should order another load of coal just yet. Mind if I check?"

Catherine shook her head. "Oh, Levi, what would I do without you? I'd completely forgotten about the coal supply."

Levi's deep grey eyes darkened for just an instant. "Looks like you might get along just fine," he said, and disappeared down the basement stairs.

Amery looked even smaller than usual lying against stiff white pillows in a large bed.

"Miss Rothe's here, Amery," Oliver said.

The large bandage covering the top half of Amery's head lent him the appearance of a pale mushroom with a lopsided smile. "Hello, Miss Rothe. I bet I look funny."

Catherine smiled. "You look just fine, Amery. Best of all, you're going to see better. Won't that be grand?"

His smile disappeared. "Only maybe, Miss Rothe. Not for sure."

Catherine raised her brows at Oliver, who said, "The doctor told him straight out the operation might not help. Amery's not expecting more than he should."

"Oh, but surely—"

"It's all right, Miss Rothe." Amery's voice seemed to have gained strength since she had last heard it. Perhaps he was more sure of himself here with no Dale Horner to mock him. "It will either be better, or it won't. We can't do anything now but just wait. Right, Father?" His bandaged head turned toward Oliver.

"Right, Son." Oliver squeezed Amery's fragile hand. "Miss Rothe is only going to stay a few minutes today, but tomorrow she'll come back and do some studies with you so you don't fall too far behind. All right?"

"You bet all right!" The mushroom's mouth took on a worried frown. "Can you, Miss Rothe? I mean, with all the other—"

"Don't you worry, Amery. I'll just give you the same amount of time here I would give you at school."

The little smile appeared again. "All right, then."

Catherine turned and nearly walked into his mother's wheelchair. "Oh! Mrs. Houle!"

"Thank you for coming, Miss Rothe." Bonnie Houle's voice was cool. To Catherine, her smile seemed pasted on. "Oliver, I have asked you time and again not to leave your work boots in the kitchen. Must you?" She had made no indication Amery was even in the room.

Catherine saw his small fists clench atop the coverlet. "Hello, Mother," he said, his voice almost a whisper.

"Yes, Amery." She didn't look at her son. "Well, Oliver?"

Oliver flushed, his mouth tightening. "I was in a hurry, Bonnie. Sorry. Of course, I'll move them."

She abruptly wheeled her chair around to leave the room. "Good evening, Miss Rothe. Did I overhear you plan to come again?"

Overhear? Evidently Oliver hadn't talked about the lesson plans with his wife.

Catherine answered, "Every day until Amery comes back to school." *To give him the attention he doesn't get from you,* she added quietly to herself.

Bonnie wheeled away, throwing her voice over her shoulder. "How very nice."

Catherine watched Bonnie's chair until it turned the corner at the end of the hall, then turned to Oliver. "I—I don't know what to say."

"Don't say anything, Miss Rothe, please," Amery pleaded.

"Just come."

"She will, Son. Tomorrow." Oliver's voice was constrained. "Please don't be offended by my wife." He led Catherine to the door, where he said in a low voice, "Amery needs you." His mouth was a tight line. "You can see how little she cares."

Catherine looked back at Amery's small, forlorn figure slumped back against his pillow. "Of course, I'll come." She called, "See you tomorrow, Amery. Rest well. We'll have a lot of work to do."

"Miss Rothe, can I ask you something? You don't have to answer if you don't want."

She smiled at his serious expression. In the past weeks, Catherine had enjoyed Amery tremendously. Away from the schoolroom and Dale Horner's taunts, Amery revealed a game sense of humor and an unexpected understanding far beyond his years. "What, Amery?"

"You are my father's very best friend, aren't you?"

Catherine was glad he couldn't see the rush of blood which rose to the roots of her hair. "What a funny question," she parried. "I don't believe I've ever discussed friendship with your father."

"I hear from your voice you're teasing. Are you smiling?"

"I always smile when I talk to you, don't you know?"

"Are you going to answer me? Serious?"

Catherine paused, her mind full of the pleasure of Oliver's company as he drove her to and from Amery's lessons, times when dusty, lonely Kansas and all the unfulfilled years before faded, and the world seemed made for talking, laughing, and sharing. "I–I hope to be his very good friend, Amery," she finally said. "We all need good friends, don't we?"

"My father needs one more than most people."

"Why do you say such a thing?" Catherine frowned.

Amery's lips pushed out. "Because my mother's not his friend. Or mine, either. She's not even her own friend." At Catherine's silence, he went on. "My father laughs with you. He even tells silly jokes. His voice is happy when he talks to you." Amery paused, tilting his bandaged head like a top-heavy bird. "Do you know what? My ears hear a lot better when my eyes don't work."

A week later, Catherine set her books on the seat of Oliver's new Ford sedan and climbed in, arranging her skirts carefully and stamping mushy February snow off her high-top shoes. "Well, that's that," she said.

She leaned back against the seat and drank in the beauty of the Houles' sunset-washed farm buildings. Two enormous white silos thrust their domes against a fading winter sky; nearby a herd of Holsteins waited patiently to be let into the barn.

"You sound disappointed," Oliver said, starting his car. "To be done, I mean. I know I am."

"Disappointed?"

"Disappointed you're done. How can I thank you? You've done so much for Amery."

She felt his gaze search her face. "You don't need to." Catherine smiled. "Amery's taught me about as much as I've taught him, I expect."

Oliver chuckled. "He's apt to if you give him a chance. It would have been good for him to have some brothers or sisters." He turned onto the main road.

She sat up. "Oliver, this is the wrong way."

"I know," he turned toward her, his eyes windows into an unknown future, "but I don't want to take you home just yet. Do you mind…Cathy?"

"Cathy?" She turned wide eyes to his. "I don't believe anybody in my whole life ever called me anything except Catherine."

"But Catherine sounds so stiff and formal. Aren't we beyond that?" He deftly steered around a soft spot in the road before he turned to look at her. "Be Cathy with me. Light and smiling, like you are with Amery. You don't mind, do you?"

Catherine was quiet for a few seconds. Mind? How could she mind? Her voice husky and breathless, her face alive with color, she said, "I think I love it."

Catherine's first winter in Middle Creek was terrible by any weather standards. One snowstorm after another kept children away from school, and fierce, relentless winds rattled the windows and whipped drifts around the small frame school building. By the middle of March, she felt certain Wisconsin had given up ever expecting spring.

The children reveled in the frosty mounds, building fortresses, sculpturing enormous snowmen, rolling in the drifts, and making new wheels for Fox and Geese games every time another storm erased the pie-shaped footpaths they so carefully traced in the snow. Cheerfully brushing each other off as well as they could outside, they stamped the rest of the snow off on the cloakroom floor where it melted into grimy slush that Catherine swept out the door at least four times a day.

As far as she could see, Amery's operation had done very little good, though she didn't voice her feelings; he seemed content with as much sight as he had. "I can see better than I could, honest," he said, his voice earnest as he peered at her through thick lenses.

"I'm glad," she said, and she was. He seemed happier than he had been; certainly, he was more at home with himself.

With a turn-about that happened so quickly tulips were startled into blooming before they should, March melted into April. The last of the snow rivered into ditches and rutted dirt roads. Catherine put away her samples of winter scenes and encouraged the children to draw spring flowers which she cut out and taped to the walls, hoping to freshen their attitudes as well as her own.

"Teacher."

Catherine looked up, frowning. It was almost four o'clock, and the shuffling of small feet told her it was nearing time to close school. "I have a name, Dale."

"Oh, yeah." Insolent, he stood too near her. "*Miss* Rothe."

"Is there something I can help you with?" She did her best to swallow her distaste for this unlikeable person.

Dale thrust an arithmetic book under her nose. "This here's kid stuff you said I should do," he complained. "Looka these pictures." He pointed with a jagged, grimy fingernail.

Catherine sighed. He wasn't stupid, just lazy. "What do you mean?"

"Baby junk. Pictures of rabbits hoppin' around. Give me a book for somebody my age, will ya?

Catherine looked up at his large, ungainly body, his blotchy skin. He should have been out of grammar school long ago, working on his father's farm where he would be in his element. She had heard he was good with animals. "Can you do those problems, Dale? Can you give me the right answers?"

"I don't even wanna try." He slammed the book shut.

"When you turn in five perfect lessons, I'll give you a harder book. Not until then." She looked down at the papers on her desk, dismissing him.

He didn't move away. She shivered involuntarily and looked up; the glint in his eyes was not a child's. "You may sit down, Dale."

"Maybe I don't want to sit down. Maybe I want to stay after, Teacher. Work on those assignments." His eyes narrowed, challenging.

She rose. "You will call me Miss Rothe from now on, and you will sit down now. You will also leave this schoolroom when the other children do." The memory of her earlier encounter with him alone was vivid. If she was going to have a problem with Dale, she would handle it in a room full of children.

He stared at her just long enough to make it a battle of wills, then tossed his head, snickered, and sauntered toward his too-small desk at the back of the room, one hand holding the arithmetic book and the other thumb-hooked in his back pocket. The other children watched him in silence. Dale had been known to lie in wait for those who laughed at him.

Catherine often kept Amery after school to help him with his lessons; he was always willing, even eager, to stay. Perhaps, she thought, he was in no hurry to go home to his mother. Often, when his work allowed, Oliver picked up Amery and gave Catherine a ride to Walker's farm. She had been thankful for his help when the snow piled drift on drift and was now even more thankful during mud season.

Things that couldn't be said with Amery between them were spoken through their eyes. Catherine felt the flush on her cheeks as Oliver swung her to the ground, quickly releasing her, should the Walkers happen to be watching. Her heart wrenched as he drove away, and she tried to keep longing out of her face. How stupid she was! First Joel, who never loved her at all, and now Oliver, who couldn't.

"What are you doing to yourself, Catherine Rothe?" she asked aloud in the loneliness of her small room. "And what are you doing to him?" She read over and over the spare poems Oliver wrote, savoring each word by the flickering light of the kerosene lamp.

Why couldn't she love Levi Sommers, who continued to ask Catherine to attend the church socials? Though he never even took her hand in his, Catherine knew he cherished her and that sooner or later he was going to ask her to marry him. What would she say? She had given her heart to another, to someone she couldn't have.

She continued to work with Amery, and to fall more deeply in love with Oliver Houle.

"Cathy, my Cathy," Oliver wrote along with one of his small poems. "When spring comes to the land, will it come to us?"

The envelope Amery gave her one soft April Friday morning was a burning ember in her pocket until the children went outside for recess. She read the short note once, and then, her throat swelling until she couldn't have spoken had she needed to, she read it again. "Run away with me tomorrow, my Cathy. Please." There was money enclosed. "Take the 9:30 train to Appleton. I have the whole day. Spend it with me, just this once? Oliver."

Catherine stuffed the envelope into her pocket and rang the hand bell, signaling recess was over. An early spring breeze gently lifted her winter-heavy skirt to let the soft April air surround her thighs with promise of a new season.

She closed her eyes. *Oh, yes, Oliver, yes. Just this once.*

She stood aside, hardly noticing the children as they piled into the schoolroom.

The Middle Creek depot was a small, soot-covered shack along the tracks. Catherine stood in the thin April sunshine, hugging her paisley shawl around her shoulders. A soon-to-be-warm breeze lifted the hem of her long print dress, perfectly suitable for shopping. She watched the 9:30 train screech and huff to a cindery stop at the rough platform. Her heart pounded with anticipation and with another, less welcome feeling. *Guilt?*

Catherine pushed that thought away and glanced furtively around, glad to find no one there but the ancient clerk. "I'd like a ticket to Appleton," she said.

"Goin' into the big city for the day, are you?" He opened the door of the small, dingy building, shuffled around behind the ticket window, took her money, and handed her a ticket. "Glad to see it's a round trip. Wouldn't want to lose our schoolmarm," he teased, his laugh disclosing mismatched, discolored teeth.

"I'm just going to do a little shopping," she said, tasting the lie. "I'll be back this afternoon."

"Don't you miss the train, neither," he said, shaking a knotty finger. "You get too busy in town, forget the time. Only one return on Sattidays."

"I won't," she promised, relieved of the worry that had kept her awake half the night. What if someone she knew, possibly even the vitriolic Widow Shimmek, would be traveling the same train, asking innocent questions about her day's plans, perhaps even inviting her to lunch?

Catherine found a seat next to a soot-streaked window that reminded her of the train she'd ridden from wind-swept Kansas, where part of her life and body—and her dreams—would always remain in the small, lonely cemetery.

The train jerked. She closed her eyes and leaned back, picturing Joel O'Brien's handsome face without rancor and even with some compassion. Amazed, she examined the ease which came with freedom from hate. She had spent months despising him, hurting because of him, and more months deliberately not thinking about him because the very thought brought bile up into her throat. Now, suddenly—because of Oliver, she realized, because of love—now she could accept Joel for what he had been and, to be honest, thank him for taking her from the safety of Milwaukee, even from the house she had lived in with her parents all their lives. Without Joel, would she have ever known the excitement of eloping, of thinking she was loved, even if it were false, of breaking into independence and starting a new life here? Without Joel, would she be in this time, this place, speeding toward Oliver Houle?

Oliver. If only they could have met before Joel, and before Bonnie. Catherine shook her head, knowing the wrong of being here, knowing she had no right to spend even one day with him, and also knowing she would have done anything, told any lie, to be right where she was. "Oliver," she whispered, the sound lost in the rush-click, rush-click of train wheels. "Hello, Oliver, my darling," knowing she would not—could not—say it aloud to him, but sure in her heart he would give anything to hear her speak those very words.

She sat forward, straining to make out the Appleton stop through the smoky window. What if he wasn't there? Then she would live the lie and spend her day shopping. Her breath caught short and she clutched her small purse in her lap as the train slowed.

There he was! Tall, graceful, hatless, his fair hair lifting in the breeze, his gaze raking each car, each window, as the train braked to a stop. Trembling, she stood, adjusted her bodice, and hurried down the aisle, steadying herself with each plush seat as she passed.

"Cathy." Oliver reached up to lift her from the high step and enfolded her in his arms. "Oh, Cathy! I was so afraid you wouldn't come."

A thrill shimmered through her and she melted against him, her cheek against his rough wool jacket, her body reveling in his lean strength. She felt cocooned; she had known his arms would be a haven. "Oh, Oliver," she whispered against his chest. She didn't know how long they stood. She didn't care.

At last he stepped back, tilting her chin up with his finger. "Thank you," he said softly. "I knew you would be like this. You belong in my arms."

Catherine took a long, shaky breath and belatedly searched the platform.

"Don't worry, no one here knows us." Still holding her hands, he flashed a boyish, excited grin. "Oh, Cathy, Cathy," he said again, as though he loved the sound of her name. "Thank you for coming, for daring. Do you realize," she heard the delight in his voice, "we have a whole day?"

She nodded, her eyes shining. Then her face clouded. "But I'm—"

"What? Scared?" His grin was infectious. "That's two of us. And guilty. But we're *here*!" He pulled her away from the depot. "Come on. There's not enough time, and we don't want to spend it all standing at a train station. I've done my work, and the day is ours."

"What work did you have to do?" She hurried along beside him.

He swung her hand as they walked. "Bought some cows. Actually, I bargained for them last week and only had to give a final okay this morning. It didn't take long."

"Then how can you justify being away a whole day?"

"Bonnie doesn't know I had already chosen them. Ordinarily,

it would take three or four hours. I'll be home before you are."

"Then let's not talk about it. Let's just enjoy being together."

"Agreed." He stopped walking. "Are you hungry?"

Hungry? She hadn't been able to even think about food this morning. She laughed. "Starved!"

"All right. It's a grand day, and I know a beautiful park right along the river. How does a picnic sound?"

"Wonderful. And private. Oh, Oliver, there is so much to talk about, so much to learn!"

"About each other." He squeezed her hands. "We'll make every minute count, won't we?

"Every single one, Oliver. Every single one."

Catherine threw her shawl off her shoulders and stretched her arms toward the sun. "What a perfect spot for a picnic." They had found a protected grass-covered knoll overlooking the spring-swollen Fox River and surrounded by thick pines blocking the still cool breeze. "I could almost believe in summer." She laughed. "There were times last winter I thought I would never be warm again."

"I think that every winter." Oliver set down the grocery bag. "I wish we had a blanket for your dress."

"Oh, I'll sit on my shawl. The ground is dry, anyway. It doesn't matter."

"It would matter to most women." Oliver reached into the bag for French bread and a block of cheddar cheese. "You're so different, Cathy. You don't waste time with unimportant things. Bonnie would have a fit if she had to sit on her shawl."

Catherine laughed. "Maybe her shawl is better than mine.

How are you going to open the wine?"

"With this." Oliver pulled a corkscrew from his jacket pocket. "I came prepared."

She watched him in silence until the wine was open. "Oliver, tell me about you and Bonnie. I don't understand your feelings toward her, or hers toward you or Amery." She hesitated. "If you don't mind my asking?"

"Mind? Of course not. I want you to know everything there is to know about me." He reached over and touched her arm. "I would like to think—and don't laugh—you and I are the past and the future and forever after."

Catherine frowned. "Quite a dream, considering our circumstances."

"Yes. I know." Oliver studied the river, his mouth a tight line. "It is, isn't it? Nothing more than a dream." Then he smiled, his face changing to boyish delight as he handed her a glass of wine reflecting sunlight from its red depths. "But today we're living it. To this day, our day." He lifted his glass to touch hers, sending a small chime floating away on the April air. "Let me in, Cathy. What are you thinking?"

"I don't know," she answered truthfully. "I'm just being, just soaking in everything about this day. I can't believe we're here. Together." She set her glass carefully in the grass, broke off a chunk of bread, and handed it to him. He sliced cheese with his pocket knife, placed the cheese on the bread, and returned it to her.

"Teamwork," he said, and grinned.

"Come on, Oliver. I asked about you. Tell all."

He leaned back against the trunk of a small birch, crossed his long legs at the ankles, and let his eyes follow a log drifting down the river before he spoke. "Where shall I start? With my mother, I suppose. Her name was Jenny, and she loved poetry. Oh, you would have liked her, Cathy. I remember her being a lot like you, interested in books and music. When she married my father, she made him promise their children would go to college."

"Really? And he promised? How unusual, for a farmer."

Oliver nodded. "But he was crazy about her. And he kept the promise. What he didn't know when he made it was he would only have one child, who might want to use the education. I wanted to be a teacher, not a farmer. Dad couldn't see it."

"A teacher?" At his nod, she exclaimed, "How surprising."

"Is it? Only because you know me as a farmer now."

"Go on. Did you teach, and what? And don't watch me eat." She blushed. "Look somewhere else. It makes me nervous."

"Look somewhere else when I can look at you? You're asking a lot. You're so beautiful." He smiled at the face she made around a mouthful of bread and cheese, and continued. "I taught for two years, in a high school near Milwaukee. English lit, poetry, Shakespeare. I loved it."

"And that's where you met Bonnie?"

"No. In college at Madison." He frowned. "Knowing her now, you'd never know what she was like then. She was sweet and loving, vivacious, fun, sociable . . ." His voice drifted off.

Catherine hugged her knees, pushing away a ridiculous jealousy toward the paragon Bonnie had been.

"We married when she graduated, right after my first year of teaching. Oh, yes, she has her degree," he said at Catherine's surprise, "and we had everything she wanted. Faculty teas, being an important person—capital I, capital P—in the community, you know? All the status things. She loved it, and she loved me because I gave her those things." He hesitated for a moment as he poured more wine. "Her family was poor. She got through on scholarships and was determined to upgrade herself. Through me, I guess." He swirled the sunlight in his wine. "But she gave, too, don't misunderstand, it was good. Until I—we—came back."

Catherine frowned. "But why come back if things were so

good?"

"Ah. There's the rub. What could a good and only son do when his father became too sick to run the farm? 'Come home, Oliver. Only for a little, until I'm on my feet again.' My mother couldn't get reliable help." He shrugged. "So, I came home. Dad died, and I was caught."

"Couldn't you have sold? Gone back to teaching?"

"Maybe. Bonnie wanted me to, worse than anything. But Amery came along. She hadn't planned for him. I believe she never planned for any children, though she never told me so. Teaching jobs weren't easy to find, and what would my mother do? It was all too complicated, so I decided to stay. Not long, not forever. It just turned out that way."

He reached for another piece of bread and sliced off more cheese. "When Bonnie got hurt, there wasn't any choice."

"How was she hurt? You said she blames you?" Catherine pushed back a wayward strand of hair the breeze had loosened from her coronet.

"She does, rightfully or not." He sighed. "Try to understand. She was so unhappy. It was like watching a flower wither and die. She took care of Amery, all right, but not much else. Then my mother took sick; Bonnie ended up being her nursemaid and hating her for it. She hated her life anyway, for my staying. Said I was a 'mama's boy.'"

"Oh, but how hard for her."

"For Bonnie, you mean. Oh, it was. And, of course, terrible for my mother. To be a burden was unthinkable to her. And to be cared for by someone who resented her for staying alive. I was too busy, working too many hours, trying to do everything myself. Now, it's different. I've got two good men and some modern machinery. The farm could almost run itself with a little supervision. It does, in fact." His eyes clouded, and he looked out over the spring-high, roiling river. "I bought Bonnie a horse, though she really didn't want one. A spirited beauty. Taught her to ride. I knew she needed something to get her away from the house sometimes. She loved it. Rode like a wild woman, too fast, as though she could outrun her unhappiness."

Catherine watched his hands clench and unclench as he continued.

"The day she got hurt, we had a terrible argument. I don't even remember now what started it. I know it ended with her shouting about my failures and her disappointments." Oliver shook his head, then looked into Catherine's eyes. "Have you ever had an argument that blows the whole top off your world, and the one person you counted on turned out to be your enemy? I guess we both felt betrayed that afternoon."

Catherine broke the leftover bread into chunks and threw them into the grass for the birds. "Not an argument exactly in the same way, but yes, I know about that person letting you down." Into her mind came the picture of Joel, naked in the Kansas moonlight. She viewed the image objectively without rancor and rejoiced that she could.

"Well, Bonnie stormed out of the house, saddled the horse herself—I'd always done that for her—and took off though the west field as though the devil himself were after her."

"And she was thrown."

He nodded. "The horse shied at a rabbit they startled. Her saddle wasn't cinched tightly enough and slid under the horse's belly. Bonnie was dragged and then dropped. The damage to her spine was permanent."

"But it wasn't your fault that the saddle wasn't tight. She put it on herself!"

"Ah. But you see, I made her live here. I bought the horse. I encouraged her to ride. I made her so mad she hurried in saddling. Oh, there were a lot of ways to make the accident my fault, and she's never let me forget that it was." He crumpled the bread sack into a small ball. "She doesn't dislike Amery, but she doesn't like him very much, either. He doesn't deserve to be treated the way he is. Not treated is more like it. Ignored." Oliver threw the sack toward a refuse container, missed, and went to pick it up.

"But why her feelings toward Amery?"

"Well, you see, if she hadn't had to stay with him, she would have left me before the accident. Meant to, but then she discovered she was pregnant. In spite of her college degree, she had no way to make a living with a child, my child, and so, you see, he's my fault, too. I sometimes wonder why she didn't leave him with me and just go. So," Oliver shrugged. "Now she's trapped not only to us but to that wheelchair. And so am I."

Catherine caught his hands in hers. "Poor Oliver."

"Not poor now." His eyes spoke even more than his words. "Not now that I've met you, Cathy."

"But there's no future for us. You *are* trapped. Even if you wanted to, you couldn't divorce a woman in a wheelchair."

He brought her hands to his lips for a moment before he spoke. "And, of course, you need a future."

Catherine made a face as Joel crept back into her mind. "Oh, I'm not looking for a husband, if that's what you mean."

"What are you looking for, Cathy?" Oliver moved closer and took her in his arms, burying his face in her neck, his searching lips against her throat. "What could I give you?"

"Give me? I–I don't know." She pushed ineffectively against his chest. "Stop, Oliver, please."

"Why?" He nuzzled under her ear. "Don't you want my kisses?"

"Yes. Yes. Yes." She pushed him back enough to see into his face, into his eyes darkening with passion. "If I could be truthful, I would say I've been looking for you all my life and now here you are. But for just one day, that has to be enough. Don't make it so hard to leave you, Oliver, my dearest love. Don't." But her lips belied her words, and he bent to kiss her, gently at first, and then claiming her mouth with his tongue. Her whole body arched toward him, asking to be caressed, even as she turned her head and murmured, "It has to be enough, doesn't it, this day?"

"No." He laid her back on the grass, his hand so lightly brushing her breast she was hardly sure he had, then more firmly, following the soft contour of her bodice. His tongue searched her mouth, asking for the response that she gave willingly, gave with all the pent-up longing of the past months.

"Oliver . . . Oliver, my darling," she breathed. Though she had dreamed of just this moment, though she had thought she knew how she would react if given the chance, she was astounded by the explosion that raced through her to her very core. She had known his kisses and caresses would be wonderful, but she was not prepared for the willful response of her body that was frightening, exhilarating, unstoppable…

But wrong. So wrong. Catherine pushed him away, breathing hard, straightening her dress, her hands unconsciously smoothing the material over her breasts.

His eyes followed her hands before he caught them in his. "I want you, Cathy. Here, now."

"No. No! It–it must be the wine." She laughed, her voice tremulous. "Let's be sensible."

"But I don't want to be sensible."

"Then...then I won't see you again," she lied, knowing she would see him anywhere, any time he asked.

"Don't tease."

Did he know that one more second, one more kiss, would have been a point of no return? And that if he had insisted, she would have been glad?

She took a deep breath and regained her composure. "Let's talk," she said, her voice firm. "Please."

Oliver sat back with reluctance, but kept her hands in his. "All right. My turn to question, if I can keep my mind focused on anything but how much I want to make love to you. Here. Now." He swallowed, took a moment, and then spoke. "All right, you win, we talk. Surely there have been other men in your life? What happened to them?"

"Not 'them,' him. Just one. For a very short time."

"Tell me about him. Was he like me?"

She shook her head. "As different as night and day. But I don't want to talk about him. Not now, on our day."

"Sometime, then. I have to know you, Cathy. I have to know all there is to know."

Catherine leaned forward and kissed the backs of his hands, feeling the soft blond hairs against her lips. "Sometime."

That night in her lamp-lit room at the Walkers, Catherine bent over her small desk, dreaming a poem onto paper. A poem for Oliver, to Oliver, to their day together.

It was the first poem she had written since Joel.

5

⁂

CATHERINE'S JOURNAL

April 13, 1938

How quickly precious minutes go. Today we met at "our bridge," so private, so remote, beyond Miller's woods. Only for an hour, all we could steal. Yet how cherished I feel. I hate lying to Amy Walker about "going for a walk," but she is so busy with her own life she hasn't questioned.

Oliver loves my poem, as though I had given him diamonds, rubies, everything precious. I love him so, I long for him so, I want so much to be together. How I want his complete love, but I will not. We cannot. Sometimes I wish I had no conscience.

How silly I am, to write like a lovesick adolescent. But who can I tell? Who cares of my desires?

April 27

Perhaps someday someone will find this journal and be shocked that Catherine Rothe, the girl who always did "the right thing," was sinfully in love with a married man. Sin. What an odd little word for something so wonderful. And so frustrating. Just the touch of his hand on mine is exciting, and oh, I long for so much more. My whole body does. I know his does, too.

Enough of that. Tonight Levi squired me to the square dance, and we had such fun. Though he must be nearly fifteen years older than I (I've never asked), no one would know it the way he "kicked up his heels," a direct quote from the Widow Shimmek who whispered to me, "You've given him back his youth, poor man." What do you suppose she meant? That he was poor for having once lost it, or now, for having found it?

Levi worships me. Before long, I'm sure he will propose. What will I say? What can I say? If marrying Levi would keep me here, near Oliver— oh! How ridiculous to think of that. And how unfair to Levi.

May 15

It's been so long since I've been with Oliver alone. To see him just at church is painful. I want more, his kisses, his touch. Spring work has kept him in his fields until long after dark, and, of course, there is no way for either of us to get away from watchful eyes. At least, I see him for a few minutes when he picks Amery up from school. But I can't touch him then…and how I want to! His eyes speak for him, as I'm sure mine must.

Poor Amery. His eyesight is getting worse, and now they tell him there is no more they can do. He may never go completely blind, but he won't be able to read for himself before long. Then what, for Oliver? A bitter, crippled wife, a blind son—doesn't he deserve the happiness I could give him? When he's with me his world comes right, he says. And mine does, too. Sometimes he brings me a "scribble." I love his *poems. Better than Wordsworth or Browning because they're for me.*

May 27

Tomorrow school will be out for the summer. The children are so excited, and I will be relieved to be free of Dale Horner. I do hope he won't return to school in the fall.

I am to stay at the Walkers through summer and tutor Amery; Oliver will deliver him each day. I would have gone to their house, but Bonnie didn't approve. Oliver says she doesn't want Amery around anymore than necessary. Of course, I don't mind, but I must be so careful, not to give my feelings for Oliver away. Amery might say something to Bonnie, though I doubt he talks much to her.

June 5

A wonderful note from Oliver to meet at the bridge tomorrow. "A surprise," he wrote. "Prepare to spend the whole day."

A whole day. I am breathless just thinking about it. To be with him, where no eyes watch. Only a day, when what I want is the rest of our lives, yet it will do. It will have to do. Of course I will meet you, Oliver my love, my love…

Catherine dressed casually as for a walk, hurrying to get away before Amy Walker could ask the usual, "Going walking, are you?" and Catherine would have to make up some answer that yes she was, and no, she didn't think she would be back for lunch, and don't wait a meal. She would take a sandwich with her.

Catherine left a scribbled note on the kitchen table and tiptoed out, carrying a large sun hat in one hand. What she did was no one's business, she told herself, and there was no reason to feel so guilty. But telling herself so didn't make a tryst with a married man acceptable.

"You know what's right, Little Catherine." Her father's voice invaded her thoughts. Had she done anything so terrible? Her friendship with Oliver was just that, never more than a touch, a need never fulfilled. Their relationship was based on caring for each other, on being able to talk freely about anything, about everything.

Besides, Oliver wasn't really married, was he? Tied legally, yes. But if love counted for anything he was married in his heart to her, Catherine.

She walked the soft June morning, feeling the fullness, the promise of its bird song and fresh breeze, yet hearing her father's voice: "If you can't be proud of what you are doing, Catherine, you shouldn't be doing it."

She made a face and walked faster. No, she wasn't proud of loving Oliver, but he needed her, and, proud of it or not, she needed him. Of course, her father was right; however, things were not as black and white in her life as they had been in his.

She turned the corner past Miller's woods and broke into a run toward Oliver, who opened his arms and enfolded her so tightly she could hardly breathe as he rocked her back and forth.

"Hello, hello! I was so afraid you couldn't get away," he said. "I've been here holding my breath for half an hour." He lightly kissed her nose, her lips.

"But how can you leave for a whole day?" she asked.

"I shouldn't, but I just did. The fields are all in. Elmer can handle the chores alone for one day with what help Amery can give him. Oh, Cathy, it's been so long! I need so much to be with you to talk, to laugh. Come." He pulled her toward his Ford sedan. "Let's get away before someone comes along."

"What's the surprise?" She clutched her hat to her head as the car lurched forward.

"Look in the back seat."

Her eyes widened. "A picnic basket? How did you smuggle that out of your house? And where are we going?"

He grinned, shrugged. His fair hair blew back from his forehead; his blue eyes sparkled with anticipation. "Oh, Cathy, who cares, who knows? We're going to drive off the end of the world and not come back until we have to." He reached across to take her hand in his. "I love you so much."

"Oliver Houle, you're acting silly as a schoolboy!" Catherine straightened her flowered skirt primly and did her best to put on a disapproving expression. "How irresponsible of you."

"I know. Don't you love it?"

She broke into laughter and moved across the seat to lean against him, squeezing his arm through his light shirt to assure herself he was real. "Yes," she shouted over the motor noise, "Yes, yes, yes!"

They drove slowly through the warming morning, stopping often to look at a pretty view, watch a bird, or pick early wild flowers from the ditch. "Are we going anyplace special?" she asked, threading a daisy into the top buttonhole of his open-collared shirt.

"Not really. I thought we might picnic on the Lake Michigan shore. It's beautiful there, and we should be able to find a private spot where we can watch the water."

"Oh, how nice! I've never seen the lake. Maybe we can find some seashells."

"They would have to be lake shells," Oliver teased. "Wouldn't they?"

"Smarty. Now that I know where we're going, let's hurry up and get there."

"You're hungry," he accused.

"Aren't you? We've been driving forever."

They turned off the main highway down a gravel road. Ahead,

Catherine could see steel-blue water at the horizon. She sat forward. "Look, there's the lake! Oh, how beautiful! It goes on and on."

"I told you we were going to drive off the end of the world, didn't I? Well, this is it."

They passed a "FOR SALE" sign hung on high stone pillars.

"Look, Oliver!" Catherine craned her neck for a glimpse of the property. "That beautiful place is for sale. What a wonderful view from those porches!" A large Dutch colonial home, sparkling white, reflected the sun from crisscrossed windows between green shutters. Its two-story screened porches faced the lake only yards from the bluff's edge.

Oliver slowed as they passed. "Looks empty, doesn't it? Well, come on."

He stopped the car at the dead end beyond the house's drive and reached for the picnic basket. "There's a strip of beach down there, I'll bet. Let's go see."

They slid and stumbled down the embankment, Catherine holding her skirts up out of the weeds. Oliver steadied her with one hand under her elbow as he carried the picnic basket with the other. The strip of sand was dry, clean, and warmed from the sun. Oliver spread out a blanket. "I'm getting better at this picnic stuff, see? You won't have to sit on your shawl today."

Catherine wrinkled her nose. "Good thing. I didn't bring one." She unpacked the basket. "Ham sandwiches, wine, apples, what's this? Chocolates! You dear." She sighed. "Perfect." The water was calm with just a ruffle of ripple lapping gently at the beach. She closed her eyes, savoring this moment out of time, trying to keep the wistfulness from her words. "Will we ever have more?"

"I can't answer that, Cathy." Oliver took her hands in both of his. "But this I do know: these stolen moments with you make my life livable. If we never have more, we at least have this day, this togetherness now."

She was silent for a moment and then smiled. "I will not—
will *not*, do you hear—spend even one minute of this perfect day
wishing for anything more or anything different. I am going to
immerse myself in this moment, this day, in you, in us, in
happiness. I love you so much, Oliver." She dropped his hands.
"Now eat."

He laughed. "All right. I see you aren't about to get serious."

"Not serious. But I am about to get thirsty."

"I'll pour the wine. We'll get lightheaded in the sun."

"Then our heads will match our hearts."

He looked at her for a long moment, as though memorizing
her face. "Oh, Cathy, how fortunate I am. You're so, so—"

Her blue eyes glinted. "Just so-so? Well!"

He grinned, poured the sparkling red liquid, and raised his
glass to hers. "To you, my love, to us, to this day."

They drank together, talked, laughed, demolished the lunch
and finished the wine, savoring every minute.

An hour later, as they scrambled up the hill, Oliver suggested,
"Wouldn't it be fun to look in that big house? Pretend it was
ours?"

Catherine shaded her eyes. "It is lovely, isn't it? Do you think
it's empty?"

"We won't know unless we look, will we? It is for sale. Surely
anyone could look at it. Maybe there's a caretaker. Everything
certainly looks well-tended. The shrubs are all trimmed, and it's
been recently painted. Come on." He took her hand as they
walked up the winding drive.

"Oliver." She turned toward him. "Wouldn't it be wonderful
if we were coming home together? For real?"

He squeezed her hand. "Remember, we weren't going to talk
like that. Today we *are* for real. This is our house. We just forgot
our keys."

They walked to the side door, preparing to knock.

A paper was tacked to the jamb: Gone to bury my father. Back Tuesday. T. Ryan, Caretaker.

"Well, it's empty," Oliver said. "Let's go around to the front and see our view."

"Our view. Why not?"

Hand in hand they walked around the house, commenting on the condition of "our garden," "our trees," and "our boathouse down there."

"I would just love to see the inside," Catherine said, standing on tiptoe at a window and cupping her hands around her temples to keep out the reflection. "It's all furnished. Nice. I wonder if they're going to sell the furniture with the house."

"Do you really want to see what it's like? Maybe we can get in."

She stared at him. "Oh, we shouldn't."

Oliver snorted. "We're doing so many things that we shouldn't already, I can't see one more making much difference. I'll try the cellar door. It doesn't seem to have a lock."

"Oliver, don't!" Catherine looked over her shoulder. "What if someone see us?"

He ignored her and pulled up the cover. Steps led down to a second door under ground level. It complained loudly, but opened at his push. "See?" He looked up at her. "It was meant to be. Come into our house, my dear, and we will see whether the servants kept it up well while we traveled in Europe."

She hesitated at the top of the steps. "You're crazy, Oliver Houle. We'll be trespassing."

"No, just deciding whether or not to buy. Come."

"Well, all right, but if we get caught, I never saw you before. You seduced me into coming here under the guise of being an eccentric absentee landlord and—"

Laughing he pulled her down the steps. "Close your mouth

and come along. How else are we going to find out anything about this place?"

They wandered through the quiet, white-walled rooms. "It's so airy, Oliver," Catherine exclaimed. "So comfortable, so obviously used and enjoyed. Look at this view!" Wicker chairs and tables faced the shifting colors of the lake.

"Let's see the upstairs," Oliver suggested.

"Oh, don't you love this place, Oliver?" Catherine turned to look down at the living area as they climbed the open staircase. "So secluded here at the end of this road, and so lovely. I wonder why the owner wants to sell, don't you? It's—oh, I'm being silly—but it feels as though this house has just been waiting for us."

"Nothing is silly if you feel strongly about it." Oliver stopped at the top of the stairs and whispered, "Maybe there are ghosts. I'll bet that's it. At night, chains clank in the walls, and the furniture flies through the air."

"Be serious." She gave him a gentle push as they stepped into the bedroom. "Oh, look at that beautiful little stained glass window between those two large clear ones. See that patch of colors it throws on the floor?" She turned around. "This is—why, this is the most beautiful bedroom I have ever seen in my life." Her face glowed. "Pegged oak floors polished to a sheen, the colors all blue and green like the lake and the sky, and look, this upper porch with cushioned wickers. Oh, Oliver, what a place!" Catherine's wide blue eyes searched every inch. She opened French doors to the upper porch and stepped into the June breeze that lifted strands of hair from her thick coronet as she walked to the screen and leaned her palms on the sill. "I could dream myself right into being the mistress of this house."

Oliver laid his arm gently across her shoulders. The fresh, wet, green smell of seaweed mixed on the breeze with the mewing of gulls. "Do you want it, Cathy?"

"Want it?" She laughed up at him. "What would I do with it?

Live here and starve without a job?"

"I could keep you here. If you wanted. I could afford to."

"What?" Catherine nearly sputtered with laughter. "A princess in a Lake Michigan two-porched tower? No, thank you, kind sir," she said, "but I think not." She curtseyed.

"I'm serious. Wouldn't it be wonderful to have this to come to, you and I?"

She smiled, shook her head, and ignored his question. "Enough silliness. We'd better get out before we get arrested." She stepped away from Oliver and walked back into the cool blue and green bedroom.

Oliver caught her arm as she crossed toward the door. His eyes held hers. "Let's not hurry away, Cathy. There's magic here, don't you feel it? As though this house has been waiting for us to claim it. Let me hold you, here, where we belong."

She hesitated and then leaned against him, loving the feel of him, loving the moment. "Yes." Moments were all they had. She tipped her head back, her parted lips asking for his.

Gently, so gently, his arms enfolded her. His lips searched hers, found response and became more eager, more demanding.

She pressed against his tall, strong frame, her breasts hurting to be touched, her whole body answering the unspoken question in his. Finally, he turned his head enough to moan, "Cathy? It's time, Cathy. Now?"

"Oh, yes, Oliver..." she whispered. "Yes!"

His fingers fumbled with the back buttons of her dress. She arched out of it, her face dreamy with want, her lips finding his neck, his softly furred chest which she had bared. Together they sank to the honey oak floor, their passion mounting in waves that loosened all their unexpressed longings. All guilt forgotten, their bodies gave and took, took and gave, colored blue and green and gold by the afternoon sun.

6

OLIVIA, 1984

The storm-lashed shore of Lake Michigan wavered through rising heat waves in the distance as Olivia walked slowly toward the point which Tim had said was a mile from Dunes House. "That's the end of the property line, that there point, Miss Livvy." He'd gestured with his gnarled index finger toward a jutting line of dark pines north of Dunes House. "Nothin' much between here and there but trees and beach."

"All that land belongs to this property? Why so much?"

He shrugged. "Came with the place, that's all. Used to belong, before Miss Cathy," his eyes softened as he said her name, "to some people over toward Sheboygan. Collinses, they were. Don't rightly know why they sold. They kept one cottage up in the woods, near the point. Used to visit there once in a while. I don't know they ever use it now, though. Never go up that way anymore."

"Where did my mother find you, Tim?" Olivia asked. "When she bought the place, were you caretaker already, or what?"

"She didn't buy it, you know. He did. For a present. She didn't know he was goin' to. There's a card around here somewheres he gave her on her birthday. No, seems now, thinkin' about it, it was *your* birthday. When you were born, that's it, he deeded it over to Miss Cathy then, I remember now, lock, stock, and barrel, as the sayin' goes." Tim sniffed. "I used to keep an eye on the place before for the Collins people. Came out from town coupla times a week is all. Then, when Miss Cathy took it over, she moved me in over the garage, and I been here ever since." His pale eyes drifted into reminiscence. "Never did partic'ly like that Collins bunch. They didn't care much about the place. I had to do a lot of fixin' at first for Miss Cathy, but I was young then, could do it. She wanted it nice. Him, too."

Olivia frowned. *So my father bought this place for Catherine, without her knowing, and then deeded it to her when I was born. But why? The farm was too demanding for them to leave it for any length of holiday. Of course, he could have gotten help to come in and do the chores. But Tim said they stopped bringing me to Dunes House when I was "just a little thing." I do remember times (How many?) when Dad said, "Your mother's gone for a little, Chicken."*

Funny, how things like the memory of a nickname came popping back to her out of nowhere. Olivia hadn't thought of Levi's pet name for her in years. "We'll be just fine, won't we, Chicken?" he'd say, swinging her up on his broad shoulder.

"Where did Mama go, Daddy?"

"Just away to rest."

"Where, though?"

"Never you mind, Chicken. When she comes back, we'll have a party."

And they always did—good food and a feeling of well-being. Her mother's eyes would sparkle, and she would reach out and touch Levi's arm with such tenderness the child shivered with happiness to see. Of course, Dunes House must have been where Catherine went. Alone? To write her poetry? There were reams of poems in the storeroom boxes, about everything, about nothing. Olivia hadn't yet gone through them.

The mystery was all so puzzling. And there must have been times Levi and Catherine had gone off together, but Olivia couldn't remember those. Certainly, they hadn't come here often enough to make owning and paying taxes on a place like this worthwhile.

"Ow!" Lost in her thoughts of the past, Olivia caught her foot in a driftwood root that stuck up out of the beach. She sprawled, spraddle-legged, on the wet sand.

"Oh! Look where you're going, Livvy Hobart," she muttered to herself, rubbing a skinned spot on her ankle and inspecting it for blood.

"Or else go where you're looking," said a deep, amused voice behind her.

Startled, Olivia stared up into a weather-burnt face framed by a curly, reddish beard that caught sunlight. Collar-length, windblown hair nearly matched the beard. He wore jeans rolled to muscular calves above bare feet. His lightweight plaid shirt, open almost to his waist, revealed a furred chest, and he carried an interesting conglomeration of driftwood under one arm. "Help you up?" he offered, extending his free hand.

Olivia grasped it and felt abrasive wet sand between their palms before brushing hers off on the legs of her tan knit slacks. "Where did you come from? I didn't see you."

"Because I was following you." He grinned, his teeth flashing through the beard. "Looking for driftwood," he explained, lifting the sticks under his arm.

"For burning?" Olivia studied him. He couldn't be much older than Pamela, she thought. Very attractive, the picture of outdoors health.

"Burning? No." Extremely light blue eyes, contrasting sharply with his sun-darkened features, were obviously entertained as he surveyed her costume, especially her city shoes. "Those aren't the proper clothes for beach walking, lady. No wonder you fell."

Feeling badly overdressed, Olivia looked down. "Probably not. But I don't have any like yours." Blue jeans? Olivia Hobart had never owned a pair.

"You must be from the big house." He jerked his head back towards the way she had come. "Visiting?"

"Sort of. You might say that." Olivia fell into step beside him, and they walked together down the beach, he stopping momentarily to pick up interesting bits of wood. "If you don't burn that wood, what do you do with it?"

"I'll show you, if you want." He flipped a final stick from the sand with the flourish of a sturdy bare toe. "Beautiful! Just the piece I've been looking for." He started toward the wooded area at the end of the sand beach. "Here, carry some?" He offered her part of his unwieldy bundle, and she tucked the sticks under her arm as they walked toward the point.

"You might tell me your name. Mine's Olivia Hobart."

He smiled, hesitating for a moment. "Would you believe Heath?"

Olivia smiled back. "After these past few days, I would believe almost anything. First or last?"

"First. Heath Collins. My grandfather one time owned the place you're staying."

Olivia stopped. "Oh. How interesting."

"Isn't it." She caught derisive bitterness in his voice. "And here I am, plucking a living out of the very sand he sold." They had come to an opening off the beach where an overgrown path led up the wooded bluff. He bowed with a flourish and waved Olivia into bushes that were just beginning to show green. A few scant leaves dotted birch branches overhead, their shadows dappling the underbrush. Here and there a late spring anemone had pushed its way through the thick leaf mold underfoot.

"Come into my parlor—"

She grinned and finished, "Said the spider to the fly? Try to stop me. I want to ask you some questions."

As she preceded Heath Collins up the narrow, wooded path,

Olivia thought of and discarded question after question. Would he know any of the history of Dunes House? It was evident he wasn't happy that his grandfather had not kept the property. Maybe—she caught her breath—maybe the "Danger! Get Out!" note was from this man?

"Ouch! Hey, let go." Olivia backed up to pull a grasping, many-thorned briar out of her knit pants, grimacing at the sharp prick in her thigh.

"Blackberries. Last year's stalks. Mean, aren't they?" Heath commented. "They're not about to let you invade their domain without telling you how they feel about it." He stopped and waited as she disengaged another of last season's brittle canes. "Don't you know they'll let go more easily if you say 'please?'"

"Oh, sure." Olivia raised her eyebrows and said in a falsetto, "Please, Mr. blackberry bush, please let me go."

"See? Wasn't that easier?" Heath said as she pushed the briar away. "You can't rule nature by force. You have to give it a chance to move over."

"Huh." Olivia proceeded up the path that wound to the top of the bluff overlooking the water. At the summit, she saw a small, obviously old log cabin, unpainted, the outer wood grey-white from years of exposure to Wisconsin weather. Unlike most original log buildings, this one had a high roof line, with a whole wall of tall windows facing the lake and reflecting the shifting blues of sky and water. There was little cleared space; the building seemed to have grown out of the underbrush, like the birch and scrub oaks around it. Enchanted, Olivia stopped. "How very—"

"Prosaic?" Heath finished, stopping beside her. His eyes met hers briefly, as though wary of the label she might put on his piece of the world.

"Oh, no! Charming, maybe?"

"Maybe." He studied the building as though he hadn't looked at it for some time. "Funny how you don't notice things after a while. You stop looking, I guess." He walked around Olivia and with a bare foot pushed open a heavy, iron-hinged door. "Come on in. It ain't much, but it's home."

Olivia hesitated momentarily. Was she crazy, following this attractive, personable stranger into this remote cabin? She stared at him, and a surprising, definitely sensual thrill ran through her body. She almost laughed aloud at herself. *I'm probably almost old enough to be his mother.*

"Well? What are you waiting for?"

"I'm not sure. I-I don't know you."

"Never will, either, if you don't start now." Heath jerked his head toward the door. His grin was contagious, and she met it with her own as she stepped over the threshold.

"You live here full time? I mean year-round?"

"I do now. It's a fairly recent development. Used to be just summers." He dropped his load of driftwood on the floor in front of the mammoth fieldstone fireplace dominating the division between two rooms. She piled her armful on top of his.

"You don't lock your cabin when you leave?"

"Lock it?" He chuckled. "What would I lock it for? There's no one around for miles, except for the place you're at. And nothing valuable to steal, anyway."

Olivia looked around the cabin's large room which ran across the whole lake side of the building and extended more than halfway back. The front many-paned window wall facing the water ran floor to ceiling with no curtains to block the spectacular view. The woods between the cabin and the water were cleared away just enough to show the tops of lower trees, the lake, and the distant horizon. Behind her, the wall was more than half covered by a stone fireplace, open from both front and back.

"Central heating, so to speak," Heath said, following her gaze. "Very modern, you know. That's my bedroom beyond."

If he wanted a reaction to that, he wasn't going to get one.

"Oh. Where do you cook?"

"Aha. One of my few conveniences. Look." He walked to the side of the fireplace and lifted a heavy, wooden cutting board from a counter to reveal two gas burners. "Bottle gas. Runs the refrigerator, too, such as it is. I never had electricity brought back here. Too far from the main line, and I don't need it anyway." He lit a burner and put a battered copper teakettle over the flame.

"You burn lamps?" Olivia asked, her eyes wide, for the first time noticing three smoky glass chimneys lined up on the heavy oak mantle. "I didn't think anybody did that anymore."

"Yep."

"Well." Dubious, Olivia shook her head. "I suppose you get used to it, smoke and all."

"You do. They're not that bad, and it's a cozy light. Comforting, compared to neons. How about coffee? I make nothing but the best instant."

"I'd love some," she said. "Old Tim Ryan brews a boiled potful every morning that I swear is either going to put curl in my hair or kill it from the roots up. I don't know which, yet."

"Old Tim." Heath chuckled as he measured dark crystals into heavy mugs. "Once in a while he used to walk up this way when I was here on vacation. I always thought he was keeping an eye on what I was doing, but I haven't run across him now for a long time. Must be at least a couple of years. I think he probably believes the cabin is empty."

The kettle emitted the beginnings of a shrill whistle. He stirred steaming water into the cups and handed one to her.

"What a distinctive mug. Handmade?"

"Yes, Ma'am. Right over there." He pointed to a potter's wheel standing in the corner near the large window.

"So you're a potter. I should have guessed, eventually, from this room, shouldn't I?" A number of clay pieces in stages of construction were scattered nearby. "But don't you need electricity for that?"

"See the balance wheel underneath? Works just wonderful with only one foot and strong leg muscles."

Olivia cradled the warm mug with both hands as she curled her tongue around the full richness of the coffee. "What about a kiln? You must need electricity to fire."

"I keep one in town. It's only about ten miles to Bayshore. I have a friend there who lets me use his electricity in return for using my kiln when he wants. He's a potter, too."

"So, what do you do with the driftwood?"

Heath picked up the centerpiece from the low, rough-surfaced hand-hewn coffee table. Gnarled and grey-white, the driftwood was pocked with open knotholes. A small, self-satisfied red ceramic snake slithered along one of the curves; a glazed chipmunk peeked from one of the knotholes through curling bunches of shaped and shaded ceramic oak leaves. He handed it to Olivia.

She turned it, sensing his creativity. "How original! And charming! Do you sell many of these?"

"All I can make, usually. Finding the right piece of wood is the hardest part. The season along the shore here starts in a couple of weeks, and I need to have plenty of stock. Otherwise," he shrugged carelessly, grinning, "I starve."

"Where do you market?"

"Anywhere I can find an outlet. Actually, not to overdo the modesty, I'm quite well known around these parts." He wasn't boasting, Olivia realized. Just stating the facts.

"I believe it." She ran a finger along the smooth snake's back. "Working with clay was something I was always going to learn."

"Seriously? I could show you, let you get the feel of it. It's wonderful. Natural, alive."

"Sometime when you aren't too busy I really would like to try." She placed the piece back onto the table. "I wasn't fooling when I said I'd like to ask you some questions."

He smiled and sat down on a low hassock across from her, leaning forward, his elbows on his knees. The heavy mug seemed tiny in his large hands. "Ask away. Of course you know the rules: asking doesn't demand an answer. That is, if I don't choose to divulge, I won't."

"Fair enough." Olivia traced the edge of her cup with her index finger. "What do you know about Dunes House? Did your grandfather ever say much about it? Do you know anything about the people who bought it from him?"

"Not much. Why? Are you a CIA spy checking on your hosts, or what?"

"My hosts?" Olivia frowned. "Oh, I see. Bad taste to ask questions? Well, I'm—"

Her voice faded as she noticed a large hammer lying across the edge of the rough table and her mind replayed the surreptitious tap-tapping that had awakened her the night before. She remembered the fear hovering under her skin to raise gooseflesh on her arms. She shivered. *What do I know about this young, winsome Paul Bunyan? Perhaps he sent the note. Perhaps he was the person with the hammer. Perhaps he knows about the emeralds and has been hunting for them.* "Well," she finished lamely, "perhaps you're right. I shouldn't ask."

Later, after finishing her supper, a solitary meal of canned noodle soup, Olivia took her coffee onto the lower screened porch, wondering whether she should have confided in Heath Collins about her mother's will, the emeralds, the note, and her fears. She shuddered, thinking of the malice behind the "DANGER! GET

OUT!" message. It would be nice to have somebody to talk to who was outside of all that intrigue. But maybe he wasn't.

Maybe he was holding a grudge because his grandfather hadn't kept Dunes House for him. It certainly was more elegant than the rough log cabin where he lived.

What an interesting man, and so attractive. Tall, muscular. And that smile—Olivia flushed, embarrassed. How utterly ridiculous! Heath Collins couldn't be much more than thirty or thirty-one, probably a good eleven or twelve years her junior!

What was it they said about older women and younger men? She shook her head, smiling, dazed at even the idea of herself with a man other than Bert. Some of her friends made no attempt to hide their satisfaction with liaisons apart from their husbands. Olivia didn't consider herself a prude. There had, for her, simply been no need.

Or, she asked herself truthfully, had there simply been no opportunity? Her mind returned to Heath Collin's mouth surrounded by his soft beard and mustache, and she wondered what it would be like to be kissed, to be held in those muscled arms close to that hard woodsman's body.

"Silly!" she chided herself out loud and deliberately thought of Bert and Pamela. I ought to go into town and call them, she thought, but in the same instant knew she wouldn't for at least a few more days. What could she tell them? That somebody wanted her out of the house? That she was no closer to unraveling her mother's mystery than she'd been when they left, and after all, that was why she was here. Nor was she any closer to making up her mind what to do about Dunes House. Every day, she fell more in love with it and the freedom it offered.

Content, Olivia cuddled into the soft cushions on the porch wicker and watched lowering sunshine reflect golden glints on the small waves moving toward shore. Her whole world seemed calm, safe, and too beautiful to be real.

Tim's angular shape suddenly appeared outside the screen. "Miss Livvy," he said, "I'm drivin' inta town to see that John Wayne movie. Want to ride along?"

"Movie?" Olivia had almost forgotten there were such things. "No, thanks, Tim." She smiled. "I have some reading I want to do. Have a good time."

"Yep. Plan to." He paused. "Goin' to stop in to see Emilie Harris, too. Won't be early."

"You old fake! You've got a date." Olivia chortled. "You didn't want me to come along at all, really, now did you?"

Tim assumed a hurt expression. "Now, Miss Livvy, would I of asked you if I didn't mean it?" He pursed his lips. "Emilie's no date. She's just a widow friend. Makes good apple pie." He turned to go. "Anyways, I did ask."

"Anyways, you did," Olivia said, smiling. "See you tomorrow."

Later, as she got ready for bed, Olivia pulled on the top dresser drawer to take out her nightgown. Stuck. She wiggled the handles from side to side, then gave the drawer a sturdy yank. The whole thing flew out. She fell backward across the bed, the drawer on her stomach.

"Well, it really came loose, didn't it?" she muttered, gathering up her spilled lingerie. She lifted the drawer to fit it back into its opening. "What's this?" she said aloud, then laughed at her habit of talking to herself just to hear a voice. She reached into the drawer space and pulled out a large, documentary-sized envelope, yellowed and dusty.

"I feel as though I should ask permission to look," she said. Hearing no thundering, "No!" from the silence around her, she shook the dust off and opened the envelope. With Tim gone to town, the house seemed not only empty, but lonely.

The envelope contained a marriage certificate for Levi Sommers and Catherine Rothe. Olivia slid it back into its case and set it on top of the dresser and put the drawer back where it belonged. "Ah, well, it could have been something to help with the mystery," she told her reflection in the mirror. "But is it? No. Just an ordinary marriage certificate, properly signed and all, and you knew they were married all the time."

She pulled the paper from the envelope again and looked at the signatures. Levi's was carefully straight and proper; Catherine's a little more feminine but just as painstakingly penned.

Olivia involuntarily sucked in her breath. The date was August 5, 1938.

"Why, that can't be right!" she exclaimed. She sat down on the bed, tucking her feet which were suddenly cold underneath her, and studied the paper. "They always celebrated their anniversary on June 5. I know they did."

It was well past midnight when Olivia turned off the light beside her bed and tried to sleep, but the conflicting date on the marriage certificate kept bobbing up before her.

If it was true her parents actually married in August of 1938, and she had been born in March of 1939, which was a fact, then she had been conceived sometime in June, certainly more than a month before their wedding.

It seemed unbelievable that of all the people she had ever met, Levi and Catherine Sommers would have had to get married. Levi was so utterly good, so—so upstanding. And her mother, well! Olivia simply could not picture her mother, so proper as she'd known her even until her dying day, wantonly making love without the blessing of the marriage ceremony. Suddenly, Olivia remembered how understanding Catherine—and even Levi— had been when Olivia and Bert had broken the news of Pamela's impending birth, far more compassionate than Olivia had expected, or even hoped. Certainly, Catherine had understood, and now Olivia knew why.

"How little we really know," Olivia muttered, climbing into bed.

She was finally drifting off to sleep when the sound came again, forcing her awake to stare wide-eyed into the dark. This night, there was no illumination; blackness swarmed in on her as fear prickled the back of her neck.

Tap-tap. A pause. *Tap-tap-tap.*

It seemed to come from somewhere underneath the house. Carefully, Olivia threw back the covers. Making no sound, she pulled on the robe lying on the foot of her bed and thrust her feet into soft slippers.

Tap-tap.

She wished she could remember hearing Tim's old pickup come back from town, but either he hadn't come home yet, or she'd been dozing and hadn't heard him. She would quietly get to the kitchen and pull on the rope to signal him in his room above the garage. She would wait until he came, and they would hunt for the sound together. He would bring a flashlight, surely.

Holding her breath, she slipped down the broad oak stairs to the living room, blindly feeling her way so not to bump any furniture. Stealthily, she moved past the dining room table and chairs—God, it was dark!—and through the door to the kitchen.

The tapping was louder down here; it definitely came from below. The basement door from the kitchen was always bolted, Olivia knew, because she bolted it herself. But there were two cellar doors outside the house leading directly into the basement.

She felt her way to the pull by the back door and gave it two sharp tugs. She didn't know whether or not it sounded in Tim's rooms, nor was there any way to know whether Tim was even there. Quietly, she slid the back door lock open.

Tap. Tap. No doubt about it. It had to be a hammer, wielded with caution by a human hand.

Holding her breath, Olivia felt her way to the basement door, and ran her fingers over the bolt. It was securely closed. She let her breath out, relief surging through her body. Then she realized the tapping had stopped, and there had been movement beyond the door. She strained to hear. Nothing.

An involuntary "Oh!" escaped from Olivia as the back door burst open and the flick of the light switch snapped the room into brilliance. She clutched her robe to her neck.

"What's the matter!" Tim Ryan demanded. His work jacket was thrown over a white calf-length nightshirt, his bony, haired legs thrust into worn scuffs, his grey hair askew. "You pulled the bell."

"That noise. The one I told you about, it was coming from the basement. Just now."

Tim, squinting in the light, stepped to the basement door and bent his head near the crack. "Don't hear anything."

"Not now. There was movement down there, though. I heard it."

"Imagination, Miss Livvy. Bet anything." Tim turned narrowed eyes to her. "Maybe the water heater cooling down or somethin' like that. Now you go on back to bed. Tomorrow we'll go down and look things over. Not 'til tomorrow."

"But, Tim—"

"Tomorrow, I said." He went to the back door and opened it. "Ain't doin' no explorin' in my nightshirt." He pulled the door shut behind him with a smart click.

In the morning, Olivia opened her eyes reluctantly. She was exhausted from spending most of the night hours listening for sounds from under the house; it had been almost daylight before she finally dropped off to sleep. She'd heard nothing more except the ordinary creakings of an old house and the refrigerator starting now and then.

She rolled her head around on her neck and stretched to relieve the ache in her shoulders. The house seemed unusually quiet. Almost every morning she heard Tim's shuffling steps in the kitchen under her bedroom. She reached for her robe and slippers, missing the pungent, acrid smell of Tim's potent morning coffee.

The kitchen was empty; the coffee pot still clean and sitting on the counter beside the sink. Olivia started to fill it herself, stopped, and tilted her head. What was that?

She turned, listening, her glance focusing quickly on the open bolt on the basement door. She had left it locked last night, she knew she had.

The eerie sound came again, louder. She dropped the coffee pot into the sink with a clatter, ran to the basement door, and thrust it open. She fumbled for the light switch and gasped as it illuminated an angular shape sprawled awkwardly at the bottom of the stairs.

"Tim! Oh, Tim, what happened?" Another ragged moan escaped from him as Olivia hurried down the steps. She barely caught herself against the wobbly wooden railing as the third stair step turned underfoot, throwing her weight off balance and nearly sending her down on top of him. She caught her breath and continued down, holding her knit robe up to keep it from catching on the rough cellar steps.

Gently, Olivia turned the old man over, careful not to move him more than necessary. His face was paler than ever, but his eyelids flickered and opened.

"Don't know…what…happened…" He stopped, breathing hard. "Came…down…to look for…"

"Don't talk, Tim. Rest."

"Must…have…bumped my head. I'm all…right. Just a little…shook up." He moved his head cautiously from left to right.

"Don't move." Olivia walked around the side of the stairs, reaching up to touch the loose step. "I know what that noise was now. Look at this! The stair is loosened. Someone had to be down here, I *knew* it."

Tim began to gather himself together, his long legs carefully bent, his arm out against the rough stone wall to steady himself. He heaved his body to the bottom step where he sat for a moment with his head in his hands.

"Are you sure you didn't break anything, Tim?"

"No. No, Miss Livvy. I'll be just fine." His voice was stronger now. "I'll fix that step. Right this morning. Wonder how it come to be loose."

Frowning, Olivia looked at him, her eyes wide. "I told you. I heard the noise. Someone loosened it."

Tim got up slowly and came around the side of the open stairway. He examined the faulty step, shaking his head. "Damnedest thing," he muttered. "Looks like the nails just come out."

"Oh, no they didn't. You *know* they didn't."

Tim didn't seem to hear her. "See? There they lay, the nails, right down on the floor. Musta just worked loose, somehow, old house settlin', I guess."

"Tim. I think we should call the police."

He turned to her so quickly she involuntarily stepped back. "No. Out here it'd be the sheriff, and he's no use atall. Now you listen! Don't you worry about nothin', hear? I'll fix that there step right this morning. I'm keepin' care of this place just like I always did for Miss Cathy. Ain't no harm going to come, not over my dead body." He pushed past her and labored up the stairs, muttering.

Olivia drew her robe closer. *Dead body* rang through her head, along with *Danger! Get Out!*

"Stop it, Olivia Hobart," she said aloud. Her words echoed off the uneven rock walls. "This is 1984;, this is not some house in a Victorian novel, and you are a sensible person. Go get dressed."

Bayshore in April looked like any other small lakeshore tourist area, thought Olivia. The snow was gone, but the winter litter scattered on the damp ground hadn't yet been picked up by the one street cleaner the village owned. The ordinance prohibiting unleashed dogs, which would be strictly enforced come tourist season, seemed to be presently ignored, and the main street was a place to be explored by any loose canine whose nose led him there. A chill wind off the lake water whipped Olivia's pants legs as she descended from Tim's ancient pickup to walk to the phone booth at the edge of the small lakeshore park.

"I'll be over there, to the genr'l store." Tim pointed to the end of the block. Olivia nodded as he revved up the clattering motor and rattled away.

She pulled the booth's winter-stiff door closed, shutting the wind out and the chill in. It should be early enough in Portland that Bert would still be at home. She shivered as she listened to the operator dial the number and heard the clicks and humming that would connect her to another world, the safe and ordinary cocoon from which she had so recently emerged. She tried to picture the phone in her kitchen's breakfast nook and surprised herself by not being able to bring it to mind. It was as though she had been away for years, not days.

"Yeah!" Bert's voice belted into her ear. Olivia flinched.

"Don't yell, Bert. You're supposed to say hello," she said. "Are you mad at something?"

"Livvy!" Bert brought his voice down to a listenable level. "Sorry. You just called at a bad time. Your daughter just burnt my eggs to a crisp in your best frying pan and," he coughed, "the smell in here is terrible."

Olivia smiled and tried to keep the amusement out of her voice. "I'm sorry."

"You ought to be. If you were here where you belong, this wouldn't have happened."

That was true, probably. "Well, I'm not, am I?"

"You sure as hell aren't."

"Look, Bert. I didn't call you to get sworn at."

"I hope you called to tell me when to pick you up at the airport." Bert sounded a little mollified. "I'm sorry I yelled. It comes from eating all the cinders I've had lately. Pam has burned everything she got her hands on, and I'm getting tired of it."

"You've only been home a few days. For heaven's sake, give her a chance."

"A chance?" Bert lowered his voice. "You know, I've been thinking. I should have left her with you. There's no telling what could happen to a dummy like her, alone."

"Bert! What a terrible thing to say. You can't talk about her like that. What if she heard you?"

"Ah, she's out of earshot. I'm serious, though. You know I can't stay home and babysit Pam like you've always done."

There was resentment in his voice when he said "Pam" that carried over the miles of telephone wire. Olivia frowned. This was a new side of Bert. Or maybe it had always been there, and she'd not noticed? He went on. "I don't know what she does all day. Goes to the park, she says. Well, you know, anything could happen in a park in a town as big as this. I tell you, it makes me uncomfortable."

"You're overreacting. Relax. Let her learn how to be alone." Her words sounded funny even to herself. When had she ever let Pamela learn to be alone?

"Well, that's enough about *her*." Again Olivia picked up the scorn in his voice. "When are you coming home? Have you answered your silly questions," his sneer was distinct through the wire, "well enough to forget this foolishness and get back here where you belong? Find those emeralds?" He laughed. "Probably about as big as pinheads, I bet."

Olivia took a deep breath. "Has it ever occurred to you that I might belong in some place other than Bert Hobart's kitchen?"

"Oh, God, that kind of talk again. Olivia, will you please come to your senses and get your ass home?"

Why had she bothered to call? She knew the answer—guilt for leaving Pamela, for messing up Bert's ordered life.

"Wait a minute! No, I haven't answered the questions. I've got more. And there's something queer going on at the house. I got a threatening note, Bert. It said 'Danger! Get Out' in big letters."

Bert snorted. "I don't doubt that. Your old Tim Ryan would love it if you got out and left the place to him. He thinks it's his anyway."

"I don't think it was from Tim. I don't know who it was from. And then somebody loosened a stair in the basement, and Tim fell."

There was a silence while Bert digested her words. Then, suspicious, he asked, "Did you see him fall?"

"No. I found him lying on the cellar floor."

"So he loosened a stair and laid down on the floor, and you think somebody else did it. Scare tactics, Livvy. Come away from there before one of his tricks backfires and you get hurt."

That could be true, Olivia thought, if Tim really wanted her out.

"How much longer, Livvy, huh? I hate having you gone. Messes everything up. And I tell you again, I don't like having Pam alone so much. You," not we, Olivia noticed, "haven't raised her to be responsible enough. She's either going to get lost or burn the house down while I'm not looking."

"Then we'll have the insurance, and we can move here," Olivia said. "Don't be a worrywart, Bert. I have to stay a little longer. I haven't found a clue to the emeralds, and there's too much unanswered here yet. Get this, this will surprise you: my mother was pregnant before they got married."

There was a humming, crackling silence. Then, "Your mother? I don't believe it. She never did anything improper in her whole life. I don't think she ever even farted when she was alone in the bathroom."

"Bert! For heaven's sake."

"Sorry. Look, I'm going to be late, and I've got to air out this kitchen before I leave. Besides, this is costing a fortune this hour of the day. Hurry up and come home."

Olivia sighed. "Yes, Bert. Listen, I'll call again in a few days."

"Don't call, just come home."

Olivia could hear some murmuring in the background. "Is that Pam? Tell her hello."

"All right. I'm not paying for her to talk gobbledegook. G'bye." There was a click.

"Bert!" Olivia stared at the humming telephone and realized she was freezing. She hung up and wrenched open the door, her mind assimilating the anger and resentment Bert had shown toward Pamela, along with his not caring about what he said in her presence. Why hadn't it been noticeable before? *Because I always was there, a buffer?*

Her thoughts swirling, she walked slowly down the street toward the general store. *I resent her too, don't I? I always have. I've kept it hidden from myself as well as from her. And overcompensated in a million ways.* Olivia took a deep breath of the wind-fresh air as she absentmindedly scuffed at a piece of paper and watched it flop across the street. And, God, yes, it was terrific to be away from Pam, let Bert take the mother hen part in the play. *But I never hurt her feelings, never. I always made sure she was protected, didn't I?*

Olivia turned into the general store just as Tim came out. "I won't be long, Tim. I just want to pick up a few groceries."

"No hurry. Got to stop at the hardware. Meet you at the truck."

A half hour later, as they bumped along the road back to Dunes House, Tim said, "Your Bert gettin' along okay? And the girl?"

Olivia sighed. "As well as could be expected, I guess. Bert's not happy. I've never left them alone before."

Tim looked at her out of the corner of his eye. "Time you did, then. Strikes me as the kind of man wants things his way."

Olivia made a derisive sound. "You've said it." She was quiet for a minute, remembering Bert's comments about Tim and the note.

"Some men ain't fit to live alone, you know…" Tim let his voice drift off into the motor's hum.

What's there to answer to that? She changed the subject. "I trust you, Tim."

His head jerked around, and he fixed her with a penetrating look. "I should hope so," he stated.

If he hadn't written the note himself, he didn't know what it said. "I mean, I think we should talk to the sheriff."

Tim's reddened knuckles turned white as he gripped the steering wheel and stared straight ahead. "The sheriff? Why? What for?"

"Because I'm frightened."

"Of what?"

"That letter you gave me the other day? The one you said was in the mailbox?"

"Yeah? What about it?"

"You don't know what it said?"

He glared at her. "You think I read your mail?"

"No, no, I don't. I mean, it was a threatening note, and—"

"Threatening!" He slowed down, looking at her briefly before he turned his attention back to driving. "What'd it say?"

"It said, 'Danger. Get out.'"

Tim rolled down his window and spat onto the road. "Whyn't you tell me before! Tell you, Miss Livvy, something queer's been goin' on ever since you come to Dunes House. Never had nothin' like it before. That note what you were lookin' for the other day?"

Olivia nodded. "That's right. Because it disappeared. I threw it in the wastebasket on the porch, and it was gone the next morning. Whoever sent it took it back."

"Then there ain't nothing to show any sheriff, is there?" Deftly, Tim steered around a pothole but hit a second one that shook Olivia's whole system. "Danger, you say? And get out?"

"And that funny pounding at night to loosen that stair, and your fall—oh, Tim! I've never been threatened before."

Tim scowled. "Scared, are you?"

"Shouldn't I be? But mad, mostly. Who's got the right? That's my house, now. My emeralds, too, when I find them. Do you know about the emeralds?"

Tim stepped on the brake and brought the truck to a jolting halt. "Ain't you got them?"

"You *do* know?"

"Know? Seen 'em more than once. Miss Cathy always wore 'em when she was here. Never took 'em off the whole time. Beautiful! A whole necklace and a bracelet, too. Musta had mor'n a dozen stones, good-sized ones, too, like this." He thrust out a bony hand, pointed to his little fingernail. "About that size. Six-eight, maybe ten on the neckpiece, another half-dozen or so on the bracelet. Color of that green glass in the little bedroom window, you know?" He pulled the truck back onto the road. "Why ain't you got them?"

"Because they're hidden. Somewhere, probably here at Dunes

House. They're mine now if I can find them, but I don't know where to look."

"At Dunes House? You think?" Tim scowled. "And you think that's why somebody wants you out? So they'll get them?"

"Doesn't that make sense? That's why I think we ought to call the sheriff."

Tim made a derisive noise through his lips. "You don't know the sheriff here. Lazy. Spends his time in his office fillin' out papers to send downstate so they'll think he's doin' somethin'. Last year he got re-elected 'cause his relatives live all over the county. Never did nothin' when those kids broke into the summer houses on the shore. You can ask him if you want, but what's he goin' to do anyways? Run around askin' people if they sent you a note? 'Sides," he turned the truck into the drive at Dunes House, "I already fixed that stair step." He pulled the truck to a stop so Olivia could step out onto the cement platform by the kitchen door and stated, "I told you I was keepin' care, Miss Livvy, and I am. Ain't no trouble going to come to you, I'll see to that." He paused and muttered, almost under his breath, "I'll fix him."

Olivia's eyebrows went up and she stopped with one leg out the truck door. "Fix who?"

Tim handed her the bag of groceries. "Whoever's messin' up around here, that's who." He glared. "Never you mind. I got some ideas." He stepped on the gas and rumbled down toward the garage, leaving Olivia on the step staring after him.

"Whoever was messin' up around here?" It was possible Tim knew a lot more about the note, the stair, and the emeralds than he was admitting.

Groceries put away, Olivia pulled a pair of jeans and a man's flannel shirt out of the plain paper bag from Bayshore's general store, along with a pair of blue canvas deck shoes. Heath Collins had been right about not having the proper clothes for beach walking, and she was going to do a lot of that. In fact, as soon as she got dressed, she was going to walk right up the shore to his cabin.

Olivia had made up her mind that it wasn't enough to talk with Tim; he was either too stubborn to admit something was going on, or was bound to keep her in some kind of mystery about it. And he had certainly left her no doubt he would resent it if she talked to the "lazy, no-count" sheriff.

Well, then, she would take another tack. There was something here which didn't jibe with Tim's honesty and loyalty about his "Miss Cathy." It was as though there were something or someone he must protect at the same time he stopped the "messin' up" around Dunes House.

She thrust her legs into the stiff denim jeans and pulled them up around her waist. A little large, a little baggy around her bottom, but they would be comfortable once the sizing washed out. The shirt was large across her shoulders, and the tail six inches too long; she tucked it in and rolled up the pants legs. Well, she wouldn't be a fashion plate, but it wouldn't matter a whole lot whether the blackberry bushes along Heath Collin's path wanted to move over or not. She laughed at her reflection in the mirror: a greying matron in her very first pair of blue jeans and an oversized plaid flannel shirt. Was that really Olivia Hobart, head of a hospital auxiliary in Portland, Oregon? The secretary of the symphony fund drive? The publicity person for the Cerebral Palsy Telethon? They'd never believe her back home.

"Goin' for a walk?" Tim hollered at her from under his old pickup as she passed him on the way to the steps leading down to the beach. "Nice day for it."

She peered under the bumper. "What are you doing under there, Tim?"

"Jest wirin' up the tailpipe. 'Bout to fall off. Rattled all the way home from town this mornin.' You be back for lunch?"

"Probably. But you don't have to cook for me, you know, Tim."

"I know. But it ain't no more trouble to heat two cups of Campbell's than one, is it?"

She smiled. "I guess not. See you later, I don't know just when."

He scooted back to stick his head out from under the truck. "I'd be careful, if I were you, you go down by that old cabin. Might be some bum hangin' around there. Believe it's been empty a coupla years now."

"Oh, but it's not. In fact, that's where I'm going. The grandson of the Collins people lives there. He makes pottery on his wheel. Didn't you know?"

"No." Tim's pale eyes widened. "Thought he went back to the city with the rest of them. You met him, you say?"

She nodded. "He seems all right. Said he'd show me how to throw a pot."

Tim shook his head, making a tsking sound with his tongue. "Never did like the Collins bunch. 'Course, he might be the best of the litter. I'd be careful what you say to him, Miss Livvy. Might be he's tryin' to figure a way to get his hands on his old grandpa's property."

"Oh, Tim." She wasn't going to admit the thought had crossed her mind, too. "Well, see you later." She turned to go.

"Yep. Jest be careful what you say. Y'know…about what's goin' on here."

She stopped. "Just what *is* going on here, Tim?"

He had slid back under the truck; his voice echoed against the metal undercarriage. "Not sure. Might be good if you went home for a little, Miss Livvy."

"Home?" She squatted down to see his face. "Why?"

He didn't turn toward her but kept working a piece of stiff wire with his fingers. "Reasons." He grunted as he snipped off the end of the wire. "Make your Bert happy, for one thing. See how that girl of yours is gettin' along by herself. Give me some time here, for another."

"Time for what?"

He still didn't look at her. "Nothin' to worry you about, Miss Livvy. Jest a few things to clear up." He gave the wire a final twist. "Yep. Believe you ought to go home."

Olivia walked slowly down the steps that led to the boathouse on the beach front. *Believe you ought to go home,* Tim had said. What did he have in mind to "clear up"?

A gull screeched overhead, and Olivia stopped walking long enough to appreciate the effortless flight of white feathers against cloudless azure. What a marvelous world, so different from her Portland closed-in suburban yard. She looked out over the expanse of Lake Michigan blending at the horizon into nearly the same color as the sky. Nothing to mar the beauty of it except a tiny puff of smoke from a far-away freighter heading toward Chicago.

How she loved being here. She took a deep breath, filling her lungs with the lake air and its bouquet of wet sand, water, and drying driftwood. Go back home? The very thought of going back even for a short time, seemed all wrong. Yet there was Pam, alone all day and Bert not being sympathetic to her...

Olivia peered into the boathouse through a dusty windowpane. It would be fun to take a rowboat out on a quiet day like this. How long had it been since she'd rowed a boat? Years.

She rubbed the pane of glass with the elbow of her shirt.

There was some kind of small boat in there. She tried the door. It swung open on complaining rusty hinges.

A small rowboat lay on one side of the room, a pair of oars across the seats. It looked seaworthy enough; she would have to take it out for a row one calm evening.

"Oh." In the dim light she noticed a cot along one wall. An old army blanket lay across it with the indentation of a head upon a dingy pillow. A glass half-full of what looked like flat beer tilted on the frayed seat of a cane-bottomed chair; a rumpled copy of a girlie magazine lay open next to it. A paper plate with what looked like well-gnawed chicken bones lay halfway under the edge of the cot. Tim's hangout? Not likely. What would he need with this when he had his own comfortable place over the garage?

Frowning, Olivia backed out of the musty boathouse, a shiver running down her spine, and pulled the creaking door closed behind her.

As she strode down the wave-washed sand toward Heath Collin's cabin, she breathed more freely. The boathouse wasn't an old man's hangout. Was it possible Tim knew somebody was staying there and even protected who it was? Someone who, or the two of them together, possibly, wanted Olivia to "get out?"

Maybe the someone was who Tim wanted time to "clear out," as he'd said. Or had he said "clear up?" She absently scuffed a clam shell ahead of her as she walked. *I'll talk to him when I get back and press him for answers. My mother trusted Tim completely, and until I learn any reason why I shouldn't, I'll trust him, too.*

An interesting piece of driftwood lay at her feet, and she reached down to pick it up for Heath.

"Hallo!"

Olivia looked up to see his hearty wave from the opening at the end of his path. As she walked closer, she warmed to his welcoming smile, noticed how white his teeth looked against his suntanned face, and felt satisfaction in looking at the trim hardness of his body. No soft potbelly on this man. A picture of Bert flashed into her mind, and she laughed out loud, enjoying her foolish physical attraction to Heath. She immediately felt guilty for the thought even though it was, she assured herself, simply a good feeling about a growing friendship.

"Well, you seem to be having a good time all by yourself," Heath greeted her. "What's the big smile all about?"

She handed him the driftwood. "Oh, nothing, really, just enjoying being here, seeing you."

"Okay, lady, keep your secrets. What an interesting piece this is," he said, examining the wood she handed him. "Thanks. Come on up?"

"Only if I won't interrupt your work. I could use a little conversation. Tim isn't much for talking, and what he does say sometimes is things I don't especially want to hear."

Heath raised his eyebrows and stepped aside for her to precede him up the path. "I could believe he's no conversationalist. Never was, as little as I remember of him. What do you mean about things you don't want to hear?"

"Well, for instance," she paused to push a bramble aside, "he thinks it would be good for me to 'go home for a while,' quote, until he, quote 'clears things up.'"

"That sounds portentous. What's to clear up?"

Heath followed her up the path and into the cabin, where she settled herself on the comfortably cushioned couch and waited while he brought two mugs of steaming coffee.

He handed her one, seated himself on a hassock on the other side of a low table, and said, "Well, for someone who could use some conversation—those are your words, remember—you aren't saying very much."

"I was putting my thoughts in order."

"Must be a passel of them to take this long." He smoothed his curly beard. "Something I can help with?" His blue eyes searched hers for a moment, long enough to quicken her breath.

She looked quickly into the dark liquid in her cup. Why not trust him? It would be good to have someone to turn to if something really did happen at Dunes House, if Tim was hurt, or God knew what. "I sort of left you with a false impression last time I was here, Mr. Collins."

"Heath."

"Heath, then." She hesitated. "Well, it all sounds crazy, but I'm going to tell you anyway."

He held up a hand, flat-palmed. "No apologies. Sometimes just talking helps. A false impression? Sounds mysterious. I haven't had a good mystery to think about since last week when something kept stealing the bread scraps I put out for the chippies, and I couldn't get a look at what it was."

"And what was it?"

"A raccoon. Big one. Rastus, I've named him. I've almost tamed him, now. Have to be sure to pull the door closed when I leave, or he comes in and ransacks the whole place. I almost wish I'd never met him." Heath's smile was relaxing. "Now, enough of that. A false impression of what?"

"Me. First, I'm not a guest at Dunes House."

"Is that what they call it now? Nice. Used to be just 'the old Collins' place.' Sorry for interrupting, go on."

"I own it."

"You?" Heath put his mug on the table with a sharp crack. "How did you come by it?"

She told him.

"Well." Heath walked to the window wall where he stood with his hands in his back jeans pockets and stared out over the water. "That's the kind of surprise everybody wishes for, isn't it? A country estate, all wrapped up with a red ribbon. Or the blue cover of a will, in this case." He turned to Olivia, but she couldn't read the expression in his eyes. "And now you're here to take up residence, just like that. Nice."

She hesitated. Did she imagine envy in his voice? "Well, not exactly 'just like that.'" In a rush she told him of sending Bert and Pam home, about the missing emeralds, the threatening note, and its disappearance.

"You're kidding. You're writing a mystery novel and want to see what I think of the plot." Frowning, Heath picked up her coffee mug to refill it.

"No, I'm not kidding," Olivia said, indignant. "Go ahead and make fun of me if you want to, but it all scares the heck out of me. You probably think I'm one hysterical woman, but I'm not." Chin up, she continued her story with the tapping noise and Tim's fall from the loosened step. She finished with, "Heath, Tim loved my mother. Simply adored her. I don't think he would do anything to me because of his memory of her."

"What a story." Heath frowned again. "And you're staying here to solve this mystery about your 'ordinary' but really very extraordinary mother's life?"

"Yes. But it's really more complicated." Olivia moved restlessly and got up to stare out the window toward the water.

"Everything is complicated until you break it down into manageable pieces. Keep talking, and I'll play devil's advocate." He rose and walked toward the counter. "Are you hungry?"

She made a face. "I'm always hungry," she confessed.

"Then while you're talking, I'll put together the most fantastic sandwich you've ever eaten, okay?"

He began to open drawers and cupboards. Olivia went back to the couch, kicked off her shoes, and tucked her feet under her, tailor fashion. "You asked for it."

She told him about Tim's reaction to her suggestion of calling the police and her discovery in the boathouse.

"Bones in the boathouse?" He chuckled, raising his eyebrows. "Now that *does* sound like an Agatha Christie story."

"Doesn't it?" She walked to look over his shoulder. "That looks fabulous. Corned beef?"

He nodded, slicing thin curls. "Cooked on my own little stove with love and lots of peppercorns. Go on with your story."

"I think Tim knows about the boathouse, and I'm sure it's not his mess. I can't picture him drooling over a girlie magazine. His biggest interest in the widow Harris is her great apple pie."

Heath laughed, handing Olivia a small plate with a three-inch high sandwich and a sturdy pottery goblet filled with rich red wine.

She peeked under the dark bread. "Corned beef, tomatoes, lettuce . . . onions . . . what's this, a slice of cucumber? Terrific! Tim was going to 'heat up two cups of Campbell's' but this beats that six ways."

They shared the couch together, their plates on the low rough-hewn table. "Ummmmm. Delightful," Olivia said around a hearty mouthful. "I really came to ask you to show me how to throw a pot if you weren't too busy. I didn't intend to tell you my life story. At least, I don't think I did."

"Is that all of it?"

"Not quite. The way Tim wants me to go home, doesn't it sound like he knows more than he's telling?"

Heath looked thoughtful as he added more mustard to his sandwich. "Maybe. Or he might be fearing for your safety."

"I suppose that's possible. And then, Bert wants me home. You see," Olivia paused, not quite knowing how to explain, "there's Pamela. He doesn't understand her. She's never been alone before . . . "

"I hear a voice full of guilt. Am I right in guessing she's handicapped in some way?"

Startled at his perception, and relieved, she nodded. "Retarded. Pretty severely. And . . . I've protected her too much, too long."

"A natural reaction, I would imagine. Tell me more about the emeralds."

Was there more than idle curiosity in his questions? "I really don't know. No clues. I've looked through some of my mother's stuff, old notes, old poems, nothing. If whoever's trying to scare me wants me gone so they can search Dunes House, why didn't they do it before I got here?"

"Interesting." Thoughtful, Heath rubbed his beard with the palm of his hand. "Most interesting. So you are an heiress. A rich and beautiful lady, jewels and all, with an unfulfilling marriage and a worrisome daughter. How old is she?"

"Twenty-seven."

"Whatever prompted you to let her go now if, as you say, she's been overprotected?"

Shaking her head, Olivia hesitated. "I don't know. I guess the realization that I never really knew my mother has shaken my foundations. I thought she was so prim and proper. Now I find I was conceived before she married. If she's not what I thought …if she kept secrets as big as these forever…then am I what I think? Is anybody? And I find myself doing things, thinking things," she felt a warm flush on her face, "completely contrary to my nature. Or at least I think they are." Her voice ran down as her forehead creased in a puzzled frown.

"Ah. So you're a child of love." Heath's light blue eyes crinkled at the corners. "No wonder you're so easy to be with." He grinned.

She grinned back. "And so are you. Now that we've covered the saga of Olivia Hobart, let's talk about Heath. Why isn't an attractive man like you married? As you can tell, wine loosens my tongue."

"Was. Didn't make it."

"Oh. And you're soured for life?"

He laughed. "Do I look soured? No. Just on 'hold' until the

right woman comes walking up the beach." His eyes held hers for a long moment before he grimaced. "Not overly likely here, but one never knows." He sighed, melodramatic. "When I'm in the city, the ladies flock to me in droves."

"Sure they do. A handsome young, single artist..." The bantering was fun. Olivia had almost forgotten how to banter. With Bert everything was cut and dried, and he was always right. *When did he become what he is? When did I?* "Oh, look, there's a grosbeak!" She went to the window. "There, see?" She pointed to the feathery fronds of a Norway Pine partway down the bluff.

"Beautiful, aren't they?" He came to stand beside her, and Olivia felt an unexpected tingling where his golden-haired arm brushed hers.

She turned to him, her clear hazel eyes wide. "I love it here. I don't want to go back home. Ever." Then she laughed at herself, thrusting her hands deep into the pockets of her still-stiff jeans. "Well. You didn't comment on my costume. Haven't you noticed? I didn't want to be accused of overdressing again."

"I noticed. Perfect. Purchased, no doubt, at the gen'rl store. I have a shirt just like that one. Might even be the same size, from the looks of the shoulders on you." He frowned. "Perhaps Tim's right. Perhaps you should go home. Maybe you could get a better perspective, reassure yourself about your daughter, do some talking with your husband. Then come back, if you choose." He looked steadily at her. "I think I'd like you to choose to come back."

He was so close she could smell his wine-sweet breath. She took a step backward. "But don't you see, that's part of it. I never knew I could make choices. I was who I was, where I was, I thought forever. Now—"

"Now a whole vista's opened up. I know. When my marriage dissolved, when Diana walked out, suddenly I had choices. I haven't regretted the ones I made." His blue eyes probed her inner thoughts. "Now I know I would have regretted not making them."

Olivia looked away to break the physical tension she felt crackling between them. "I'd better go. My gosh, I've kept you from your work for over two hours."

"Not really. I wasn't much in the mood, and I miss conversation, too. Some days I talk out loud just to make sure I still have vocal cords." He pulled open the door. "Come on. I'll walk you down to the beach."

At the water's edge, Olivia held out her hand. "Thanks."

"For what?"

She wanted to reach out and feel the warm softness of his beard in the palm of her hand, but she didn't. *Should I thank him for adding to my life? Waking feelings I thought were for other people, younger people? No.* "For listening, I guess."

"Any time. Any help I can give." His eyes focused on a point behind her. "Say, isn't that old Tim hot-footing it this way?"

"Miss Livvy! Miss Livvy!" Tim's thin, crackly voice wafted to them on the lake breeze as he hurriedly scuffled over the wet packed sand, waving a yellow paper. "Telegram!"

Olivia broke into a run, Heath beside her.

"Thought you should get it soon's they ran it out from town," Tim panted, thrusting the paper at her. "This the Collins boy?" He shaded his faded eyes with a weathered hand. "Ain't seen you for a coupla years or more."

Heath acknowledged his greeting, watching Olivia's face whiten as she read the message.

"Oh, no!" She gasped, turning to Heath, her eyes clouded with anguish. "Bert was right, I shouldn't have let her go, I shouldn't. Pam's been attacked!"

7

"Catherine, Levi Sommers is here to see you." Amy Walker's cheerful voice pulled Catherine from her drowsy half-sleep savoring of yesterday at the beautiful house on the dunes.

Levi? Here? Early Sunday morning? How unusual for him to come unannounced. Perhaps something had happened at the school? "I'll be right down," she called, shrugging into her pale pink robe and thrusting her feet into matching satin slippers. With a quick brush over her long golden hair, she hurried down to the Walker's sunny kitchen. "Levi. Is something the matter?"

His weathered face broke into pleasure as his deep grey eyes caught sight of her. "No, no, Catherine. I know it's forward of me. . ." He held his good felt hat by the brim with both hands. He was dressed neatly in his Sunday-best navy, with a quiet tie and black dress shoes, his grey hair carefully parted. "But I thought, if you haven't any plans, of course, perhaps I could drive you to services, and then we could go for a little ride." He hesitated, his work-solid body tensed for her answer.

Amy Walker's eyes twinkled as she bustled from the sink to the table and placed a full sugar bowl on the checkered blue cloth. "How nice, Levi. And it's going to be a perfect day for just that. I could put up a lunch in no more than a minute. "

Levi's amused glance caught Catherine's; she read "matchmaker" into it before he said, "That's kind of you, Amy, but I brought a lunch. In case."

"Well." Catherine smiled. It was going to be a perfect day for anything out of doors, and there would be no chance to be with Oliver; Sundays were impossibly lonely. "Of course, Levi. I'd love it." She raised both hands to her heavy, loose hair. "But I'll have to dress. Could you come back in a half-hour?"

"No need for that, Catherine." Amy Walker hurried to the stove. "I've just made a pot of coffee. Levi and I will have a cup while he waits." The expression on her motherly face clearly stated her pleasure in fostering Catherine's future, if even only for a day.

Catherine hurried up the stairs. She had planned to walk to services, though the distance was more than a mile. It was nice of Levi to come by; she loved riding in the shiny black surrey behind his matched roans. She reveled in the earthy smell of the horses and the rich jangle of their brass harness fittings moving musically with each step.

She threw off her robe, pausing to study her slim unclothed body in the cloudy mirror on her dresser and to remember Oliver's touch. It would be good to do something, anything, to keep her mind off him, off that magical yesterday on the dunes, off the final, wonderful fulfillment of their love, the anticipation of it only a fraction of its reality. Had loving ever been that way with Joel? If so, she couldn't remember it. No. Not like that.

She cupped her breasts with both hands for just a moment, remembering Oliver's tenderness as he held them in his palms. She stepped into her underthings, chose a soft plaid summer dress fitting for a picnic, yet not too casual for services. She felt light and happy, bubbling with love and sunshine to match the day. Oliver's name sang through her thoughts, through her very being, as she braided her heavy hair into its coronet.

Oliver, Oliver. His very being surrounded her whether she was near him or not.

"Ready." She stepped into the kitchen, her face coloring as she met Levi's obvious pleasure at just seeing her.

"And so you are. So quick. And so pretty." Levi stood and took her arm. "Thank you for the coffee, Amy." He tipped his hat toward Mrs. Walker before jauntily putting it on.

"Oh, Levi, I'm so glad you stopped," she simpered, patting Catherine's arm. "You two have a lovely time, now."

As they walked together into the small white church on top of the hill, Catherine smiled comfortably up at Levi. There was a lot to be said for feeling easy with another. Not that she wasn't easy with Oliver, but there was always the underlying current of sexual tension, the wanting of him and the equal excitement of knowing he wanted her.

The Widow Shimmek nodded with a meaningful look toward one of her friends and whispered just out of earshot something Catherine couldn't hear, but the words weren't necessary. A dark flush spread over Levi's features, and Catherine snuggled just a little obviously against his arm as, conspirators, they grinned at each other.

"Every village has to have one," Catherine whispered, her eyes twinkling.

"A matchmaker? Or a widow?"

"Probably both." Catherine laughed. "Sometimes in the same body. Levi, have you ever thought maybe all these years she's been just waiting for you to ask her to go for a ride after church?"

Levi gave Catherine a sideways, surprised look and then laughed, his strong teeth white against his sun-darkened face. "No. No, Catherine, I never did."

They sat together, her clear soprano and his deep bass blending together over other voices. Catherine's mind was not on the hymns, however; it was on Oliver and the afternoon before.

Could it possibly have been real?

Oliver and Amery sat four rows ahead of Catherine and Levi, Oliver's fair, smooth hair and Amery's, even whiter, making light halos in the dim sanctuary. Bonnie wasn't with them. Catherine's breath caught lightly whenever her gaze fell on Oliver. Was it possible she had actually committed adultery with him and now they were sitting piously here in the same church as though nothing had happened? As though they were not sinners before God? Was Oliver thinking those same thoughts? She lowered her head. Surely, her face must show the effects of them.

"Stand, Catherine." Levi's voice brought her to the present.

"Oh." Catherine almost jumped to her feet; she hadn't even heard the minister.

As they left the sanctuary, Levi said quietly, "A good sermon, Reverend. Thank you."

Pastor Winslow nodded and smiled. "And do you agree, Miss Catherine?" he asked.

"Oh, yes, certainly," she replied, shaking his hand, glad he hadn't ask her any pertinent questions. She hadn't the foggiest notion of what he'd preached about. "It is a beautiful day, isn't it?" she added, thankful the minister was already greeting someone behind her.

She and Levi walked down the church steps to where Oliver and Amery Houle stood on the old stone walk.

"Hello, Miss Rothe," Amery said, peering at her through his thick lenses. He was a smaller, slighter version of Oliver, except for his eyes. Her breath caught in her throat. Was it obvious she had become, in body as well as soul, Oliver's forever?

Consciously keeping her face calm, she held out her hand to Oliver, resisting the impulse to reach up and smooth his fair hair lifting in the summer breeze. "How is your wife, Oliver?"

His eyes windowed yesterday's passion, though his voice was matter of fact. "She's well, thank you. And you, Levi?"

"Just fine. On a day like this, with Miss Catherine at my side, how could I be otherwise?"

Oliver's eyebrows raised, but he kept his voice noncommittal. "Oh? You have plans for the afternoon?" Though he smiled, she felt the tension in his grip.

Levi's voice was kind, almost fatherly. "Only a picnic." He turned to Catherine. "Shall we go?"

"Of course. Have a good day, Oliver." She gave his fingers an impulsive clasp before letting go. "And you, too, Amery." She bent toward him. "Are you going to do something exciting today?"

Amery's pale owl-face stayed sober. "No, I don't think so. We never do, unless with you."

"Why Amery, how nice of you to say that. We'll do something special tomorrow, when we have your lesson, all right?"

He nodded, his expression brightening.

"Come on, Son," Oliver said. "Dinner will be waiting."

As they pulled away, harnesses jangling, Catherine pictured herself riding home with Oliver to the large house on the farm with double silos, to a Sunday dinner which she would prepare with care. Would they do "something exciting" together, were she there instead of Bonnie Houle? It wouldn't matter; just being together would be excitement enough.

She looked back as they rounded the corner onto the main road to see Oliver standing beside his car, staring after them. She lifted her hand in a small wave. He raised his to return the gesture.

After a quiet moment, Levi said, "Now, Catherine, I have a spot picked out that will be perfect."

With a start, she realized that she had completely forgotten Levi; his voice called her to the present.

"You've been woolgathering all morning, and now it's time to come back." Levi smiled, slapping the reins on his horses' shining rumps. "Are your daydreams really all that wonderful?"

"What?" She stared at him, color rising to her hairline. "What do you mean? Why do you ask such a question?" She busied her hands straightening her skirt.

"Because your whole face grew even more beautiful each time you drifted away."

Flustered, she bit her lip, but before she had to answer, he turned the team down a small, almost overgrown path near a quiet brook. "Levi, how lovely!" she exclaimed. "I didn't know this was here."

He leaped down from the surrey with the exuberance of a man half his age and came around to lift Catherine down. "Yes, it is lovely," he said, his gaze soft on her face.

Catherine reached quickly for the picnic basket, handed it to Levi and picked up the blanket. "We're being altogether too serious, Levi, for such a grand day." She spread the blanket under a tree and dropped to her knees to open the basket. "Let's see, now, what you've brought. Smells like chicken." She pulled out a casserole and uncovered it. "And it is. Wherever did you get fried chicken on a Sunday morning?"

His weathered face lit with pleasure as he lowered himself to a tailor's position across from her. "I fried it. I haven't been a bachelor this long without learning how to cook."

"Dill?" she sniffed a crusty wing.

He nodded. "From my garden."

"But Mrs. Smith cooks for you, doesn't she? Couldn't she have made it?"

"Of course. She would have if I'd asked, but I don't have her come on the weekend when her family is all at home. Besides, I wanted to do it myself." He paused, then leaned forward, holding her gaze with his. "You see, Catherine, you are so very special. I wanted to do this for you."

"Oh, Levi. I don't deserve—"

He held up a palm to stop her words. "I've learned people

seldom get what they think they deserve and often don't know what they deserve even when they've been given it." He covered her hand with his own, his touch light but firm.

The weeks had been building up to what she knew was coming next. She had thought about it for a long time, but she was still not prepared to deal with the generous love she knew Levi would offer. Love and devotion that included protection, care, and a good living, nearly everything any woman could want. She knew he was going to ask her to share his life, today, probably right after lunch here in this bower of beauty. What would she answer? What *could* she answer?

Catherine kept her eyes on the plate of chicken and potato salad she fixed for Levi and handed it to him without speaking, without looking into his eyes, though she felt his gaze following her every movement. She sensed the beauty of the lacy leaves above her, the sunshine dappling mossy undergrowth, heard the swishing rustle of the creek as it whispered through tall grass at its edge, but it all seemed as if she were watching herself from a great distance. How could she say yes, knowing and loving Oliver Houle, caring more for him than she had ever thought she could care again after Joel?

Joel. Should she tell Levi about Joel? That she was not the virgin he probably thought, that she had born children and buried them? That she had not been married to their father, but only thought she was? That Joel had not been legally free to marry? That he had been her first lover, but after yesterday, not her only one?

No. No, not now, at least not now. *Say something. Anything.* She searched the basket. "Levi Sommers, don't tell me you made this apple pie."

"Oh, yes, but I did," he said, "with my own two hands. Even the crust."

They ate in companionable silence until finally Catherine put down her plate and sighed with content. "Ummm. Delicious." She shook her head and smiled. "Levi, you have made my life so pleasant here. You've taken so many of the worries of the school off my shoulders. Just to know you were watching over the coal supply this past bitter winter was worth more than I can tell you."

"It gave me pleasure, Catherine." His gaze and the low timbre of his voice penetrated the very core of her being. "To know that you were comfortable. I want to see you comfortable for the rest of your life."

Not looking at him, Catherine busied herself putting the picnic things back into the basket.

Leaning forward, Levi tentatively touched her hand. "There's a place I'd like to show you. Walk with me, Catherine."

"Oh, yes, let's." Relieved, Catherine almost jumped to her feet. "But will the horses stay? You didn't tie them."

"Dropping the reins is all that's necessary." Levi stroked one velvet nose and got an answering nuzzle. "They won't move as long as the reins are down."

Catherine stood beside him to scratch one of the horses between its ears. "Such beauty," she said. "How long have you had them?"

Levi's eyes darkened. "Since before my life began," he said, his voice unsteady.

She stared at him, blue eyes wide. "What an odd thing to say."

"Is it, Catherine? Not so, when you know my life began when you came into it. I don't remember much before then."

"You're—why, you're serious!"

"Oh, yes, I'm serious. You've brought sunlight into my life. I measure all my days by whether I will see you and what you will say to me when I do. It matters to me that I do well now and have something to offer you."

"Let's take that walk." Catherine turned and began slowly down the path that followed the bank of the small, whispering creek. A few soft leaves, loosened by the summer breeze, floated down to ride the current. Catherine felt the pain of the day, a June day to remember forever, a declaration of unlimited love from the wrong man.

She slipped her arm through his and changed the subject. "Levi, tell me about yourself. I don't know very much about you at all."

"Anything. Just ask."

"All right. What about your family? Did you always farm? Are you on your father's land? Were you never in love? Did you never want children? Why didn't you marry? Tell me. Let me understand you."

The canopied path was lush, splashed with splotches of midday sunlight. No animals were to be seen in the lazy afternoon; even the birds had quieted.

Levi chuckled. "My, what a lot of questions. Have I loosed a monster?" He tilted his greying head toward her, catching her hand in his own as they strolled along. "Where to start? My father farmed here, and I carried on. Not that I wanted to, at first."

"Did you have brothers? Sisters? Or are you truly alone in the world?" She wished her hand in his could transmit some feeling toward him other than the friendly interest she felt for any acquaintance. He deserved so much more.

"Alone? Not anymore." He patted her hand and moved his own up to hold her arm gently. "I had a brother. He was older, and I thought he would be the one to take the farm. But he died when I was fifteen. Fell under a horse. That's been a good many years ago."

"My sister died when I was eleven. It sounds bad to say so, but sometimes when I look back I realize I wasn't even really sorry for her when she died. I was sorry for *me*."

Levi nodded. "I understand. You had to take over for her, didn't you? I didn't want to farm, either, but I had to. Aaron's death made it expected of me. There was no choice."

"And are you sorry?"

"Not now. Now that you're here."

"Levi, that doesn't make any sense."

"Oh, yes it does, Catherine. Watch that root." He helped her step over a large exposed growth. Only leaves rustling overhead broke the charged silence around them.

"Levi, shouldn't we be going back?"

"I have nothing to do until chore time. Unless, of course, you have some plans." Disappointment flowed through his voice.

Catherine thought about the poem for Oliver she had intended to write. "No, nothing really," she said. "I was just going to do some writing."

"I'd wish to hear some of your poems sometime, if you'd share them. I never had time to learn those things, you know. There aren't enough years to learn the things you must, let alone what you want to. Do you agree?"

At her vigorous nod, he continued, "And if you meet someone who will let you into a part of the world you won't get to by yourself, well, it's wonderful. You are that for me."

A small woods mouse skittered across the path in front of Catherine, but she hardly noticed. "I hadn't ever thought about it," she said, realizing she felt that way about Oliver, had even felt so about Joel, though the worlds they let her into were very different, full of new excitement, new relationships. And, in the case of Joel, new pain.

Catherine caught her breath as they rounded a small bend where a clear waterfall cascaded over layers of limestone ledges to fall a few feet below into a deep green pool. "Oh, my!" she exclaimed, stopping to stare. Along the edge, plants shifted and swayed with the current; sunlight sparkled off rivulets that made hollow, musical sounds as they fell gaily to the next level. Overhead, enormous oaks and cottonwood leaves whispered as they shifted in the slight breeze. "Levi, it's so beautiful." She turned to him, her eyes shining. "Like–like a church for God himself."

"Yes." Levi looked up at the thick, leafy canopy, his voice hushed. "I used to come here when I was young to work things out in my mind, to make peace with my life. Later, I came to just enjoy, to be part of nature and to make sense of the world, if I could. Sit here, Catherine." He led her to the base of a large oak bordering the water; one of its exposed roots became her chair. He seated her carefully, as though on a throne. "I've been waiting for the right time to bring you. Now, let me speak. Don't stop me. Let me say my piece, and then, if you want to talk, we will. If you don't. . ." His voice fell away as he twisted his hat brim in both hands, watching her.

The reality of Levi opening his heart to her in this special place brought tears to her eyes. Her mouth opened, but he stopped her words with upraised palms.

"Hush," he said. "Hush."

Catherine bit her lip.

Levi laid his felt hat on the tender shadowed grass and dropped down on one knee in front of her.

She blinked back tears. *There won't be any going back from this.* "Stand up, Levi. You'll ruin your suit." She patted the wide, rough root beside her. "I can listen just as well if you sit by me."

"Hush," he said again, still kneeling. "I have rehearsed this many a time, and I am still not sure of my words. Let me say what I will. Please." He waited for her nod. The music of moving water behind him mingled with a far-away jay's call; time stood still. The moment engraved itself on her mind, so beautiful.

So wrong.

"I offer you a solid, comfortable living. I offer you a house which was my mother's, and you can do anything you want with it. I can afford to give you the finest clothes, the finest dishes. I can, I *want* to give you so much you will never need look for anything more. I want you to know all that, and take it into account." He looked down at his work-worn hands and then back into her eyes. "But I also want you to know that to me, those things are not important. What I offer you today is my devotion in the hope my caring for you will someday bring you to caring for me."

Catherine watched Levi's steady, weathered face become boyish, almost shy. "I know people say you're too young for me, maybe I'm looking for a daughter, or I'm nothing more than a randy old man trying to relive his youth. They'll say I never found a woman and wouldn't know what to do if I had one. That's not true, Catherine. I had a love once, and I lost her. She was much like you, light and laughing, and she was everything to me."

"Truly." Catherine leaned forward. "What was her name? What happened to her?"

"Beth. Elizabeth." Levi shook his heavy head of grey hair. "It doesn't matter now. Let me finish." He cleared his throat and studied her face. "Do you think I'm blind, Catherine?"

She flushed, looking down at her hands crushing her skirt into wads. "What do you mean?"

"Ah, Catherine." He gave the impression of patting her arm without touching her. "You don't understand, do you?" He shook his head slightly. "I ask, do you think I'm blind? I see the softness in your face when you look at Oliver Houle and his when he sees you."

Catherine twisted her hands and bit her lip.

"I know his marriage is not a marriage. I know you love him and that he feels the same for you."

"Oh." Catherine closed her eyes and bowed her head. "Is it really that obvious?"

"It is to me."

"Levi—" she leaned toward him, but he held up a hand.

"Don't say it. You don't have to say anything. But most of all, don't deny it. Love denied," he paused, his voice drifting into memory, "love denied dies. Believe me, I know." His strong, square hands stopped the writhing of hers. "Let me finish. Nothing else matters now except my feelings for you." He waited until she raised her head and looked into his eyes. "Catherine, I ask you to marry me. Don't answer me now." His hands holding hers were strong, yet tender, as though holding a precious, breakable treasure. "I offer you my hands, my heart, and all my worldly possessions, and I offer you the rest of my life."

Her troubled eyes filled with tears. "And what do you ask in return?"

He searched her face. "Your loyalty. I ask you to care for my things and never shame me." He smoothed the skin on the back of her hands with his thumbs. "I don't want your answer now, Catherine. Not until you are ready, when you know your own heart and whatever decision you make is one you can live with for the rest of your life. For once I have you, if I ever do have you, I will never let you go."

Catherine sat, head bowed, tears falling onto their hands. It would be so wonderful, and so settled, to love him with the kind of love he deserved from the woman who would share his home and the rest of his years.

She raised her head. "Thank you, Levi. I can't say yes now. I don't know if I ever can."

"But you can't say no?"

She shook her head. "I can't say no, either." Of course she couldn't. To marry Levi would assure her staying here near Oliver, and to be Mrs. Levi Sommers would be a prestigious position in this community. There would be lots of advantages, but without love? How unfair to Levi.

"I do understand, Catherine. About Oliver."

Her thoughts must have blazed across her face for Levi to

have read them so clearly.

"And I know," he continued, "part of your decision to marry me, if you do, would be to be near him."

She sucked in her breath.

"I want you to know, if you decide to marry me even for that reason, I still offer you my life and my love."

That night in her room, Catherine's pen hovered over her journal for a long time before she wrote: What answer will I, can I, give? And when?

More than a month later, Catherine walked slowly toward their bridge through long ribbons of late July afternoon sun, her forehead creased from the burden she carried. What could she tell Oliver? Could she leave without giving him the reason? What if he persisted in knowing why? Then should she tell him what she suspected—knew, not suspected, she corrected herself—that she had to leave or ruin him here in his community?

Pregnant. What would be his reaction?

Her thoughts flipped back to Joel O'Brien, standing naked in the moonlight in that stark Kansas room, the image of his milk-white skin against the dark wall forever stamped in her memory, with the shock in his voice as he repeated her word, "Grand?" in horror. Perhaps all men felt the same? *No, surely not, not Oliver.*

But there could be no place for her here, not now. She would make an excuse to leave, not tell him at all, just explain she knew they had no future and calmly—it would have to be calmly—point out there was no use in her staying.

As she walked, she rehearsed the moment to come. Could she say something brave, like "Goodbye, my love. Remember our good times." They had been so few. Or, "It's too painful to be here and not belong to you."

And then what? What if he said, "But you do belong to me. How can you leave? Why would you want to?" Would she, could she, then speak the truth? That she had no choice?

Oliver was pacing near the bridge. *Thank God he came.* She broke into a run. He opened his arms, crushing his cheek against her hair, kissing her eyes, her throat.

"Oliver." She pushed away. "I had to see you. I'm sorry. Did you have trouble getting away?"

He made a face and shrugged his shoulders. "Some. I always do. It's all right, but I can't be gone long." He held her away to look into her face. "Something's the matter. Tell me."

She looked down. *This was what I brought him here for. Can I do it?* She lifted her chin, squared her shoulders and blurted, "I'm leaving Middle Creek, Oliver."

"What?" He pushed her away, roughly, with both hands.

She met his eyes, calmly, with purpose. "You must understand there's no future for me here, Oliver, or for us. I'm going away." She saw his face go white; a streak of sun lay gold across his eyes, lighting the tips of his pale lashes.

"For God's sake, Cathy! What do you mean?" His voice was confused, anguished. "Why? For God's sake, why?"

She shut her eyes and took a deep breath, willing herself to do what she planned. But she couldn't lie to Oliver; he was too important. He deserved honesty. *I can say it. I will.* The words spilled out: "I'm pregnant." She raised her head to watch the kaleidoscope of emotions race across his face.

"Pregnant?" He took a step back. "Are you sure? How do you know? You can't be!"

"Oh, Oliver, I know," she said. "I do know."

An eon passed. A bird chirruped, another answered; water gurgled against the bridge's wooden pilings. Unable to bear his silence, Catherine walked to the railing and watched bits of foam catch at the edge of the creek. The sun had disappeared behind the trees along the stream, and even as she watched, the world seemed to darken. *Will he never say anything?*

She heard his footsteps, felt his arm across her shoulders as he led her to sit on soft grass beside the water and gathered her into his arms. "Oh, my Cathy, my Cathy." He rocked her slightly, like a child in need of comforting. "You're mine, don't you know? Mine. God! Leave? Oh, no. No. No."

Crickets, crickets, loud in her ears. Her mouth found his; she tasted the salt of tears on his lips. Finally she pulled back. "For your sake and mine, and most of all for our child's, you *know* I can't stay. Not now."

He shook his head, his pale hair shining in the dusk. "Our day on the dunes. It was so beautiful. I wasn't thinking. I should have—I'm so sorry, Cathy."

She stiffened. "I'm not."

"No, no, I didn't mean. . ." His eyes held hers. "Cathy, you can't leave now. Any child of ours has got to be so wonderful. You can't take that away from me." He tipped up her chin. "Surely you won't do anything foolish."

Her eyes burned into his. "Do you think I would? Even if we never have anything else in this world, we will have this child. Nothing or no one is going to take it from me." Her thoughts went back to two small bodies wrapped in white inside a small pine box. "But I won't have it here and shame you and Amery. And Bonnie." She took a deep breath. "I've already told Mrs. Walker I might go."

"You have?" Oliver pulled his long legs up in front of him, elbows on his knees, his head in his hands. His voice was rough. "There has to be another way. I can't lose you. I can't lose our child. I want to see it grow up."

She stared at him. "Are you crazy? You want me to stay? Just hold my head up and pretend no one will ask who its father is? And let our child live with that? And where would I live, pray tell? Do you think Mrs. Walker would keep a 'fallen woman,' for that's what I would be, in her house?"

He was silent. Shadows lengthened into muffling darkness. "Of course you're right," he said finally, his voice low. "But where would you go? How would I ever see you? See our child?"

"I don't know. I haven't thought that far ahead." Her voice dropped to a whisper, and he had to lean near to hear her words. "I wasn't even going to tell you. I was just going to say our relationship was too difficult and I had to get away." She looked at him, her face soft. "But I couldn't. I can't lie to you, Oliver, of all people. Certainly not about this."

"I'm glad." He held her hands as though he would never let go. "Oh, Cathy, Cathy. Come here."

His arms cocooned her. For just a moment, she resisted, then surrendered herself once again, body and soul. "Love me, Oliver. Love me here, now."

The rustle of leaves stirred by whispering evening breezes mingled with the music of the creek, surrounding and settling over them like a blanket sealing them in a private world where love sealed their commitment once again, promising the one thing not to be denied: their entwined futures, no matter what decision.

That night in her room, Catherine found a note propped up by her lamp: "Sorry I missed you, Catherine. Levi."

Catherine undressed slowly, her thoughts a jumble of people: Oliver, Levi, Mrs. Walker, Bonnie, Amery, the school children, even the Widow Shimmek. And herself, becoming a matter of public scorn if she stayed. Because of her, Bonnie Houle becoming even more an object of pity. What would Bonnie do? Miserable already and vitriolic at her best, hating Oliver for what she had become. Oh, she would be vindictive, no doubt, and with reason.

Catherine stood in front of her clouded mirror, the flickering light from her small kerosene lamp throwing changing shadows across her alabaster body, sinking her eyes into dark sockets, her mouth into a shadowed frown as she studied her betraying flesh which would make her pay for just one never-to-be-forgotten afternoon, an afternoon she had never planned but one she realized now had been inevitable from the first moment she met Oliver Houle. And from that glorious afternoon, the ladies of the Middle Creek church would brand her wanton.

She ran her palms over her smooth hips, over her stomach, slim as yet but cradling something so precious, so glorious: Oliver's child, their child.

The solemn mirrored woman met her eyes. You could get rid of the child, Catherine. Oliver would never know you had caused it. You could, couldn't you, if you chose? Her own eyes answered: More death from this body? Another child never to live a Christmas, never to run, to laugh, to know the joy of a spring breeze, a summer dawn, a winter sunset?

No! She shook her head violently and pressed both her hands protectively over her stomach, as though her fingers could touch the living being already there. I will hold you, child. I will. Somehow, I will make this all right for you, without shame, without bitterness.

I will.

But how?

Catherine wasn't sure when the plan took place, whether in a dream or waking thought. She didn't look for the answer which came. She simply let it come and accepted it, because it, like

Oliver, like the child to come, was inevitable.

"Levi?" They were leaving services; his matched roans stamped and swished their tails under the big elm outside Middle Creek's white country church as they waited to be driven home.

"Yes, Catherine?" he answered, his eyes as always memorizing her face, seeing her as though there were no crowd around them.

"Let's take a drive. To your waterfall. It's such a glorious day and it will be cool there." *Why am I speaking so fast?* She had rehearsed what she planned to say over and over last night in her quiet room. "And I-I want to tell you something." There, she had said it; she was committed.

"But of course. Whenever you want." He chuckled as she squeezed his arm for the obvious scrutiny of Widow Shimmek who "harrumphed" under her breath but pasted an imitation smile on her wrinkled face and commented on the weather.

Catherine nodded. "Yes, it's lovely, isn't it?" She turned to Levi. "Shall we go, please?"

"You're all out of breath, Catherine. Of course, we'll drive. You knew we would if you asked. Tell me, is what you have to say so serious? Should I be afraid to hear it?"

"You'll have to be the judge." She smiled as though she hadn't a serious thought in her head. *But this is serious. More than anything I've ever done or thought of doing.*

The trip to Levi's woods was far too short. It seemed only minutes before Catherine reached the same root where she'd sat when Levi, so quixotic on one knee, proposed. Now he sat beside her. She could feel the tension in his body though they didn't touch; she knew they wouldn't unless by her invitation. She was sure he expected her to say no to his proposal; she suspected by this time Amy Walker had spread the word that Catherine intended to leave Middle Creek.

The canopy above was the same cool sanctuary it had been

the afternoon they had spent here; sun-dappled, the cascading waterfall seemed as clearly intent on performing its duty in the world's business. The grass was as soft and green, the sky as blue, but Catherine felt as though she stood on the edge of a great precipice. The words she was about to say would forever change the very colors of the sky, the trees; she would never see anything the same way again. Always the world would be shrouded in a haze of deceit.

Never before had Catherine deceived anyone deliberately. Now she was to compromise her whole life, her whole being, just to remain near Oliver, to be close enough to see him even from a distance, to keep his child where he could watch it grow.

Her father's voice intruded as it had through the years whenever she was uncertain about something. "Pray on it, Catherine." His voice seemed to come at her from the trees, the grass, the water. "If you're not sure, pray."

And she had. Last night she had prayed for the first time in years, for the first time, actually, since the day she watched dirt splatter on her babies' coffin and she had been sure there was no God. Or, if there was, He was not the kind of God she wanted to rely on.

Catherine stared up into the canopy above her, almost expecting to see her father's stern face looking down like some mythical figure, even forgetting for the moment that Levi sat beside her, his solid figure waiting quietly, patiently, for whatever she chose to say, whenever she chose to say it. Her thoughts swirled. *His adoration is for a graven image. I am a graven image. Should I have prayed for permission to do what I am going to do? Or for forgiveness?*

"Catherine?"

She started. "I'm sorry, Levi. It's—it's just so beautiful here, as though anything could happen, any magic."

He nodded, smiling, his eyes first searching hers before looking toward the crystal waterfall. "Yes," he said.

She took a deep breath and turned her face to his, knowing he saw her blue eyes intense, darkening, knowing he found her face lovely under the rich coronet with leaf shadows moving across her features. Could she? How credulous would he be? And, most of all, could she be fair in what she planned to do?

Yes. This act was necessary for everything she wanted, for everything she must have. She moved perceptibly nearer until her body touched Levi's from shoulder to thigh and ran her fingers through his, teasing, touching his work-hardened palm ever so lightly. She felt the involuntary shiver that quivered through his body and whispered, "Levi, take me." Her eyes burned into his. "Take me now, here, in this place of yours, and make me yours forever, too." Her eyes deepened with the passion she so wanted him to feel.

He sat motionless for an endless moment. There was no smile on his face, only astonishment. "I–I can't, Catherine. You are not mine."

"But I will be. Yes, yes, I am yours. I was the moment you first brought me here. That's what I wanted to tell you. Come."

She urged him to his feet and stepped lightly over the roots, pulling him with her to a patch of soft, tender grass near the lower, quieter part of the brook. There she turned to him, pressing the length of her body to his, lifting her lips to meet his, arching her back until she knew his yearning body would have to answer.

Levi stood with his arms down at his sides, his hands clenched, holding himself away from her by sheer will. "Catherine, wouldn't you want–shouldn't we wait—"

"Wait for what?" She slipped her hand under his tie, loosened his shirt, and lightly touched the crisp greying hairs on his muscled chest, hairs so unlike the soft, silky ones on Oliver's body.

"For the marriage." Levi's breath was coming in soft gasps,

his eyes closed as though he were afraid to open them. "You will marry me, won't you, Catherine? Say you will. I can't touch you if you won't."

She tilted her chin and looked up at him, her eyes wide, her smile an invitation to love. "Of course. Do you think I would give myself to you otherwise? It's just that today...today is so perfect." She let her body shudder and felt the answering thrill in his. "Oh, Levi, why should we wait for a minister? Here in this place, our place, before God, who is our witness. . ." She ran her hands down his arms and gently unclenched his fists, placing their palms over the thin cloth covering her breasts, straining toward him and lifting her face again to his. "Take me, Levi. Please. Take me."

She closed her eyes and imagined Oliver's hands undressing her, caressing her, Oliver's tongue asking hers for response, as Levi gently lowered her to the grass and reverently explored her body, more and more intensely.

As she helped Levi out of his clothes, she teased him with her tongue, imagined Oliver's slim, lanky hardness against her as she felt Levi's stocky body upon her, relived the tremendous explosion she had experienced on the sun-colored floor in the empty house on the dunes, and pretended she felt it again as her body brought Levi's to culmination, his passionate moans rising raggedly in the sweet summer air, until, exhausted, they lay entangled, moist and quiet on the crushed grass.

"Catherine." Levi's voice held wonder. He nuzzled against her, his eyes closed, his lips pressed against her warm breast.

She cradled his head, her fingers entwined in his thick greying hair, and stared up into the breeze-tossed canopy. *It's all right now. Use me, Levi, use me. You deserve every happiness I can give you because I am using you.* She held his head gently and caressed his cheek. *I am using you, but you are never, never going to know it as long as I live.*

"On Saturday? You're getting married on Saturday? That's not even a week away." Amy Walker's voice rose in delight. "Well, I never! And you said you were going to leave."

"I was."

"Oh, I see. Levi couldn't let you go. Can't say as I blame him. What a change in that man since he's been squiring you. But Saturday, already? What will you wear?"

"It doesn't matter."

"Doesn't matter? Child, what do you mean? Your wedding dress should be special."

I'll have to show more interest. Catherine smiled. "I'm sorry, Amy. I just meant—well, it doesn't matter because it's the wedding that's important, you know?" Whatever she wore, it was the wrong groom; what difference would the dress make?

"You could wear mine. That's it, I have mine still, and it would fit you just fine."

Catherine shook her head. "No, thank you. I want my own clothes to start my new life." She smiled. "I'll be fine."

"Well. A wedding should be pretty—"

Catherine started upstairs, laughing gaily until she escaped into her room, sank down on the bed, and dropped her head into her hands. She had done it; she had lured Levi into marriage. Though their child would be born a little early, there would be no cause to question.

Levi, Levi. You are so fine. I will never shame you, never. She buried her face in her pillow and sobbed until there were no sobs left. The decision had been made, the road taken, and she would never cry over it again.

"Oh, God, Cathy!" Oliver's voice was choked as he paced the ground near their bridge. "Did you have to do this to me?"

"Yes."

"But to marry someone you don't love? Is that fair to him?"

"No. But was there any other way?"

Oliver closed his eyes and took a deep breath. "Of course not, not for you to stay."

"I won't meet you here again, Oliver. And the child will be his." In her determination her voice sounded cold and hard, even to herself.

"Yes, I know."

"And you must come, rejoice with the celebration of our marriage."

He closed his eyes. "I will come, though the sight of it will kill me. But I wouldn't dare not be there. My absence would be noticed. And," he paused to search her face, "Levi is my friend."

Catherine nodded and held Oliver's face between her palms for just a moment before she said gently, "More than he will ever know."

8

OLIVIA, 1984

Olivia deliberately kept her hands quiet in her lap as she stared at the clouds below, her mind projecting vignettes of Pamela: at six, at eight, at ten, fifteen, twenty, her loving, affectionate, open expression pleading, expecting, and—almost always, at least from Olivia—getting approval.

I shouldn't have sent Pam home with Bert. It wasn't fair; Pam wasn't used to being alone. Olivia remembered with guilt the tone of Bert's voice the morning Pam had burnt his breakfast, a rejecting voice, an open non-acceptance of Pam's inabilities.

Inabilities that I fostered. And a need for approval that I fed constantly and which probably went hungry while I've been away. Has it been only six days, not even a week? A lifetime, a whole world's worth. Whatever happened to Pam was the result of my decision to send her home. She was always protected, loving, afraid of no one, cautious of nothing, because I was always there. I had no right to let her go. Like throwing a baby to a pack of dogs. But our neighborhood was so safe. I thought it was. I was so sure it was.

Olivia looked up at the Stewardess' questioning face.

"You seem disturbed. Is there anything I can do for you?"

Olivia shook her head. "Thanks, no. How long to Portland?"

"Half an hour, maybe forty minutes."

And then what? Bert had said so little over the phone. Maybe, and the thought had occurred to her more than once in last night's wakeful hours, maybe what he'd said wasn't even true. Maybe he just wanted her home and…no. Surely, Bert wouldn't do that. Would she be able to talk with him alone first, or would Pam be at the airport with him? Certainly, he wouldn't have left her at home alone, not now, would he?

Her mind replayed Bert's accusations in yesterday's totally unsatisfactory conversation which had resulted in her taking the next plane home.

"Of course, you must," Heath had said as she stepped out of the Bayshore phone booth, his blue eyes dark with concern. "Did he say what happened? How is she?"

"I don't know. Bert wouldn't talk over the phone, just insisted that I get there. He made it quite plain that whatever happened—and I hope at least that it isn't as serious as he seems to think—is my fault for sending her home with him."

"That's heavy." Heath opened the door of his jeep for her and walked around to the driver's side.

"I didn't thank you for bringing me into town," she apologized, leaning back and closing her eyes.

"No trouble. I knew I could get you here quicker than Tim with his old pickup. He might have had to wire something together first." Heath pulled a swift U-turn in the middle of the intersection, surprising a mongrel that streaked for the sidewalk. "I'm glad to see you aren't going to pieces."

"Pieces?" Olivia considered. "I never had much patience for women who fall apart. I couldn't see it served any purpose." Olivia closed her eyes. "But Pam *was* too protected. I know, I did it myself. If somebody offered her affection, and I'm sure Bert hasn't been—oh, God. What a complicated situation!"

Heath reached over and covered her hand with his, and in spite of her concern over Pamela, Olivia felt an answering tingle. "I'm sorry," he said. "You've told me a little about Bert and Pamela, but not about their relationship. Evidently it's not good?"

"Anything but, I would say. He resents her far more than I ever realized. Always has. Either I was blind, or he kept it hidden really well." She pulled her fingers from the warmth of his and clutched her purse with both hands. "Bert said some pretty awful things today about Pam. And about me." She looked blindly out the window.

"Want to talk about it?"

Did she? "Not yet, okay?" Some late spring flowers bloomed in the ditch. Olivia didn't recognize them, but took some comfort in realizing that whatever happened, the world and all its wonders just kept happening. "He was upset, you know?"

"I didn't mean to pry." Heath capably steered around a watery pothole, the crisp light hairs on the back of his hands catching shards of sunlight. "It's just that sometimes burdens seem lighter when two people carry them."

Grateful, Olivia smiled at him. He was a solid treasure. And to think she had suspected, even for a minute, he might have anything to do with the mystery at Dunes House.

Bert was inside the Portland terminal, pacing nervously before he spotted her. "God, Livvy, I thought you'd never get here. Am I glad to see you! Where's your luggage?"

Olivia handed him her small suitcase and searched the waiting room for Pamela. "Where is she, Bert? You didn't leave her home?"

"No, no. I told her to sit in the car. I wanted to see you alone, first. God, Livvy, I don't know what to tell you, what to do. If anything."

"What to do? You mean you haven't done anything? When

did this happen? What exactly did happen? You haven't notified the police?" Olivia's felt her eyes widen at the guilt on his face. "You've taken her to Dr. Brault, surely." Her voice dropped off. "You haven't. Oh, Bert!"

He took a step backwards, closing his eyes. "God, Livvy, what can I say? To her? I can't even ask her what happened, can I? She's your baby. I don't fit in, never did, not since you first laid eyes on her." He pleaded, "Ah, c'mon, Livvy, understand, will you? I didn't want to scare her, you know, and I didn't know what I ought to do. If it's really done, there's no stopping it now, and what's the use?"

Olivia took a deep breath, caught between compassion for Bert's inadequacy and anger at his non-action. "Bert." She kept her voice calm, almost the same calm she used with Pam when Pam was upset. "Before I see her, what do you mean, 'if it's really done.' Isn't it? *Was* she raped? Tell me what happened."

"I can't." Bert looked at his feet. "Listen, Livvy. All she said was, 'Why don't you touch me here, Daddy? Hold me tight, like that man in the park.'" Bert rubbed his fingers over his eyes. "And then she pointed to herself, you know, there." His voice trailed off before he continued defensively, "Well, I told you we shouldn't leave a dummy like her—sorry, leave Pamela alone, and I was right, wasn't I? If you'd been here where you belonged— what have you accomplished, anyway," his voice rose, "except to screw up everything for all of us? Where's the rest of your stuff?"

"That's it." She pointed to the small suitcase he held. "I left the rest."

"Left it? You aren't going back!"

Was that fear in his voice? Olivia started through the door to the parking lot. "Lower your voice. People are staring. Of course I'm going back and taking Pam with me, but I have to know what happened."

"Ask her yourself. Here she comes."

Pamela was trotting awkwardly toward them across the brightly-lit asphalt parking lot. Her rumpled skirt had worked its way between her overweight legs and she stopped momentarily to tug it free. She surged toward Olivia and pulled her into a fierce bear hug. "Momma! Good see you."

She hadn't called Olivia "Momma" in years.

Olivia held the soft, yielding body tightly. "Pam. Are you all right?"

"All right." Pamela grinned and nodded her head up and down, up and down. "Sure. Why you stay away so long?"

It was nearly midnight, far too late to contact Pamela's doctor. Olivia was pleased to see that the house was dusty, but neat.

"I did good, didn't I, Mom? Everything's clean!" Pamela shouted, waving her pudgy arm around the living room. "See!"

Olivia had forgotten how loud Pam's voice was, as though by sheer force she might make it transcend her difficulty in expressing herself.

"It looks just fine, Pam. Really fine." Olivia hugged Pam's shoulders, noticing Bert evidently hadn't been insisting their daughter remember to use deodorant. "It's late, Honey. Wash up and go to bed."

"I'm not sleepy!" Pamela declared, although her lids drooped over her grey eyes.

"But I am. Scoot."

Pamela went upstairs, dragging her feet all the way.

"At least she does what *you* tell her," Bert said, tossing his jacket over the back of his La-Z-Boy chair. He loosened his tie and jerked it over his head as he moved toward their first-floor bedroom. "Come on, Livvy, it's been a long time."

"Long time?" She stared after him. "Bert. It hasn't even been a month. Don't you want to know what I've learned?"

"Sure. In the morning. Let's go to bed."

From the tone of his voice, she recognized what he wanted wasn't sleep. She followed him into the bedroom, slowly. "Bert. I really don't feel like having sex."

He had thrown his clothes over the cedar chest under the window and was already under the covers, his soft shoulders bare above the blanket. "Think about me, then." His tone was testy. "I've been living like some monk, and you're finally here. What do you expect?"

Olivia rubbed her forehead. "It's not what I expect, Bert. It was a long flight, and I worried the whole way. I can't just forget everything else and turn on like tap water."

Bert dropped his belligerence and sighed. He threw back the blanket on her side of the bed in invitation. "Ah, Livvy, give me a chance, will you? Let me back into your life."

Later, after Bert was asleep, Olivia lay wide-eyed in the dark. The room, the house, even Bert's deep breathing, all of it was familiar. Let him back into her life? She didn't even fit there herself. Not any more.

Sitting behind his desk, Dr. Brault ran both hands through his sheaf of white hair before he pressed the tips of his fingers together and narrowed his eyes. "I'm so sorry to hear about this, Olivia. And you don't know what really happened? If anything."

"No." Olivia sat forward on the edge of the leather chair across from his cluttered desk. "Dr. Brault, you've known Pam ever since she was born. You know her limitations. Should I ask her for a play-by-play?" She gripped the wooden handles of her purse. "Couldn't that bring on a trauma? At this point she doesn't seem to be upset, just wondering why Daddy doesn't 'touch her like that,' whatever 'that' is. Should I ask you to examine her? You could tell, if she'd been…violated…couldn't you, even after this amount of time? What if …God, what if she's pregnant?" Olivia straightened up, her eyes wide. "That's frightening."

He held up his hand. "Wait a minute, wait a minute." He rose to put his hand on her shoulder. "There's no point in worrying. If she should be pregnant there's no question an abortion would be performed. No question." He frowned. "Do you want me to examine her? Now?"

"I don't know. I'm seeking your advice. You know her temperament. She's happy. Shall I just take her away? Or shall I report this to the police and subject her to all the harassment, the publicity, the…I don't even know what all. Does she deserve that?"

"Of course you have to consider the possibilities, though the police might be compassionate to someone like Pamela."

"And Bert. Bert would do anything to keep this quiet. He resents her so already. If what happened to Pam reflected on him, and he'd think it would—"

"But shouldn't the man be punished? If there was a man?"

"If?" Olivia raised her eyebrows. "If?"

The doctor held up his hand. "Perhaps it was a fantasy. Perhaps—and this may be distasteful to you—but perhaps she masturbates and fantasizes, maybe even about your husband. Those things happen, Olivia. The limitations of her mental capacity do not preclude her sensuality, her physical maturity, you know."

Olivia sank back into her chair. "I hadn't thought—hadn't even considered. . ." She got up and walked the length of the office before she said, "Perhaps it's better, then, to not make more of this than I should. I'm planning to take her back to Wisconsin with me." She gave him a quick run-down of the situation at Dunes House.

"And how would Bert feel about your going back? Or would he go, too?"

"No, he wouldn't go, and he won't like it. But I have to finish what I've started there."

Dr. Brault sat down again and put his fingertips together. "How are you and Bert getting along?" He waited for her answer, which wasn't forthcoming. "I ask with the privilege of a long-time friend as well as the family doctor, so don't call me nosy. I haven't seen Bert for his annual checkup yet. He should come in."

Olivia stopped walking and half smiled. "This is becoming a psychiatry session, not a medical consultation." She faced him. "But, in answer to your question, I guess this chance to be away from both Bert and Pam, even though it hasn't been very long, has given me some time to evaluate my own life. And learning that my mother was a very different person than I thought, even evidently led a different—not just different, but *secret*—life, has led me to question my own motives for doing what I do, being who I am, where I am."

Dr. Brault nodded. "Has discovering that caused you to make some changes?"

Olivia did smile then. "Not yet, at least. I do realize Bert and I haven't really had much between us for a long time, partly because he resents my relationship with Pamela. I'm not so sure, right at this moment, whether I could come back here and be only Mrs. Bert or Pam's mother now. I have new dimensions."

Brault nodded. "I could see that when you came in. A 'personhood,' to borrow a word from the libbers, that hasn't been evident before. Be careful of bursting out of your cocoon before your wings are ready, Olivia. I've seen it happen." He glanced at his watch. "I have another appointment. Have you made a decision about Pam? Do you want me to examine her? It would prove whether or not she was molested to the point of physical intercourse."

"And if she was raped?"

"Then you would have to decide to prosecute, if you could identify a perpetrator, or not. I can't answer for you. Pam has been too protected for too long to go through the possible legal procedures unscathed."

"I understand." Olivia paused, bit her lip, then continued, "This is my fault, and why I couldn't see it earlier, I don't know. But now I'll have to deal with it, won't I?" She held out her hand. "Thanks, Dr. Brault. I guess I can't stop protecting her just yet, can I? I should have before, and didn't. Now it's too late."

CATHERINE, September, 1938

Catherine basked in the warm contentment of Levi's deep grey gaze following her movements across the comfortable farm kitchen while he savored his richly creamed morning coffee. She picked up their breakfast plates and smiled at him over her shoulder as she placed them in the old kitchen sink. Had it really been more than a month since their hot, early August wedding?

"But don't you want to even see the house first?" he had asked, shaking his grey-laced head, bewildered by her hurry to marry. "It's old. You might hate it, want to change it to your liking."

"I won't hate it. And there'll be plenty of time to change it later. A whole lifetime." Catherine declared passionately. "Life is so short, Levi, so unpredictable. We have to make every moment count."

Levi had hesitated there in the green sun-dappled cathedral on the day Catherine had sealed her fate with their flesh, his eyes feasting over her silky, love-warmed skin. He said slowly, "But I don't want you to hurry now and wish to change your mind later, Catherine." He leaned up on one elbow to look deep into her eyes, staring beyond the clear blueness of them, searching her very soul. "Because I will never let you change your mind."

"Never let me?" Her smile belied her treachery and hid the inner cringe she felt at the sudden realization that his words held more than a promise. They held eternity, an eternity away from Oliver Houle. "Oh, Levi." She gently cradled his head to her breasts to keep him from seeing her anguish as she stared wide-eyed up into the green canopy above her and asked her heart to forgive.

Levi groaned softly as his lips captured one taut nipple, and he moved his strong, work-hardened hand reverently to cup her other breast. His touch was so tender she was unaware of his calluses and felt only his caring. "I only mean I will see you'll have no reason to want to change your mind…ever."

"I believe you, Levi," she said, refusing to think beyond this day, claiming the lie she would live from this moment on.

Now, mid-September frost had browned the fields, and it was time to admit aloud what her body would soon begin to proclaim visibly: her child. Oliver's child.

Catherine poured more coffee for them both though its rich, pungent aroma nauseated her sensitive stomach. She pulled her chair close to the table so she could steady her elbows while she spoke the words she had so carefully chosen during the past nights' wakeful hours. "Levi, have you time to talk?"

"Time?" He smiled gently. "Of course. We will always have time to talk, won't we, Catherine?"

"I hope so," she answered fervently, thanking God for Levi's fine solidness, his caring commitment. Could she ever make herself worthy of the depth of this fine man's love?

She would. Forever.

"Is it so important?" His smile was boyish as he pushed away his sturdy coffee cup and leaned back in his chair. "You want to tear the whole house down and build a new? Go ahead."

"Oh, Levi. Be serious. I am."

"Yes, ma'am." He rubbed a square, work-worn hand across his face, literally wiping his smile away, and replaced it with a make-believe frown. "Serious. All right."

His growing playfulness was new to both of them, a surprise to him and an unexpected joy to her. He reached over and traced the line of her flushed cheek with the back of his finger. "Serious I'll be. I'm listening."

She breathed deeply, looking away. How should she begin? "There are things I must tell you. About before I came here to Middle Creek."

"No," He broke in, slapping his palms on the table. "You needn't."

"But I must, Levi."

"For my sake or for yours?" Leaning forward, Levi took her hand and curled it inside his two larger, calloused palms. His grey eyes captured her, bathing her in exquisite tenderness. "Listen, Catherine, and listen well. I've told you before, my life began with you. There were other people, other years, for both of us, but we began. Do you understand? You needn't go beyond. It isn't necessary."

With a rush of understanding, Catherine realized Levi was protecting her through this gallantry about the past. He had to have known she was not a virgin on that fateful day by the waterfall. Grateful tears formed in her eyes, making the blue even more luminous.

"Please, Levi. Listen." She had to tell him about Joel O'Brien, about the two tiny babies lost to Kansas earth, about this new, this oh, so precious child who must not be lost.

The story came, all of it, in spurts and rushes, from her parent's death to the tiny pine box in the graveyard on the windy plain.

"Oh, my dear." Levi kept her hand in his, nonjudgmental and compassionate through her recitation. "And you had no one. I'm so sorry." He brushed the tears from her cheeks with his blunt, caring thumbs. "But it's all right now. It's all past."

"But don't you see, Levi?" Her eyes serious, still awash with tears, she pressed on, "The babies came too soon, only six months, and they didn't live…and now…" She hesitated, fearing his reaction. Did he even want a child? At his age?

"Now?" Levi waited patiently, his mind gathering Catherine's past to the woman he knew.

"Now…now I carry your child and," she leaned toward him and unconsciously placed her hands across her stomach as she pleaded his understanding, "and oh, Levi, I'm so afraid for it."

"A child? Catherine! So soon?" The joy in his voice was unmistakable.

"So soon." She lowered her head. He had a right to answers, if he chose to ask the questions. "I'm sorry."

"Sorry? Sorry?" He leaped out of his chair and pulled her up into his arms. "Oh, my dearest, my sweet Catherine, my love…"

"Looks to me she's a mite bigger than she ought to be," harrumphed the Widow Shimmek behind her hand to Mrs. Dodge as Catherine and Levi walked down the aisle for an early December service.

"Wouldn't have said so myself, though you might be right," nodded Mrs. Dodge. "But don't spread gossip. I always did think Levi'd make a fine family man. At least now we know he's not too old." She chuckled, winking one fading eye. "Anyway, he's hardly the first fella around these parts that might have rushed his wedding night a little."

"But Levi Sommers?" Widow Shimmek pursed her lips. "Of all people?"

"He is only human, Agatha." Mrs. Dodge sighed. "And she's a lovely girl."

The first winter of Catherine's marriage wore on interminably, it seemed to her, milder than some years for a few days at a time, then hitting hard with storms swirling snow tornados around tightly-battened farm buildings with a vengeance and covering the drive with four-foot drifts.

In furious bursts of activity that astounded and worried Levi, Catherine tore the old farmhouse apart, painted its dreary rooms with clear, winsome colors, made lighthearted chintz curtains, baked all his favorite dishes, and cleaned their home from top to bottom. At night, while Levi rested and read in his chair by the stove, she sewed tiny garments for the coming child and tried not to remember another time when the garments she had sewn were never worn.

Catherine never felt better, or, sometimes, lonelier. Except for snatched moments when Oliver found an excuse to come to the farm for county business, or a dangerous public exchange at a church function, she was unable to see her love, unable to touch or speak to him about themselves, their needs, and their growing child who was a constant source of wonder. Catherine became more beautiful, more glowing, day by day.

"God, Catherine, you have to tell me. Does he know? Has Levi ever questioned?" Oliver anguished one hurried moment when he stopped to see Levi about an exchange of silage work. His tormented eyes lay bare the emotions he must always hide when he and Catherine were not alone. His hands gripped hers so tightly she would have cried out had she not so hungered for his touch.

"No, no." Catherine pulled his light head down to hers. "Oh, Oliver, kiss me, kiss me quickly."

The always simmering fire would erupt and envelope them then for fleeting moments to hold them until another stolen time, a stolen touch. Caught up in the ecstasy of being together, able to speak without codes, they never realized that Levi always managed to give them time alone before coming from the barns to greet his neighbor.

Levi was her warm companion and her tender lover, and his delight in the child he would father was a constant joy in both their lives, but for different reasons.

As the months wore on, Catherine, more secure for herself and the child, felt less guilty because of the happiness she brought to Levi. She basked in her husband's solicitation and returned his love in every way she could. The willing gift of her body to the needs of his was her way of repaying him even while she dreamed of Oliver's hands, his mouth.

One January night as the Wisconsin winter surrounded the house with cold, screaming, snow-filled winds, she and Levi lay cocooned in the warmly quilted bed scented by their lovemaking. Levi moved a reverent hand across her swelling belly, delighting in the movement of the fishtailing child within. He was silent for a moment, then searched her face. "No matter how we love, my Little One…"

"Yes?" She gazed up into the warm grey of his passion-contented eyes.

"There is still a part of you I cannot reach."

"No. No." She shook her head fervently, denying the truth of it.

He smiled gently. "Don't be upset. I'm not complaining, nor chastising. I knew it would be so."

"It's the baby. That's all, you'll see—"

He touched her mouth with his finger to close off her words, and traced his way down her slender neck, over her breasts, to her swollen belly, where he splayed his hand over the tightening flesh.

"No. It's not the baby. But I've enough, more than I ever thought to have." He moved, laying a strand of her heavy hair across her shoulder and stroking its silkiness. "I love you so much, Catherine. So much."

"I know. Oh, Levi, I do know." She brought his head to her breasts, offering him all she could, not bothering to wipe away the tears that ran unheeded to her pillow.

Oliver, she thought. *Oliver.*

Vignettes of Oliver stayed and glowed like shining jewels in Catherine's mind: Oliver's barely-veiled eyes meeting hers across the crowded hall at the monthly Church meeting; Oliver's swift, tormenting kiss. His lingering touch in stolen moments in her farm kitchen; his spoken and unspoken concern for her health and welfare, and the anguish in his face as he pleaded for some time, any time alone with her, even an hour.

Though unfulfilled love for Oliver was an underlying thread in the daily fabric of her life, Catherine was wrapped in the richness of Levi's caring for her and the coming child. As her time drew nearer, she rejoiced in every movement, every stirring that proved the child within her lived. She never voiced her concerns to Levi, but she knew he understood her fear that this child, like her twins, might come too soon.

Contrary to the proverb of a winter month that comes in like a lion will go out like a lamb, this February burst in with a terrifying snarl of blizzard, bludgeoned the Wisconsin farmland unmercifully for days and went out the same way.

"What if the baby comes now?" Catherine worried as they stood in the window of Levi's ancient farmhouse one early morning and watched the drifts swarm up against the grey outbuildings. "Dr. Hays won't be able to get here."

Levi's large, blunt hand held hers tightly to his chest as he comforted, "It won't. It's too early. The child won't come until spring, you know."

But Catherine knew differently and began to be more careful, quieter, hoping by her inactivity to hold the child within her past its time. Remembering the angry pain her body had endured when her twins were wrenched from her womb before they could survive, she spent hours humming wordless songs and speaking soft words to this frail baby nesting inside her whenever Levi was busy outside with chores. She wrote short scraps of poems to the child, poems that revealed nothing except her overwhelming love. Every uneventful day was a blessing, keeping her secret safe from the world, but even more important, safe from Levi.

"You know I want to be a part of our child's life," Oliver said one morning in a stolen moment before Levi came in from the barn. "You must know, Cathy. I want to claim our child."

"But you won't." She reached up to touch his winter-cold cheek with her fingertips, memorizing the line of his face, mindful that Levi, having seen Oliver's truck pull up to the house, would come in from the barn in a minute. "We know. It has to be enough."

"For now. Maybe for you, but—" He turned as the door opened. "Hello, Levi! I brought your sharpened saw blades from Elmer's shop as long as I was picking up my own."

"Oliver." Levi's welcoming nod was appreciative. "Thanks for saving me the trip on these drifted roads." His eyes stayed on the younger man's face for just a moment and then shifted lovingly to his wife. "Catherine, should you be standing?"

"Oh, Levi, I'm fine. Shall I make some coffee?"

"Not for me, thanks," Oliver said as he pulled up the collar of his heavy mackinaw. "I'll get on home before dusk falls. This wind is still whipping up snow and that spot by the bridge closes off quickly." He stopped at the door, his shoulders slumped. "If you need anything, let me know." Then he was gone, enveloped in a swirl of flakes off the roof that fell like stars to melt on the kitchen floor.

Levi turned to Catherine before she had time to compose her face. She quickly looked away, but with a swift step he was beside her, his finger tucked under her chin to turn her toward him. He said quietly, "Is it so hard, Catherine?"

She didn't answer his question directly but threw her arms around him, burying her face against the warmth of his neck, unmindful of the snow-wet coat he still wore pressing against her coming child. "I love you so, Levi Sommers," she said. "Do you know that? Do you?" She took a deep breath and raised her eyes to meet his. "I do love you so."

9

CATHERINE'S JOURNAL

February 28, 1939
February is past, filled with storm and precious moments,
fleeting moments, and such meaningful ones. Oliver was here today
and then gone, but never gone from my thoughts for long as our child
grows, steadily, surely, into being.

Catherine leaned back against her pillows, thought for a
moment, then closed the book, picked up a piece of paper from
the bedside table and wrote, "To have given me hope, to have
given me this future, to have given me your love…Levi, thank
you, thank you. Catherine."

She laid it on the pillow beside her own and, smiling, fell
asleep.

An hour later, Levi stood staring down at her dream-caught,
defenseless beauty, her note in his hand, a bemused look on his
face. Her journal lay carelessly on the bedside table. Levi picked
it up and held it for a long moment before shaking his head and
laying it down. No. Her thoughts, her secrets were her own, to
share only if she wished. He turned off the light and slipped into
bed carefully, not to disturb her, but she turned in her sleep and

nestled against him, her breath soft against his chest.

He smiled into the dark. His world was in his arms. He had more than enough.

February moved into March during the night with a final roar of sleet and snow that laid a coating of ice over everything first and covered that with a layer of frothy flakes making footing treacherous.

"You'll not go out until this clears," Levi stated. "I'll not have you fall."

"Oh, but Levi, I was to help Amery Houle with his reading today." Amery's eyesight was progressively worse, and the small country school was crowded with an unprecedented twenty pupils, leaving no time for the new young and inexperienced teacher to spend extra minutes with Amery. It had been natural for Oliver to ask her to tutor his son and she had agreed gladly, as much for the boy himself as for the opportunity of time with Oliver as he drove her to his farm and back. "Amery really needs the help."

"Then Oliver can bring him here."

As her time of confinement came nearer and nearer, Catherine's constant prayer was for her child to go full term. Or, for Levi's sake, even be late. It seemed that God intended to cooperate as the first week of March came and went uneventfully, and as she marked each day off on the calendar she breathed a sigh of relief.

In fact, in spite of her ungainly shape and weight, Catherine had never felt better, and the longer her time stretched the happier she was. A hint of the coming spring filled the air at the height of day, and the high-piled drifts softened into shapeless mounds around the buildings and fences.

"Cathy, isn't it time? Is something wrong?" Oliver's words were low and laced with concern, spoken only for her. His enigmatic expression gave nothing away to the other Sunday churchgoers.

Her smile was genuine. "There's nothing wrong, Oliver. Dr. Hays is taking good care of me."

"But when?"

"Soon." The baby had already dropped. Catherine knew it to be only a matter of days, and she was sure that the Widow Shimmek and the other calendar-counters of the parish would be well aware it was much too early. She put up her chin. "I think very soon."

"You're even more beautiful now. Do you know that?"

"Levi tells me so."

"I wonder sometimes…does he know how lucky he is?"

"It isn't luck, Oliver. Levi deserves everything I can give him."

"And will that include other children?" Oliver's eyes pleaded her denial.

"I hope so. If he wants." Catherine smiled up into Oliver's serious face. "Don't you wish your child to have brothers and sisters?"

"Don't tease, Cathy. You break my heart."

"I'm sorry, Oliver, but we must look ahead, not back. Mustn't we?"

Oliver muttered, "Look ahead to what?" and turned to greet his neighbor as Levi came to claim his wife. Catherine welcomed her husband with a smile and thrust her slender arms into the warm coat he held for her.

CATHERINE'S JOURNAL

March 9, 1939

The baby is quiet, so quiet, yet I know, I must know, its heart is beating. It must be alive, it must! Today I rested, listening, waiting for a movement, but nothing. Nothing! Until I thought I must go wild! Then, miraculous, a flutter, a kick, and finally she (I know this child must be a she, for Levi will so treasure a daughter more than a son) turned, slowly, as though awakening from a deep drugged sleep. The relief, the thankfulness that flooded through me is indescribable! God is with me, with this child, I know. I know.

March 10

Dr. Hays came today. "The baby is almost ready," he said. "Are you?" Oh, yes, I am. But nothing is happening. I rest perhaps too quietly, but every day belongs to Levi's happiness, and every day I can carry this child within me makes that happiness more possible. The child rests, too, only fluttering, not rambunctious as she was a week ago, as though she's conserving her strength for the effort we must make together. If only she will be small!

March 11

My back aches, no matter how I sit or stand. But no pains yet to bring this child, just little twinges that don't last any time at all. Yet I know she's near.

The weather threatens. Though it's early morning, the sky in the west is as dark as dusk. There's snow coming, surely. I hope not a storm, not now.

Three o'clock. Levi has gone out to close the barn tightly and make the animals ready for the night. Flakes are falling oh, so gently, large drifting flakes, the kind you see on Christmas cards. The sky is slate dark, heavy. My body is heavy, too, and ripe. Still, nothing.

Later that night, in bed, Levi gently pulled the covers over her shoulders. "You're restless, Catherine. Can I do anything for you?"

"Rub the small of my back, please, just for a minute?" Catherine shivered with pleasure as his gentle massage eased unfamiliar pressure.

"Does that help?"

"Mmmmmmm. Wonderful." She turned to look up at him, declaring, "Levi, whatever happens, you know I love you."

"I do hope whatever happens is a baby." He smiled, his grey eyes crinkling at the corners before he sobered and all the tenderness he felt spilled over her. "I do know, Catherine."

She slept intermittently, conscious of the ever-increasing wind keening around the eaves, but unaware the dense heavy snow had now changed to fine, driving sheets. She awakened momentarily more than once without really knowing why until suddenly a not-to-be-ignored contraction gripped her into consciousness. "Ohhh!" she moaned, arching her aching back and stretching to meet the pain.

In seconds, the light was on, and Levi was leaning over her, his grey gaze penetrating her distress. "What is it, Love?"

Her sleep-drowsed eyes widened as her hands involuntarily pressed against her taut belly, recognized its uncustomary hardness. She felt the tautness fade as the contraction waned. "Levi, it's the baby!"

"But it's too soon!" He smoothed her heavy honey-colored hair from her forehead and placed a soft kiss there. "You're sure?"

She nodded and put her arms around his neck, clinging to him for a moment as her eyes darkened with the beginning of another contraction. "Call Dr. Hays, Levi, Please!"

He wasted no time crossing the room to the chair where his clothes were piled and hurriedly pulled his denims up over his sturdy body, thrust his feet into boots. He was out the door in a flurry, his loose shirttail flapping behind him as he clattered down the stairs to the telephone on the kitchen wall.

It seemed to Catherine she had suddenly moved into another dimension, that the familiar bedroom grew unreal, larger than she remembered. A new pain started in the small of her back and fingered its way up over the mound of her belly, gripping her and the child within with a ferocity that seemed too great for such a short while of labor. The contraction didn't abate as fast as the first one had.

Had it been like this with the twins? Hazily, Catherine tried to remember as the pain released her. No, this was different. That had been slower, much slower, each contraction much longer in coming. Not like this onslaught, this avalanche of pain she could not control.

She drew in a ragged breath as another whirling, tightening, vortex swept her in. "Levi!" she screamed, frightened. "Where are you, Levi?"

"Here." He strode through the doorway, his face contorted. "The phone is dead. The storm winds. . ." He came to the bed and sat beside her, taking her hands in his strong, work-hardened palms. "The doctor couldn't get through even if I could call. The storm has made the roads impassable."

"Oh." Catherine lay back on the pillow and shut her eyes for a moment. "Oh."

Then as another pain began to build, she gripped his hands as hard as she could and fastened her wide blue stare on his face. "Then it's just the three of us, Levi. You've birthed calves and colts," her breath caught and she held to his strength, "now birth your daughter. She's not going to wait for better weather." Catherine tried to smile before the pain took over again and she cried, "I have to push, Levi. Oh, God! The baby's coming. Help me!"

He added his pillow to hers and placed her hands around the rungs of the headboard behind her. He stripped off the heavy coverlet and folded a sheet across her breasts and stomach for warmth. He kicked off his boots and climbed onto the bed, spread her legs and knelt between them, massaging her taut belly, crooning, "It's all right, Catherine. Save your strength until the pain demands it. Breath deep...come on, now, Catherine . . . we can bring this baby . . . carefully . . . carefully."

Through intermittent swirls of pain coming one on top of another without enough time between to catch her breath, Catherine felt caught in a moving, all-encompassing pain even as Levi's deep, soothing voice penetrated the haze around her.

"It's all right, love, all right...everything is all right...I love you, Catherine...remember I love you...here, now. I can see the baby's head...breathe deep...it won't be long now...now, push! Push, push! That's good, that's good, the baby's coming. Now rest."

He leaned back for a moment, smiling encouragement, his grey eyes full of love. "The baby has lots of hair, Catherine, lots of dark hair …now, push…push…you don't have to be quiet, scream if you want…that's right, let go…relax just a moment…now push…once more…"

Pain mushroomed through Catherine, blooming into a terrible pressure, stronger, more monstrous than any she could remember. She felt stretched beyond belief but the baby would not, would not come. Her arms were numb from gripping the headboard and her head was bursting from her efforts. "Help me, Levi!" she cried. "It's too hard. Help me!"

With a final, groaning shriek she felt release and knew the baby's head was born.

Levi's soothing voice blanketed her. "Breathe deep now…that's right…we're almost there…ready now, once more, my love…just once more."

"I can't. I'm so tired, Levi." Catherine moved her head from side to side, back and forth. "Just let me be…." But the pain built again. "I can't help, Levi," she cried, tears streaming into her ears. "Take the baby! Please take the baby!"

"It will come, Catherine…" Levi's calm voice was strong and vital. "Once more…here, now…" He leaned forward and placed one strong, blunt hand atop the mound of her belly. "I'll help you now, breathe deep…and push…push! Catherine, you must. Now!"

His command was imperative, and she caught her breath, biting her lip so hard she tasted blood. She shut her eyes and gathered all her strength, grunting as she pushed hard, down, down unaware of anything but her effort and Levi's strong hand helping.

Suddenly she felt a slippery rush and heavenly release. The

pain was gone. She opened her eyes to look up at Levi, kneeling between her bare knees, his face awash with the silent miracle he held in his big hands.

Tiny, wrinkled.

Quiet.

Blue.

"Oh, God. The baby's dead, too, isn't it?" Catherine's voice was flat, exhausted. She clamped her dulled eyes shut against this new, fresh pain that was untold times mightier than any other.

She couldn't breathe.

All for nothing. Nothing!

She closed her mind against Levi's murmured words and the resounding slap he administered to the baby's tiny bottom.

No, no! Not another shallow grave…not for this child of love… Catherine's head moved back and forth, back and forth on her sweat-drenched pillow, railing against fate, denying its reality.

Suddenly a faint, mewling wail seeped into her senses and blossomed into an angry, gusty resistance at having been thrust from a warm nest into this cold and drafty room. Catherine's eyes flew open in wonder to meet Levi's triumphant smile.

"Your daughter, Catherine." Levi moved off the bed carefully, wrapped the baby in a warming towel, and laid the child in Catherine's arms.

"*Our* daughter, Levi." Her eyes spoke more than her words. "Thank you," she whispered. "Can you—"

"Yes. The cord. I know." He deftly tied and cut the fragile lifeline, so similar and yet so different from that of the animals he'd tended. As they waited for the afterbirth, Catherine counted small fingers and toes and then smiled up at him through her tears. "She's beautiful, isn't she, Levi?"

But his eyes were on his wife. "Yes," he said quietly, "She is."

"She's nearly a week old, and you haven't a name for her yet," Levi said, letting a tiny fist curl around his calloused finger as he stood near the rocking chair and looked down with pride at the small, fuzzy head nuzzling and sucking contentedly at Catherine's full breast. "Don't most mothers have a name ready for either boy or girl long before it's born?"

"I was afraid to," Catherine admitted. "I didn't want to tempt fate."

"My dear Catherine, you can't tempt fate. You can only deal with it." He touched the dark fuzz on the baby's head. "The plow's been by and I've shoveled the drive, so today we can register her birth. Now our daughter needs a name and," Levi paused and smiled, "if you haven't one to give her, I do."

Catherine looked up with surprise at her husband's solid, weather-worn face. "You have? And you never said a word?"

"It was my grandmother's name." His expression was enigmatic. She couldn't tell whether he was teasing or not.

Catherine wrinkled her nose at him. "Is it a perfectly horrible name?"

"You can be the judge of that."

The baby lost her nipple, and Levi gently turned its head back to suckle again. "I love to watch," he said. "It's something I've always dreamed of."

She caught his hand. "Levi, Tell me."

"What?"

"The name, Silly. Remember?" She laughed up at him, her clear blue eyes sparkling. "What if I hate it?"

"Then you think of one, and I'll hate that."

"Levi Sommers! If I wasn't nursing this baby I'd hit you with the frypan. Tell me!"

His smiled disappeared, his deep grey eyes met hers and his voice was so quiet she had to strain to hear it. "It's Olivia."

Startled blue eyes widened. She swallowed. "O–Olivia?"

He nodded. "No questions, no answers. Do you hate it?"

"Oh, Levi." She looked at him, perplexed. Was he telling her he knew? "Was that really your grandmother's name?"

"No questions. Do you hate it?"

"No." She blinked to hold back tears. "I–I love it."

"I thought you might." He started for the door. "That's settled, then. And I have a request."

"A request?"

"Perhaps a demand."

Catherine stared at him. He had every right, but what would he ask of her?

"I've waited so long to have a child, and I do not want her ever to be hurt, to question her birth. We will celebrate our marriage anniversary in June each year."

Her eyes widened. "But others know."

"They'll forget, lose interest. And who is more important?"

She nodded. "Of course. Our child."

After Levi had gone to the barn to do chores, Catherine rocked the baby slowly as dusk seeped into the comfortable, flower-papered room, trying hard to understand a love so complete, so selfless as Levi's.

He'd named the baby Olivia. Surely he knew.

No questions, no answers, he had said. Catherine held her daughter fiercely to her breast. "Olivia Sommers," she whispered to the baby's fragile ear. "You are going to have—you do have—the most wonderful father in the world."

"She's exquisite." Oliver Houle was the first neighbor to reach them after the snowplow cleared the roads. As Levi had driven into town to register the baby's birth, he'd met Oliver on the road, flagged him down, and given him the news.

"Stop by and see her," Levi had finished, and Oliver wasn't sure whether he meant the baby or Catherine until he added, "She'll be glad for the company."

Now Oliver and Catherine stood together, looking down into the white-painted, ruffled wicker basket that stood near the stove in the kitchen, the warmest room in the old farmhouse.

"What have you named her?"

Catherine's wide blue eyes met his. "Olivia."

Oliver took a quick step backwards. "You named her that? How could you?"

"I didn't. Levi chose it."

Oliver frowned. "Just like that?"

"'No questions, no answers,' he said. He told me it was his grandmother's name."

"He knows. He must know."

Catherine touched the sleeping baby's head lightly. "Nothing's been said, and nothing will be. It doesn't matter. She's his daughter. Now and forever."

Oliver turned his head away. "Of course. How could it be otherwise?" He took a deep breath and straightened his shoulders. "I brought you a gift, Cathy."

She smiled. "Oliver, you're supposed to bring the baby a gift, not the mother."

"Perhaps I have. Here." He reached into the inside pocket of his mackinaw and handed her an official-looking paper.

"What is it?"

"Look."

She frowned. "A deed? To what?" She read on, puzzled, finally drawing a quick intake of breath and raising startled eyes to his. "The house on the dunes. The lovely house? In my name? Oliver, you can't. What have you done?"

"Bought us a retreat, a dream…a chance at time…a memory…I don't know. It's yours, Cathy. And has a man to keep it up. When we can steal away, it's ours. Oh, Cathy, say you'll work it out somehow. Say we'll have time there alone even if it's only an hour." His eyes pleaded even more passionately than his words.

"But we'll never use it."

"I need to think we will. And it's only fitting that someday Olivia, our daughter, will have it as her own. The place she was conceived."

She shook her head. "Oliver, you're crazy. I'm married. There's Levi and the baby—"

"Our baby."

"And your own family. How? Oh, Oliver."

He pulled out his pocket watch and frowned. "I've got to go. I'm late, and Bonnie will be furious. Oh, Cathy." He pulled her into his arms, held her so close she could barely breathe, as though he would never let her go, and then tilted her face to meet his kiss.

It was a poignant kiss, a sweet tasting of each other, a longing for what should have been, a kiss of remembrance and promise.

Catherine's body arched to meet the longing in his, and she clung to him, relishing his love, memorizing his arms, his tongue, his very being for the lonely times ahead.

Then, shaken at her brazenness, her disloyalty to Levi's goodness, she stepped away. "You'd better go, Oliver."

"Yes." He nodded, swallowing with difficulty. "I'll keep the deed, but the house is yours to do with as you like. Tell me when to be there, and I will." He drew her to him again, holding her as though he would pull her body into his own. "It's our insurance against fate, Cathy."

Her voice was muffled against his chest as she repeated Levi's recent words. "You can't tempt fate, Oliver. You can only deal with it."

Early April spread spring's promise over Wisconsin. Against the south foundation of the house, purple and yellow crocuses Catherine had planted in the fall pushed up to greet the sun. Drifts that had seemed too high to ever disappear melted into snow-cold rivulets that warmed and ran down the hills to feed the valley streams. The sun teased buds from early trees and shrubs, blanketing Wisconsin farmland with the hope of another rich growing season.

After shaking dried mud from the entry's throw rug, Catherine stood on the small back porch and breathed in the clear sweet promise of the new season. She shaded her eyes to watch Levi competently straighten a wobbly fence post near the barn. The muscles of his sturdy arms rippled as he worked, and he whistled a lively tune that came across the distance to her in a thin, lilting melody.

She had it all—Oliver's child, healthy and happy, a home and respect as Levi Sommers' wife, and Levi himself, surrounding her with love and care.

As though he felt her presence, Levi looked toward her and smiled. "Do you need anything?" he called.

"Nothing," she called back, shaking her head. He was too far away to see the tears that filled her eyes.

Full spring came, finally, with pale budding leaves and soft winds, fields plowed and planted and rows of vegetables seeded into summer gardens. The season flowered into the sweetness of plum and apple blossoms that wafted across the fragile green spears of grass surrounding the Sommers' farmhouse.

Catherine looked up into the early summer sky from where she nursed tiny Olivia in the sunny south porch. Weeks had passed since she'd seen Oliver; full weeks of spring farm chores and plantings that should have, but hadn't, driven thoughts of him from her mind.

Had Oliver's farm work driven thoughts of her and Olivia from his? Where was he, now, at this minute? Busy in his fields? Talking with Amery? In town perhaps, buying supplies or feed? She longed to know. Was he thinking of her? Did he wish he could see how Olivia, the daughter he so longed to claim, had grown?

She ran a finger over the soft dark hair on Olivia's head and smiled down into the child's blue eyes that were already turning toward hazel. Catherine reveled in the sweetness of the baby's gurgling smile that returned all the love showered on her.

"You lucky, lucky little baby," Catherine crooned, slipping her finger into the small, grasping fist. "Spoiled little girl."

The baby gurgled again, and a bubble of warm milk dribbled from her little mouth before she suckled again.

"Such manners." Levi chuckled from over Catherine's shoulder.

She flushed as though he might have heard her unfaithful thoughts. She hadn't heard him come in.

"You'll have to teach her to use a napkin," he teased.

She laughed, raising the baby to her shoulder. "There'll be time enough for that."

Levi lowered himself to the opposite rocker, his expression thoughtful. "Catherine." He paused and then leaned forward to run his knuckle over Olivia's cheek. "I have something to say."

It was unlike Levi to spend time in the house during the day, especially now at planting time. What could be so important he would stop his afternoon work? She waited, busying herself with the baby.

"Look at me."

Almost reluctantly she raised her eyes to meet his. He sounded so serious, and all too often he seemed able to plug into her innermost wishes or fears. "Yes? What is it?"

"A gift."

"Oh, Levi! You've given me so much already."

He cut her off with a raised palm. "Things, perhaps. But not what you need most."

She frowned. "And what would that be?"

"Time."

"Time?" Puzzled, she searched his face. "I don't understand."

"To go away."

Olivia nuzzled Catherine's neck, and she brought the baby to her breast again before she could raise her questioning eyes to his. "Levi, what are you saying?"

"Take her and go."

"Go? What do you mean? Are—are you sending me away?" Her eyes were wide with apprehension. What could he mean? Where should she go?

"I know your need, and I'll be here when you come back. An

hour, a day? I hope not more." He rose heavily, suddenly looking older than his years. "Say nothing. Now or ever." He left the porch as quietly as he had come.

Stunned, she shut her eyes, and, as he asked, said nothing.

The dream was powerful. To go away. To Oliver, with Oliver? Could that really be what Levi meant? She knew it was, and she knew what it must cost him to offer.

Promise me you'll never shame me. His words that fatal day in the woods cathedral came into her mind as clearly as though Levi spoke them aloud. *Oh, Levi, Levi...*

Where could they go that wouldn't be known, wouldn't bring shame to Levi Sommers? A day, more? And could Oliver get away now, at such a busy season? Thoughts jumbled over and over through Catherine's mind as her stomach churned with the exciting possibility.

In an hour, Amery would come for his tutoring. Could she send a note? No. She shook her head. That would be all wrong, wrong. Hadn't she put that part of her life away? Yet Levi was offering. She shut her eyes, and Oliver's sensitive face appeared as it had so many times. *See me, Cathy. Anytime. Anywhere.*

Her note was short. *The house on the dunes. Thursday.* She knew Amery would deliver it without Bonnie's knowledge. The train would take her into Bayshore; Oliver had given her the name of someone who could be hired to take her to the house and he would let the caretaker know they were coming.

"We're going to see your daddy, Olivia," she whispered, holding the baby so tightly she burped and bubbled milk down onto her lace collar.

The station was empty for the 5:30 morning train, and Catherine looked soberly through the dirty window at Levi, standing quietly on the platform, a warm wind tugging at his grey hair as they chugged away, his expression nonjudgmental, one sturdy arm raised in farewell. She knew he would be there the next evening when she returned.

"Come back happy, my Catherine," were his farewell words. "Take good care of the child."

Not "my" child, but "the" child. Blinking back tears, Catherine leaned back against the plush cushion, holding bundled Olivia asleep in her arms. "Oliver, Oliver, Oliver," the train's wheels seemed to whisper.

10

OLIVIA, 1984

"The girl okay?" Tim whispered as Pamela waddled ahead of them toward the door of Dunes House.

Olivia reached into the back of the old pickup to get her suitcase. "I think so, Tim. Well, I didn't ask her all about everything. I just brought her back with me."

He nodded, his Adam's apple bobbing with each movement of his head. "Right thing to do. No use digging around in things can't be changed. Just sticks them in a body's mind."

"You're very astute, Tim." Olivia smiled and lifted her head, taking a deep breath of clear Lake Michigan air. "It's wonderful to be back. I do love it here."

Tim nodded. "The very words Miss Cathy used to say when she came, every time. The very words." He pointed to Pam's back. "You know, a person ought to take better care of a girl like that one," he said as they walked toward the house.

Olivia stopped, frowning. "Meaning?"

"Now, don't get your dander up. I don't mean pertect, exactly. That's prob'ly not so good."

"You're right about that. That's something I've finally learned, too late. I shouldn't have protected her so well, but what do you mean by 'care'?"

"Well…" Tim chewed his lower lip for a moment. "A girl like that ought to be given the know-how that'll keep her safe, you know? To know what to do, I mean. You didn't find out what really happened to her? Think best left alone?"

Olivia nodded. "I do think it's not too late to put in some of that know-how now. I'm just not quite sure where to start." They reached the kitchen door. "Thanks for picking us up, Tim. Oh, I meant to ask, would you be able to teach Pam to row the boat? I'm sure she could. It would be good exercise, give her something to do."

"Sure thing. Fish, even. She might like that."

"Of course, she would. She's never been fishing. Bert's not much of an outdoors man." Olivia laid her purse on the kitchen table. "And I thought I might let her do some of the cooking, if you think you can stand a few burned dinners."

"I was tired of cookin' anyways. You just tell me what you need. Otherwise, we'll let her be, all right? Let her feel her way around for a bit. Then, well, we'll see."

"Thanks, Tim, I appreciate it. And the fishing. I think she'll really enjoy that."

He nodded, cleared his throat, and fixed her with a determined look. "Now listen, Miss Livvy, I want you to know that I locked the boathouse up good and tight, and there's been nobody hangin' round there since. Prob'ly was some college kid lookin' for a place to bum free. But you don't need to worry any more about somebody hangin' round." Every word punctuated by a nod and the bob of his Adam's apple. "You ain't to worry any more. Subject's closed." Tim turned and headed out the door toward his apartment, calling back over his shoulder, "Good to have you back anyways."

Olivia stared after him. She'd learned there was no use talking when Tim closed a subject. Anyways, it was good to be back.

Later that day, Olivia and Tim sat with iced teas on the lower porch, looking out over the lake where gray skittered over blue as breezes played with the surface. "Tim, did my mother ever say anything to you about keeping things over at the farm?"

The familiar closed look came into Tim's face, the look Olivia had seen whenever she tried to dig into her mother's past.

"Can't say that she did."

Won't say, she thought. "I'd like to run over to the farm one afternoon and pick up a box or two the renters said they found in the attic and pack up what's left in the little house there. Okay?" At Tim's nod, she went on, "Tell me, Tim, did my mother write a lot when she was here?"

He nodded again, the soft look coming around his eyes at the thought of Miss Cathy. "That she did. Evenin's they would sit around the kitchen fireplace there. Quiet, like, both of them, rockin.' Reading or writing. Like they was just happy together, not even talking."

Olivia tried to picture Catherine and Levi, simply reading or writing around the fire. Somehow the picture wasn't clear. The evenings she remembered at the farmhouse brought the image of Levi simply resting in his armchair, his gaze following her mother as she sewed or read, or cooked a meal in the open farmhouse kitchen.

"Sometimes I'd find papers lying around in the morning when I cleaned up after they left. Those I put in the box I gave you the first morning you were here. If she had other stuff, I didn't see it, 'cept for the notebook she was always writin' in.

Wonder where it went." He put down his glass and stood up. "Got to fix one more thing on the pickup. Heard another darn rattle on the way home today. I'll be around. You want something, give me a whistle."

Olivia watched Tim make his slow way through the kitchen, her mind chewing on the tidbits he'd thrown her, wondering once again whether Tim was not only part of the conspiracy of odd things going on around Dunes House but was perhaps the instigator.

Pamela waddled onto the porch, one leg of her shorts pulled higher than the other. She looked disheveled, as usual, but not unhappy. She seldom looked unhappy. Olivia remembered reading a poem about retarded adults which asked whether it was fair to bring them out of their comfortable world into the author's uncertainty. For Olivia, Pam was one of those people. Whatever had happened to her in Portland hadn't seemed to disturb her. "Pam, I want to ask you something."

"O-kay." Pam jerked at her shorts leg. "What?"

Olivia studied Pamela's blotchy cheeks and wide grey eyes. There was no apprehension there, no expression at all. Olivia opened her mouth, but stopped. What could she ask this overgrown child? Tell me about the man in the park. Where did he touch you? Did he hurt you? She sighed. "Oh, nothing special, I guess. I was wondering if you'd like to learn to row the boat."

"Row the boat?"

"Move it around on the water. Out on the lake. And Mr. Tim said he would teach you to fish, if you want."

"Fish?" Pamela grinned, dovetailing a hand through the air.

"To catch them. To eat."

"Catch? Like this, in my hands?" Pamela snatched at the air.

Olivia smiled. "I think that might be difficult. Mr. Tim will show you. I'll have him open the boathouse and take you out.

You'll like that."

"Yes!" Pam stated, smiling as she studiously tugged her shorts legs even around her pudgy thighs. "I'll like that," she repeated.

"Livvy!" Heath's voice, deep with pleasure, called to her through the open window beside his potter's wheel as she climbed the briar-lined path. "Come on in. Delighted you're back."

Olivia's breath caught at the sound. She'd been surprised at how much she'd missed talking with him, actually missed looking at his tautly muscled body, even in the short time (Had it really been only a week?) she'd spent in Portland. She'd been surprised, too, at how often he'd been in her thoughts, even when she was dealing with Bert and the problem of Pamela.

Olivia opened the door and was greeted by a warm bear hug and a hello kiss that began as a greeting but turned into something considerably longer and more special. Heath's arms around her were strong and affectionate even though he held his clay-wet hands away from her back. She stepped into his embrace as though she belonged there at the same time she irreverently thought what a pleasure it was to be hugged by someone whose stomach didn't get in the way. She drifted for a heady moment.

"Look, Ma, no hands!" Heath grinned as he let her go. "Let me finish this piece while we talk, and then I'll kiss you properly." He sat down at the wheel and gave her a studied, one-eyebrow-cocked leer. "That is, if that's the way you want to be kissed."

"How else?" Olivia fell into his banter easily, experiencing a world suddenly lighter, brighter, more real.

"Improperly, of course." Heath's expression sobered as he kept his eyes on the tall, slippery pot his deft hands formed as he spoke. "How is your daughter? Did you find out what happened?"

Olivia, still a little breathless from his kiss, gazed out over the wind-tossed treetops and beyond to the shimmering water that shifted grey, then green, as she brought Heath up to date.

"She's here with you?"

"You sound surprised." Olivia went to stand beside him, appreciating the authority which guided the sleek grey clay into graceful symmetry. "What else could I do?"

Frowning, Heath wire-cut the pot off the wheel and placed it on a bat to dry. "Nothing, I suppose. Of course not. I guess I just hadn't considered you would."

"Oh, Heath, I had to. I've made so many mistakes with her."

He stood back to examine his pot, nodding satisfaction. "Thing is, have you learned from them?" He turned to her. "That is, will you be any different now? Will she?"

She tried not to take offence. "My hindsight's twenty-twenty. I'm not so sure about my foresight. God, Heath, I don't know! Of course I love her, but now…she's like a millstone. I never felt that way about her before." Olivia absently fingered the little snake in the coffee table arrangement. "And if I thought I felt guilty before, I didn't even know what guilt was!"

"Have you considered what you'll do if she's pregnant?"

"That's a bridge I'll cross if I come to it." She wandered aimlessly around the room, touching various pieces of his art. "All I really want right now is to keep this experience, whatever it was, from damaging her somehow. I don't know. I'll just have to wait and see."

"And wallow in guilt. You're good at that."

"Thanks. But you're right, of course, I will." Olivia straightened her shoulders. "New subject. Tim says he 'cleaned him out' of the boathouse."

"And who is 'him'?"

"I don't know. The chicken-bones man. This isn't the first time I've thought Tim wasn't telling me everything. He said once he had a nephew 'somewheres,' and I'm beginning to wonder if maybe 'somewheres' isn't right under my nose."

Heath finished sponging up the mud spatters around his pottery wheel. "Coffee?" Before she could answer, he shook his head and answered himself. "Nope. Time for wine. Well, I think you shouldn't worry. If Tim says he took care of it, he probably did."

One way or another, Olivia thought as she watched Heath's capable hands uncork a tall, slim bottle and pour two rough goblets of clear red wine.

"To your return. God, it's good to have you back, Livvy. I hadn't realized..." His eyes held hers for a long moment as she lifted her goblet to answer his toast.

"Thank you," she whispered. "I feel as though I've come home."

He took her hand and pulled her toward the couch.

"You have come home, Livvy," he said as he took the wine from her hand and set it on the table. "I think you know you have."

She wanted to tell him she'd missed him. "Heath—"

Her words were cut off as he gathered her into his arms without preamble. For a split second she pushed her palms against his chest, telling herself this was wrong, she was married, she belonged to Bert...but Heath's lips were on hers.

His kiss was first an asking, then a searching and finally a demand, sensuously testing, tasting her response. Olivia caught her breath as her mouth greedily accepted his tongue, as her body moved against him of its own accord.

Heath nuzzled her neck. "Livvy? You feel it too, Livvy?"

Olivia arched her neck as his tongue moved slowly down into

the V of her shirt, giving him her answer without words.

"I want you, Livvy." His voice was husky with desire as his caress slid up from her waist to her breast, the warmth from his palms burning through her clothes as he kissed the beating hollow at the base of her neck. His fingers sought the buttons on her shirt.

She caught his hand to stop him. "Heath—"

"I want the pleasure of undressing you, beautiful lady."

The thought struck her as funny, and she laughed aloud. "Nobody but me has undressed this body for God knows how many years."

"Don't spoil the mood," he chastised, grinning. "Though I haven't exactly practiced a lot lately, I think I still can manage buttons and buttonholes." His hands, light but insistent, brushed against her breasts as he undid the front of her shirt.

Olivia stared, mesmerized, into his blue eyes, now darkened with passion, before his heated gaze moved slowly to her uncovered, heaving breasts. She reveled in his warm, wine-rich breath against her skin.

Her lips parted, her eyes closed and she fell into an abyss of simply feeling, not thinking. Relearning. "Yes," she whispered into his tousled hair. "Oh, yes."

Barefoot, Olivia swung her deck shoes in one hand as she walked slowly back up the beach in late afternoon sunshine, her thoughts tumultuous with the tantalizing excitement, the fulfillment of Heath's lovemaking.

"Lovemaking." She said the word aloud. How long had it been since she and Bert had found more than physical release in each other? And how many times, for her, no release at all? She couldn't remember. Like the scene a few nights ago in Portland, sex had all become so...so dutiful and so dull.

Olivia grinned at herself, strutting along the sand in rolled-up blue jeans. She skipped lightly and kicked a small shell into the water with a bare toe. She felt about 20 years old. Ridiculous! Playing sex games, at her age, and with a man years younger than herself. Well, speaking chronologically, yes, but most assuredly not younger in experience or in the ability to make the ordinary act of sex a white-heat episode that consumed them both. Her face flushed. She had thoroughly enjoyed every second, every single sensuous second.

She could feel guilt hovering like a small, dense cloud above her, ready to descend. Good grief, was she going to become paranoid over everything she did? Other women had lovers. She pushed the guilt up and away, mentally tossing it along with a real pebble out over the ever-changing water. The whole grand world was bright and beautiful, and her personal world was, for the first time in years, interesting and exciting beyond words.

She stopped short. *Do I love Heath Collins?* Love? She examined the word and all it should mean. *Probably not.* Did it matter? She did love his fantastic, taut muscled body, even his backside. She grinned. So different, so much more sensuous than Bert's soft, droopy flab. Olivia snorted aloud, remembering her friend Andrea's comment on younger lovers: "Really, Livvy, you should try one. They're wonderful!"

Try one. Like a new blouse, or a sexy pair of shoes? Olivia began to walk again, watching soft, foamy riffles of water lap at her bare toes. Good old sex, she mused, chuckling. Done right—*and Heath definitely knows how to do it right*—what it can do for a person is really something.

She calculated how long she'd been gone from Dunes House

and another blanket of guilt hovered overhead, then descended. Probably Tim and Pamela thought she'd fallen in a hole somewhere along the shore.

"Come back, you sexy vixen," Heath had said as he kissed her goodbye. "As soon as you can. Later tonight?"

Olivia opened her arms wide to the sky, embracing the world and everything in it. Today. Heath Collins. Living.

A piece of driftwood perfect for Heath's work caught her eye. She marked the spot; she would carry it back to him when next she went.

"Why do you bother to wear a bra?" Heath had asked, loosening her breasts, nuzzling them as he held them gently together. "Here, I mean. You wouldn't have to."

"I guess I'm just used to being conventional."

He leered. "Lady, you don't look very conventional right now." He ran his finger down her tingling diaphragm and inside her belt line. He leaned forward as he unsnapped her jeans and lightly, oh, so lightly, caressed her stomach and threaded his fingers into the soft triangle above her thighs. Her nipples stung, wanting more of his soft moist mouth, the sensuous opening within his fuzzy, nuzzly beard. It had felt the way she'd imagined it would, against her mouth, against her breasts.

"I should be embarrassed," she said, cradling his head in both her hands as her body arched toward his teasing lips and her thighs pressed to his.

"Should you? Why?"

"That I'm with you like this. All the old ethics come to the surface."

"Ah." His light blue eyes danced with laughter as he teased her nipples. "You and I might be the end of the world here, you know? Or the beginning. Adam and Eve." He caressed her smooth bare shoulders, down her arms.

"At least they were the same age."

He raised his head. "Does that bother you?"

"Shouldn't it?"

"Not unless you think I'm looking for a mother figure, which, lady, I assure you I am definitely not." He moved his hands to cup her breasts and push them together so his tongue could favor them both. "What else bothers you?"

"I've never done this before," she said. "And never with anyone but Bert."

He grinned. "And aren't you serious about it."

"Well, I mean–I don't–oh!" Her whole body shuddered as he tugged her still-stiff jeans and underwear off her hips.

He stood above her for a moment, just looking. "Livvy, you're beautiful. Definitely, yes, definitely, not a mother figure. But did anyone ever tell you that you talk too much?" And then his lips claimed hers once more.

Now she smiled, reliving as she swung along the waterline, her bare feet making shallow water-filled indentations. She stopped for a few seconds at the boathouse to check whether the rowboat was in and continued slowly up the steep steps to the top of the bluff.

With Pamela here, Olivia's feelings about Dunes House weren't the same, as though the house didn't exactly belong to her any more, as though her too-recently acquired private space had been narrowed, invaded, even surrounded.

"Mum! Where you been?" Olivia looked up to see Pamela's round, freshly sunburned face behind the screen of the second-floor porch. "I been waiting and waiting. I caught a fish. Big!" She held her hands up, more than a foot apart.

"Oh, very good, Pam. What kind?"

"I don't know. Mr. Tim is peeling it for our supper." Pamela grinned happily and dropped her chin into her palms, propping her elbows on the sill. "What're we goin' to do tonight, Mum? I'm so glad you came home."

Olivia squinted up at the silhouette of the house against the brilliant late-afternoon sky, seeing Pamela not as someone on the inside looking out, but as someone from another life with the power to change Olivia's whole new-found world.

"I don't know what we'll do, Pam." Of course she wanted to go back to Heath tonight, to savor again the glory in his hands, his mouth, his aroused body. And of course, that was impossible. She shook her head and sighed. "I really don't know."

11

CATHERINE, April, 1939

At Dunes House for over an hour before Oliver drove in, Catherine put away the food she'd bought in Bayshore and got acquainted with Tim Ryan, the taciturn man who lived over the large garage. With no idea about what was in the house, she found to her delight Oliver had repainted the whole house and furnished it completely.

"How lovely!" she exclaimed, fairly dancing onto the lower porch to gaze out over the deep grey-blue water. "Oh, Mr. Ryan, you've done a wonderful job."

He grinned, his Adam's apple bobbing with every nod of his head. "Wanted to have it ready any time. The mister said you wouldn't come much, but he didn't know when, and I was to keep it ready as if you'd walk in any minute. Everything okay, then?"

"Oh, yes." Catherine impulsively took both his hands in hers and stood on tiptoe to kiss his cheek. "Thank you!" Her eyes glowing, she ran to the screened porch. "Oh. I never dreamed…" Flushing, she bit her lip, embarrassed at what she felt needed saying. "We'll…we'll not want to be disturbed."

"Figured that." Tim Ryan looked amused at her discomfiture. "Need me, pull that bell rope by the kitchen door. Otherwise, you're on your own."

The minutes before Oliver finally drove into the yard seemed endless. She nursed Olivia and put her to sleep on colorful cushions from the porch wicker, hoping she would nap at least until Catherine and Oliver had some time alone together.

Time. *The one thing you need,* Levi had said.

Pensive, Catherine stood on the lower porch, her thoughts turning from Levi and their home to Oliver and this house. My house on the dunes, she thought with wonder. It was all too much to comprehend: Levi's unselfish generosity and Oliver's gift of the house to her and eventually to Olivia. She shook her head with the enormity of all she had been given and caught her breath at the sound of a car turning in between the stone gateposts.

She met Oliver at the door in a swirl of happiness and dissolved into his arms, unleashing all the passion held within her for so long, thrusting up to meet his demanding lips, arching her trembling body against his lean strength, asking for and promising everything all their months of unfulfilled desire had denied.

There were no words at first, only tender murmurs and endless moments of electric rediscovery, until, finally, capturing her hands in his, Oliver pulled her toward the open stairs.

Later, in the quiet aftermath of love, Oliver raised on one elbow, frowning, to look down into her ardor-filled eyes. "How, Cathy? How were you able to come? What did you tell Levi?" Olivia heard concern for his long-time friend and neighbor even through the joy and wonder of being with her at last.

She paused for only a moment. "Levi sent me, Oliver."

"Sent you?" Oliver pulled back. "You can't mean that. Sending his wife to another?" He scowled. "Is the man trying for sainthood, or what?"

"He loves me, Oliver. It's that simple. He just really loves me." Catherine closed her eyes for a moment, remembering Levi's sober wave as the train pulled away. It hurt too much to remember such longing and such forgiveness as had been written on his face. She put the memory away. "Let's not spoil our precious hours with our other lives. They're there. This is here, now." Her clear blue eyes were soft; her love-swollen lips invited his to claim hers, to possess her again.

Levi sent Catherine and Olivia away again that fall and the next spring, only for a day each time, but that was enough. There were no questions asked; she understood he didn't want to know where she went, and she was sure he never asked anyone whether Oliver was also gone, though it would have been easy enough for him to find out. Like her journals, these days were hers alone. Whatever she needed, if Levi could give, he gave.

For Catherine, each stolen day was a precious pearl strung with love so strong nothing could have shaken her from Levi's side. Contrary to what anyone might have believed had they known, Catherine's marriage to Levi grew stronger as he nurtured that strength with everything within his power. He had more than he had hoped to have, and he could wait for the rest. Forever, if need be.

Every hour at Dunes House was too short, filled with Oliver's passion for Catherine and his wonder at Olivia and how she grew and developed in unbelievable spurts.

"I wish she knew I was her father," Oliver said one Spring day as, wistful, he watched Olivia toddle across the buffed oak floor, tempting her to take one more step, then another, by holding out a tiny, soft teddy bear he had brought.

"No!" Catherine cried, her eyes wide, clutching his arm. "You wouldn't!"

The sadness in his voice was unmistakable. "You know I wouldn't, Cathy," he reproached. "I'm just wishing."

"I'm sorry." Catherine was immediately contrite. "But Levi is so good to her—"

"Levi!" Oliver exploded, slamming his fist against the arm of his chair, sending tiny Olivia tumbling, howling, to her mother's knees. He rose and strode furiously across the room. "Levi.

Sometimes I'm so damn sick of Levi Sommers! He's got everything I want and he glories in it."

"He does not," Catherine declared before she bent to sooth the little girl. "It's all right, sweetie…it's all right." She raised her eyes to meet Oliver's. "And you couldn't have it all anyway. You know I'd be gone if it weren't for Levi. We wouldn't even have these times."

It was his turn to apologize. "Sorry." He sank down on a chair, elbows on his knees, his head in his palms as he stared at the floor.

"Oliver." He looked up. "We only have another hour."

"I know. God, how I know…. "

The fall when Olivia was two, Levi spoke into the darkness above their bed. "You won't take her any more, Catherine."

She had been almost asleep. "I'm sorry, Levi. What did you say?"

"The child. From now on she stays with me."

His meaning was clear, and sensible, for Olivia was beginning to talk.

"Oh." The darkened room was charged with things unsaid. "Yes, Levi. Of course."

And a week later, Olivia boarded the train alone, looking soberly out the dusty window at Levi on the station deck holding a whimpering Olivia. A moment's hesitation before the train began to move gave her time to change her mind, get off and go home with them, but the pull of Oliver's love, the thought of his face, his arms, was too strong.

The stolen days were a taste of heaven for Catherine and

Oliver, with golden hours spent walking the beach below Dunes House, with quiet, wine-rich dinners on the lower porch when the weather was fine, or inside by the fire, cozy against rain and wind. It never seemed wrong for them to be in the one place in the world where they belonged together, and it never seemed they were different in any way from the two dream-crossed lovers who wandered into the house so long ago.

Years when it was impossible for them to be away with each other were torture, and Catherine found herself gazing out windows for long moments at the changing seasons, drifting in her mind to the place she longed to be if only for precious minutes.

But when they did come together, even fleetingly, Catherine's life took on a special sheen, a serene and loving happiness even young Olivia felt when her mother returned from her "renewals." And they *were* renewals for all the Sommers in their quiet family life, which held very little socializing outside of community church functions. The three of them were a content, close-knit circle as Olivia grew into a bright young girl who excelled in school and became more attractive every day.

"I wish you didn't all look so damn happy!" Oliver remarked at one church potluck supper as he filled a plate to take to Bonnie.

"But we are," was Catherine's answer. "I only wish you were."

"I am, when we're at Dunes House."

Seasons passed, approached and passed again, sometimes happily, sometimes less so. Catherine's and Oliver's separate lives continued to intertwine whenever they could, through the growing-up years of Amery and Olivia, through Bonnie Houle's continual unhappy niggling, through Levi's steadfast loyalty in spite of tiring muscles and arthritic pains and other physical problems of simply growing older.

Crop seasons were good, year after year, and the Sommers prospered, but not to the extent of the Houles. Oliver, his life empty except for the short and passionate hours with Catherine, threw himself with fervor into making more and more money, extending his lands and crops and delving into investments and futures.

"Can't you get away from those everlasting books of yours, Oliver? Talk to me!" Bonnie demanded often, especially after Amery had gone to the University at Madison, but Oliver's home hours were spent planning how his investments could make his considerable fortune even larger.

"We don't need anything more, for heaven's sake!" Bonnie cried, waving her arm to take in the sumptuous furnishings of his library office. "Look around you. We live in a palace!"

The farmhouse, solid and ample in the beginning, had been enlarged, carpeted, re-windowed, the kitchen remodeled to meet every need of a wheelchair-bound woman.

"I thought you wanted everything I've given you." Bemused, Oliver looked up from his desk. "Have I forgotten anything?"

"Forgotten anything?" Bonnie repeated, her voice choked as she turned her chair to leave the room. "Just living, that's all."

Oliver bent his head back to his ledger.

Catherine was pleased that Amery, now almost blind, kept in contact with her as he finished his studies at the University of Madison with high honors, married, and moved to Connecticut, where he taught in a school for the blind. His classes revolved around the love for English literature which Catherine had fostered. The announcement of his only child, Kurt, was accompanied by a short note to Catherine from Amery's wife, with thanks for all her help to him, and included the wish that Kurt would someday know a teacher as dedicated to his future as Catherine had been to Amery's.

Catherine took the note to Dunes House and showed it to Oliver one quiet evening as they sat on the lower porch watching the water fade to blue-grey in an early dusk.

"He always loved you, Cathy," Oliver said after reading the note. "He asked me once—remember when his eyes were bandaged that first time and you came to the house with his lessons?—he asked me why I couldn't marry you instead of his mother." Oliver's voice trailed off.

"Oliver! You never told me. What did you say?"

He shrugged. "What could I say? That it was impossible. But oh how I wished." He fastened his eyes on the blurred horizon.

"So many wishes." Catherine covered his hand with hers. "So many years."

Oliver's deep blue eyes, fanned now with wrinkles from years of outdoor work, looked steadily into hers. "When, Cathy? When will there be time for us? Real time, not these pretend hours?"

She didn't look at him. "Someday, maybe. When it's right."

The year that Olivia turned fifteen, October was a myriad rainbow of color at Dunes House. The birches behind the house swirled brilliant yellow to the ground; the red oak near the side yard transformed into rich wine; the pines took on an even deeper green against the oranges and russets.

"Oh!" Catherine drank in every spectacular as she stepped from Tim Ryan's pickup into the late afternoon sun. "It's so beautiful! I do love it so." Grinning, she spread her arms wide to encompass the whole world of Dunes House and all it meant to her.

Tim smiled, nodding, his protuberant Adam's apple bobbing. "Color waited for you. Leaves just began to turn this week. Mr. Oliver said this time was goin' to be special."

"Special?" Catherine raised her eyebrows. Wasn't every time special?

But not like this. After a quiet candlelit dinner and a second glass of the very expensive sherry Oliver had brought, he took her hands and pulled her to the loveseat. "I have something for you."

She laughed, delighted. "Tim told me this was going to be a 'special' time. Is it something foolish?"

Oliver smiled. "You'll have to be the judge." He pulled a long, slim leather box from his pocket.

"Oh." She raised her eyes to his. "That doesn't look foolish. It looks very expensive."

He laid the box across her lap. "Open it, Cathy, my love."

She hesitated.

"Please."

She lifted the cover and gasped. Displayed on grey velvet were a necklace and bracelet of the biggest emeralds she had ever seen. There were nine in the necklace, each set within two sparkling diamonds, with the center, larger emerald surrounded completely by more diamonds, all held together on a shining gold chain. The six stones in the bracelet matched.

"Oliver. These…these are worth a fortune!" Catherine's eyes were wide. "You're crazy. I couldn't wear these."

"Yes, you can. You can wear them here. Let me." He lifted the wisps of hair straying down her neck from the upswept coronet braid she still wore, its strands now laced with grey. He clasped the necklace first, then circled her slim wrist with the bracelet. "Look." He pulled her to her feet toward the long mirror at the entrance hall.

Catherine stared. The necklace fell perfectly to the low vee of her rose velvet robe. "Oh, Oliver, they're exquisite! But—"

"I know what you're going to say, and don't. All these years I've wanted to do this. Remember? I promised."

"Promised?" The carefully-scripted line from his long-ago card appeared in her memory, and she laughed. "You did, didn't you? 'Someday I will give you emeralds,' you wrote. I kept the card, but I didn't intend to hold you to it." She stared into the mirror, mesmerized by the beauty of the jewels. "But I can't—"

"No buts. It's very simple. We'll keep them here, and you will wear them when we come. Count them. There are fifteen, one for each year of our daughter's life. And when the wonderful someday comes she can know the truth, they will belong to her." He moved behind Catherine and laid his cheek on her hair, his arms cradling her as he looked at their reflection in the mirror. "You are so beautiful, my Cathy."

"Still?" She met his eyes in the mirror, and instead of seeing two middle-aged people the image was of dream-caught lovers, as they had been on their first day in this house so many years ago.

He saw the same image. "Still," he answered.

CATHERINE and OLIVIA, 1955

"Mom, there's somebody I want to ask to dinner." Olivia Sommers, sixteen, her crew-necked sweater matching the pale green heather in her plaid skirt, smiled with a far-away look across the kitchen table where she and Catherine shared their after-school ritual cup of tea and fresh-baked cookies.

"Really. Is he tall, dark, and handsome?" Catherine teased.

"*I* think so." Olivia's hazel eyes lit with excitement as she tossed her light brown hair back from her face.

"Like that, is it?" Catherine smiled. Olivia had begun to show an interest in boys only recently, and most of those the Sommers had met were, like Olivia herself, members of the farm and church community of Upper Creek. "Let me guess. Terence Richy."

Olivia convulsed in giggles, almost choking on her ginger cookie. "Him? Oh, Mom, not tongue-tied Terry."

"Is that what the girls call him? I thought he was rather a nice young man."

"Nice, maybe. But wow, it's one-sided conversation all the way with him. Guess again."

Catherine loved these special moments of Olivia's transition between her day at school and home, when she heard all the gossip of the girls' locker room, who was dating whom, who wore what to where. It was such a wonderful contrast to her own convent-like teenage years when she'd become a surrogate Aurelia to fill the void in her parents' lives.

"Hmmmmm. Willy Dodge."

Giggles again. "Silly Willy? Not a chance!" Olivia leaned over the table, serious. "Mom, this man is *older.*"

"Man?" Catherine frowned. "I guess you'd better tell me more."

"Well," Olivia grinned around a mouthful of cookie crumbs. "His name's Bert Hobart. He's visiting his cousin, you know, Merle Thomas? He's from somewhere out west, Oregon, I think. He picked Merle up from school today." Her eyes sparkled. "He's got his own car."

"Does he?" Catherine didn't miss the enthusiasm in her daughter's voice. "Just how old is he?"

"Almost twenty."

Catherine laughed. "Does that mean nineteen?"

Olivia's face fell. "I guess it does. But that's what he said, 'almost twenty.'"

"I'm not sure your father's ready for an almost twenty." Catherine poured a second cup of tea.

"Daddy will like him, I know he will. Please, Mom, can Bert come for Sunday dinner? If he can?"

Catherine thought about it for a moment. "I don't see why not."

Bert Hobart was not really tall, not really dark and not really handsome, but he certainly had an aura of future success about him, and displayed a totally charming, differential manner toward Olivia's parents, especially her mother.

"Salesman type, wouldn't you say?" Levi commented later. "Seems nice enough, though." They were getting ready for bed after staying up to outlast the long goodnight Bert had said to Olivia on the front porch.

Salesman type? Catherine's eyes widened, remembering Joel O'Brien and how he had swept her off her feet, even though she had been years older than Olivia. "Perhaps we ought to discourage him," she said.

Levi sank onto the bed beside his wife and smiled gently as he leaned over to kiss her. "And wave a red flag before the randy bull of first love? He's only going to stay a few months." Levi reached to turn out the light and gathered the wife he cherished so deeply into his arms.

Bert Hobart did only stay a few months. But when he left, he took their pregnant daughter with him.

"You let her go? All the way to Oregon? Without telling me?" Oliver paced the lower porch of Dunes House.

"Oliver, how could I not? And what could you have done? The boy has work out there. There's nothing here, and his uncle has a place for him."

"You're taking it mighty easily. What kind of a 'boy' is he? Don't you give a damn? Doesn't Levi?"

Catherine whirled from the window where she had been staring out over the darkening water, the soft folds of her velvet evening robe swirling around her still-slim body. "You can't believe that. Not of Levi, especially. He's devastated. You know Olivia is the light of his life!" The diamonds surrounding the magnificent emeralds Catherine always wore when they were together captured flashes of fire from the setting sun and sent tiny rainbows spinning around the porch.

Oliver raked a hand through his thinning, greying hair that even yet was determined to fall over his brow. "No. Of course I don't. But all these years…I've watched her grow…in my mind I made such plans for her…for the three of us. . ."

Catherine turned back to the wide expanse of Lake Michigan. Her voice was flat as she said, "It's her life, Oliver. God knows we've made enough mistakes in our own."

He came slowly to stand beside her. She took him in her arms, holding him close, comforting him.

"You're so strong, Cathy. You've never faltered." She shut her eyes and sank her teeth into her inner lip. Never faltered? Sometimes it seemed as though she had done nothing else.

12

OLIVIA - 1984

"*I*'d like to go over and pick up the rest of my mother's things, Tim, if you'll drive us," Olivia said over Pam's burnt breakfast pancakes and coffee. Bert had been right about Pam's cooking, but Tim was patiently holding his tongue and slathering the stack on his plate with plenty of butter and warm maple syrup to counter the taste of charcoal.

"These are good? Not too burned?" Pam asked, her forehead furrowed.

Tim nodded. "Not bad. Takes a while to get it right."

Pamela fixed him with a blue stare, nodding solemnly along with each bob of Tim's prominent Adam's apple. "Next time better."

"Sure."

Glad she'd never been heavily into breakfast, Olivia sent Tim a look of thanks. "So could you take us over to the farm later?"

He pushed his plate away. "Any time. How much stuff you think is there?"

"I'm just going to bring back boxes. I'll rent the little house out furnished, that's easier. We don't need any of my mother's things here, and I won't haul it all back to Portland."

Tim's pale eyes narrowed and he pursed his lips. "You going back, then?"

"I suppose I'll have to," Olivia said.

"Why?"

"My daddy's there," put in Pamela, "and my house." Seeing Olivia's frown, she added, "But it's nice here."

Olivia tried to find an answer to Tim's "Why?" and couldn't honestly think of a good one. More and more, the realization was clear: she didn't want to go back to Bert. Now away long enough to get a distance perspective, she found him boring, pompous, and didactic. She didn't need his financial support any more. She was tired to death of her committees and volunteering. She loved it here, and she accepted a new reality: she cared about Heath Collins. She enjoyed his lighthearted banter, his fascinating personality, his real interest in her life and its problems. *And his sexual attraction.*

"Why? I'm beginning to wonder myself," she said finally. "Come on. Let's clean up this kitchen and go over to the farm."

As they jounced up the long lane to the farm where she'd grown up, Olivia viewed with pleasure the neatly painted barn and outbuildings, the carefully tended flower gardens around the main house, and the freshly painted, sturdy old house itself. Evidently the tenants were worth keeping.

"I remember this place," Pam said, leaning forward. "I was here!"

"That you were. Many times," Olivia said. "Swing around to the little house, will you, Tim?"

"Sure thing." He braked to a squeaky stop at the side of the small home Catherine and Levi had renovated and moved into when he retired and rented out the farm. Originally built as a home for a hired hand, the building had stood empty while Levi ran his farm without help. When he stopped farming, he threw himself wholeheartedly into making the little house perfect for Catherine.

Olivia remembered her mother's letters. "Your father is

working harder now than he did when he farmed, but he won't
listen to me say so. He's determined this house be everything the
big house wasn't. It's wonderful to have such a modern kitchen,
but I keep telling him he's killing himself ..."

But Levi had thrived on the work until, at eighty-two, when
the house was everything Catherine could possibly want, he slept
peacefully into the next world with his arm around the woman
he'd so loved. Olivia recalled coming home for the funeral—with
Pamela, of course. Bert had been "too involved in a business
deal" to make the trip.

"Can't do anything for him anyway, can I?" Bert had said.
"You go."

Olivia mourned her father, mourned the closeness they'd
shared during her childhood and the sad but quiet steadiness Levi
Sommers had shown when she and Bert declared their need to
marry. And she mourned his tender understanding about Pamela.
Sometimes, even after so many years, a picture of her father's
steady, caring face as he took her hand came into her mind: "Your
mother's gone for a little, Chicken. Come with me. We've lots to
do."

"Where did she go?"

"Oh, just away. To renew herself."

"Why, Daddy?"

"Because she needs to." There was never a real answer.

"But can't I go with her?" Olivia remembered asking.

"Not this time," was all he ever said, and there had been other
"not this times," perhaps once or twice a year, which Olivia
learned to accept as a part of the very private lives the Sommers
lived, a worthwhile part because the warmth and love that
Catherine showered on them when she returned more than made
up for her short absence.

"There was somebody here asking about Catherine's things a
few days back, Miz Hobart," Doris Hugh said, the farm tenant

who met them near Catherine's—now Olivia's—little house.

"Really! Who might that have been?"

"A young man. Blondish. A little mustache. Thin. Let me think, now, did he say who he was?" Doris Hugh squinted, her arms akimbo on heavily padded hips encased in denims suited to the garden work she'd been doing when Tim's rattling pickup rambled into the farmyard.

Catherine had been such a retiring, quiet person, even more so after Levi's death, from Olivia's understanding. Who could have been asking about her things? "Didn't he leave his name?"

Doris frowned. "If he did, I don't recall. He wanted me to let him in the little house, said he was supposed to pick up something belonged to his father." She shook her head. "Used to live around here, he said."

"He did? Or the father?"

"I'm real sorry, but I just don't know. But anyways I didn't have a key. There were only two, and the real estate man took the other one, you know, so the young fellow went away. Didn't say where he was staying or if he'd be back."

Olivia thanked her and turned to Tim. "Give me a hand, will you, Tim? It won't take long to pack these boxes."

"Sure thing."

There wasn't a lot. Catherine had evidently been clearing things out for some time; only a few clothes remained in her closet. There were some scattered, unmatched dishes in the kitchen cupboards—nothing worth keeping, really. Olivia left them where they were. The real estate agent had already been contacted to handle the rent of the house; he could worry about those things.

The attic storage room yielded three boxes of memorabilia: Olivia's baby pictures, school report cards, yellowing photographs. After a quick glance through those on top, Olivia flapped the boxes closed and asked Tim to put them on the truck.

A few linens and towels from the bathroom cabinet would be useful at Dunes House; Olivia directed Pamela to box them along with her mother's clothes.

"Oh, Mom! Something's here!" Pamela's voice was muffled from inside the linen closet in the bathroom.

"What is it?"

"A package. All tied up."

"Put it in. We'll look in it at home." Olivia smiled to herself. How easy it was to call Dunes House "home." She finished emptying Catherine's dresser, glancing quickly through a small jewelry box heaped with costume baubles. Who could have been asking to be let into this house? Olivia's mind searched through the people she might have known, but she'd been away for so long.

"I wish you'd come out and live with us, Mother," Olivia had pleaded after Levi's death.

"No."

"But you're all alone here."

Catherine's voice carried a soft smile. "Not really, Olivia. This is my home. I'd just rather be here."

Why hadn't I visited my mother more often? Gotten to know her as a person? Olivia's life had seemed full, and Bert hadn't wanted her to leave for any length of time. Driving all the way from Portland took too long, and was grueling to do alone; Pamela was no help. Bert wouldn't agree to the cost of flying the two of them, so she and her mother had been strangers, more than less, after Olivia's early teen years.

Would I have liked you as a person, Catherine Sommers? As a woman? Olivia mused as she went through the meager offerings of Catherine's closet. A long, warm coat. Woolen pull-on hat. High-top rubber boots, scarfs, worn woolen gloves. Nothing frivolous, everything serviceable, nothing likely to belong to a woman who owned Dunes House. Nothing to be worn with emeralds "big as your little fingernail."

Olivia finished closing the last box and took it into the small living room where Tim was waiting.

"Not takin' any of these furnishings, Miss Livvy? Some pretty nice things here."

"Nothing except that little wooden writing desk, Tim. Let me put this box on the truck and I'll give you a hand with it."

She was turning from piling the box on the others in the pickup when Tim came bumping out the door sideways, carrying the desk. His foot caught on the doorsill and he lurched, lost his balance, and dropped the desk down on one fragile spindle leg that splintered off. Tim caught the desk just before it toppled off the cement step.

"Dag nab it all!" he muttered. "Pesky step!"

"Oh, Tim, why didn't you wait? Are you hurt?"

"Not me. But the desk leg's broke." Tim righted himself. "Sorry, Miss Livvy. I'll glue that good as new once we get home. Couple of days clamped it'll be fine."

"I'm sure it will."

They put the desk into the pickup. "Drive over to the big house, will you, Tim, and we'll get those two boxes Mrs. Hugh found in the attic. I'll close up here."

"Sure thing." He motioned Pamela into the truck and rattled off.

Olivia took a last slow walk through the little house, wondering what she might have missed. Surely there were no emeralds here, and Catherine Sommers had left very little of herself to tell any kind of story.

Quietly, with an overwhelming sadness, Olivia pulled shut the door of this home which had held her mother's last years, smiles and tears, wishing there was some way to know, to understand the hopes, the dreams, the feelings that couldn't be packed into any pasteboard box.

A whole life ended and I never even knew what it was really like.

"You goin' to put this stuff somewhere, Mom? Now?" Pamela, evidently bored with the prospect of staying indoors on such a beautiful afternoon, tugged at her wayward shorts legs and looked disgruntled.

"I thought I would. Why?"

"Oh." Pamela sucked on her front teeth for a minute, a habit she'd learned from Bert. "Can Mr. Tim get me the boat?"

Olivia, already concentrating on the boxes before her and deciding what she would do with their contents, said absently, "I suppose. If he's not too busy." She looked up to see Pamela's heavy backside disappear through the door. "And don't forget the life jacket," she called. "Always!"

She turned her attention to the larger carton of her mother's clothes, nothing worth keeping. Catherine Sommers certainly hadn't been a clotheshorse in her last years. Olivia would box them for Goodwill.

That decision made, Olivia began unpacking bathroom linens and came across the package Pamela had included. Hesitating to open another private segment of her mother's life, she sat back on her heels to examine it.

The size of a fat notebook, its brown paper covering was bound with ordinary string. More poems? Olivia left the porch and foraged in the kitchen drawer for a pair of scissors to cut the tie when a strange sound reached her through the open window. She raised her head to listen.

There it was again, a muffled moan. A cry for help? Pamela! Heart in her throat, Olivia rushed outside to the bluff above the boathouse, one hand shading her eyes against the water's brilliant reflection of the afternoon sun. With a sigh of relief, she focused on the small craft which Pamela was studiously rowing in a wide circle on the water, and lifted a momentary hand in return when Pam waved happily at her mother on the bluff.

Tim, then? Olivia heard another muffled moan.

Hurrying, she rounded the house to where, in the wide drive turnaround, Tim's old pickup tilted crazily to one side. A deathly stillness hung in the quiet afternoon air and she gasped as she saw one booted foot protruding at an awkward angle from under the truck.

"Oh, Tim!" She dropped to all fours, peering into the pale shade where the old man lay. Another, softer moan told her he was alive, but his forehead was bleeding profusely, evidently struck by a jutting piece of undercarriage when the truck had fallen from the jack. In the half-second of analyzing the situation, Olivia wondered what he was doing there without the wheels blocked.

She didn't have time to think about it. Carefully shifting the old man's thin, fragile body away from the jagged metal, she pulled him from under the truck. Strange how heavy he was, dead weight. She shivered at the thought. He was only unconscious, certainly not dead.

She ran for the house, snatched up a kitchen towel, wet it, and hurried back to press it tightly over the still oozing wound on the old man's forehead.

Cradling his head in her lap, her mind in turmoil, Olivia shut her eyes. What to do? The pickup was obviously not serviceable. Did Tim need a doctor? She carefully pulled the towel away just a little to see whether the bleeding had stopped. It hadn't quite, but with its first flow stanched the cut didn't look quite as serious, though it certainly could have been.

"Need some help here?"

"Oh!" She flinched, unnerved at the unexpected deep voice as a strong hand gripped her shoulder and a tall, muscular figure squatted beside her.

"Heath!" Relief made her voice squeak. "Thank God you're here!"

Tim's eyes fluttered, opened. "Cussed truck!" he muttered. He looked up at Olivia. "Shouldn'ta fell like that! Had it propped good. Shouldn't!"

Heath knelt down beside him. "Okay, Tim? What were you doing under there anyway?"

Tim struggled to sit up, but fell back.

"Stay still for a little, Tim," Olivia said. "You've got a nasty cut, and it's still bleeding." She pushed his head back onto her lap and pressed the towel tightly over the gash. "Just wait a few minutes."

Tim's pale gaze fixed on Heath. "How come you're here? Was that you I heard walkin' round the truck?"

"There's nobody else here, Tim," Olivia said. "I came when I heard you call."

"No! I mean before." Tim shut his faded eyes. "Somebody was here. I heard footsteps, thought it was you comin', Miss Livvy…and then the truck came down." He broke off. "Never mind. Musta just slipped."

Olivia frowned up at Heath. "Footsteps? Slipped?"

Heath raised his eyebrows. "Those things do happen."

Perhaps they do, Olivia thought, but remembering Tim's fall from the loosened step in the basement, questioned that this had just "happened." Someone was certainly out to hurt Tim.

With Heath's help, Olivia installed Tim on the bed in his apartment over the garage, with strict instructions to stay put for at least the rest of the day.

"Treat me like I don't have no sense," Tim grumbled, but sank wearily back on his pillows. "I'll just rest a minute." His eyes were closed almost before Olivia and Heath were out of the room.

"Thanks. I didn't even ask how you happened to be here." Olivia's voice trailed over her shoulder as they went down the outside stair leading from Tim's apartment, pushing to the back of her mind Tim's reference to footsteps. Could they have been Heath's? No, it wasn't possible. He had come only after she had run to the house for the towel.

Shaking away suspicion, she said, "Come over to the house." During the few moments of anxiety and activity over Tim's accident, she had reverted to being calm, efficient Olivia Hobart of Portland. Now, suddenly, she was Livvy of Dunes House and her breath came faster in awareness of the strong, lean, younger man who walked beside her. Who might have caused the truck to fall? Surely not Heath. She shook her head. Foolish.

"I was just going into Bayshore for a couple of things," Heath said, "and thought you might like me to pick up something for you. Didn't you hear the jeep?" He pointed to where it stood at the end of the drive. "Or—" he paused, his grin appealing, "— well, actually, I came to convince you to come along with me."

"Oh. Thanks, there's nothing I need, and I couldn't leave Pam here." She took him into the kitchen. "Iced tea? Beer?"

"Beer. Bring her along. I want to meet her anyway."

"She's out rowing." Olivia loaded a tray with frosty bottles and two glasses and led him to the lower porch. "There." She nodded toward the small boat bobbing on gentle swells below them before she turned, frowning.

Heath held out a hand, palm toward her. "Hold on. I know what's going through your mind. Tim said the truck was "propped good" but I didn't see any blocks. Did someone take them? I certainly didn't see anybody. And if there was, why? Tim's a harmless old man."

"He may be harmless, but if he weren't here, I'd be alone,

except for Pam, now." Olivia put the tray down on the small wicker table and stood staring out over the water. She sensed Heath's presence just behind her and felt the animal magnetism flowing between their bodies, pulling her toward him.

On a brilliant, sunshiny day like this one, the idea of danger to anyone at Dunes House seemed totally improbable. An accident, that's all it had been. Nothing serious had come of it.

She turned into Heath's arms, hungrily lifting her face to his, wanting, needing his tongue, his warmth, the indescribable electricity that sparked through every fiber of her body at his touch.

Hours later, in the cooling dusk of early evening after Heath had gone and Pamela trudged sturdily along the small strip of beach looking for unbroken shells, Olivia sank down into one of the wicker chairs on the lower porch and opened the brown paper package.

It held a fair-sized composition book and a dozen loose scraps of paper. Unexpectedly, a shiver ran through her body, and she rubbed gooseflesh from her upper arms.

An omen of some kind? She pushed away the thought that she was about to learn something she perhaps didn't want to know, something about herself. It was here, in these mementos of her mother's life, Olivia could feel it rising from the writings in her lap.

She looked through the paper scraps first.

My child, fruit of love
I sing to you. Listen, Listen.
Hear my heart. Float safe.

Stay. Stay.

Olivia shrugged. If there was a meaning, she was missing it.

Child, child. Had our lives
Been unencumbered, free—
What then would the difference be?'

Whose lives unencumbered? Were anyone's? She put the scrap aside, picked up another written by a different hand that looked familiar, and she realized it was the same script as the note that had promised emeralds, "someday."

She is three. And beautiful.
A princess, caged. And she is me.
Thank you, my love.
For staying.

Olivia frowned, surmising that the poem was about herself at three. "A princess, caged. And she is me." What did that mean? What did any of it mean? A final scribble in Catherine's fine script told her even less:

Go, my child. Your mistake is mine. I understand
and yet I cannot tell you why.
Go in peace and live your life.
I cry. I cry.

A tiny penciled date on this paper corresponded to Olivia's own wedding date. She stared through the screen to the far horizon. My mistake? Which one? Pamela, of course, she thought. And the mistake of pregnancy, the careful keeping from Olivia that she herself had been conceived before the marriage. To keep me safe from hurt, Olivia realized. Everything they did was to keep me safe from hurt.

Olivia shut her eyes, remembering the kindness in Levi Sommer's solid, caring face and his never-failing steadfastness.

She opened the composition book and was surprised to see

that the narrative began in 1925:

"I begin this journal with a heavy heart," wrote Catherine Rothe in a meticulous script. *"For I am forced to stay… "*

Olivia read slowly at first, then avidly, through Catherine's cryptic entries: frustration at living at home through normal school and after; descriptions of her aversion, held inside, to participating at Irene Rothe's sewing circle and church work (the wry sense of humor describing vignettes of Irene's friends caused Olivia to chuckle aloud); through Catherine's narration of Olivia's grandparents' deaths and funerals, and her honest, joyous delight about at last having attained the freedom she had wanted for so long. Finally, the hope, the joy, and the tragedy brought to her life through dashing, handsome, unscrupulous Joel O'Brien.

Olivia put the notebook down on her lap and stared across the lake, astounded by the knowledge that her mother had in fact married—or thought she had—a brush salesman, run away with him, been deserted and birthed twins that hadn't lived. Olivia was even more astounded that none of this had ever been mentioned. Perhaps Levi never knew?

Olivia turned back to the last page: "And so I quit this dry and windy place, and leave here buried in one small pine box, a part of myself, my life, my unwise love. What does the future hold? Thank God we never know."

Olivia laced her fingers through her hair at the back of her head and closed her eyes, her mind boggling at this new realization that her mother had kept secret more, much more, than just some emeralds and the house on the dunes.

"I'm coming out there, Livvy, and you damn well better be

packed up and ready to come home with me. I'm dead sick of living like this!" It was impossible to mistake the anger in Bert Hobart's voice, even over the miles of wire between Portland and the dusty little telephone booth in Bayshore.

I shouldn't have bothered to call. Olivia held the receiver away from her ear, shut her eyes for a moment, and took a deep breath before she spoke. "Come ahead, Bert. I'll be glad to have you. So will Pam, but I'm not ready to come back to Portland." *I don't know if I ever will be.*

He tried another tack. "There's old Pam, you know. She ought to be home, here."

"Why? She's learning to survive somewhere else. This has been good for her."

He paused. "Is she…do you know…you know?"

"Pregnant, you mean."

"Well…yeah."

"It's too soon to tell. She's learning a lot of things, Bert. She likes it here. She's tanned and content."

"Hell, Livvy, she's content wherever she is as long as you're there to baby her!"

Olivia winced. *That's probably true.* "Bert, the answer is no. I'm not coming back with you. I love it here."

"That's your problem."

Only one of them, Olivia thought. *You're another. So is Pamela. And…Heath is the biggest of all.*

"I'll be there next Saturday. You be ready."

Surprised by the sudden dial tone abruptly ending the conversation, she hung up the receiver and walked to the jeep where Heath and Pam waited.

"Things okay?" Heath asked.

"Not hardly. Bert's coming next Saturday."

"O-kay!" Pam clapped her hands and bounced up and down on the back seat. "Take us home!"

Olivia turned and studied her daughter's bland smiling face for just a moment. "That's what he thinks."

Heath covered her hand with his on the seat between them. "And what do *you* think?"

Olivia sighed. "I honestly don't know."

Each day the hours sped by far too fast to suit Olivia, who was definitely not looking forward to what Saturday might bring.

Tim was back on his feet and busy around the house and yard. Pam was either fishing, rowing, or looking for shells. Olivia finished unpacking the boxes of keepsakes from the farm, touched by the mementos her mother had kept of Olivia's accomplishments—pictures she'd drawn, cross-stitching she'd worked. There were snapshots by the dozen: Olivia with a black lamb, Olivia with her first bicycle, Olivia with Levi, group shots with her schoolmates and her Sunday School teacher.

But there was nothing to tell Olivia more about her mother, only things about herself she already knew. She went through the house again, room by room, nook by nook, searching for anything that might tell her more about her mother's life. If she had so meticulously kept a journal before she came to Middle Creek, wouldn't she have kept one after, through all the years she lived there? Tim said she had written often in a book, but Olivia found nothing more.

On Friday afternoon, she stood idly at the lower porch screen, watching Pamela, who looked even pudgier in her thick orange life jacket, row the boat in an ever-larger circle. I'll have to tell her not to go out so far, Olivia thought, remembering how suddenly the weather could change from a balmy, calm afternoon to a wildly dark and windy storm. Something like the way her life was going to change tomorrow when Bert arrived and demanded her return. And what would she do? Her life in Portland was like a half-remembered movie now, a movie, she thought with a sigh, that she wouldn't want to see again.

A peremptory knock on the kitchen door broke into her thoughts. She wondered as she moved to open it whether she had inadvertently locked Tim out.

However, the thin, blond man at the door was unfamiliar to her, though for some reason she felt she should have known him. He pulled at a slight mustache that was as unfulfilled as his body. "Mrs. Hobart?"

"Yes?" She took in his appearance: tailored brown suit, shined shoes, heavily knotted red-striped tie, acne scars pitting his face. His brown eyes were so dark she couldn't see where the iris left off and the pupil began; looking at them was like staring into marbles.

She immediately didn't trust him. How did he know who she was? Who even knew she was here?

"May I come in?"

Though his words were polite, his tone was unfriendly, and Olivia felt a shiver of apprehension. Where was Tim, anyway?

"Is there something you want? I don't buy anything at the door." How did these salespeople think they had the right to invade the privacy of her home?

"I'm not selling anything, Mrs. Hobart. I'm here to claim what's mine." He stepped forward and put one shiny brown shoe over the doorsill.

Olivia involuntarily took a step back. "What's yours?" She frowned. "I'm quite sure you have the wrong house and the wrong person. Who is it you're looking for?"

"You, Mrs. Hobart. I ask again, may I come in?" He moved forward and put his other foot in the door.

Olivia's chin came up. "Move your foot and state your business. I'm not in the habit of inviting men into my home without knowing who they are and what they want."

"What I want, Mrs. Hobart, is to regain what rightfully belongs to my family."

Olivia sighed, exasperated with this game. "Look, whoever you are—"

"The name is Houle. Kurt Houle."

"Houle!" Olivia frowned. "From the Houle family over at Middle Creek?"

"He was—is—my grandfather. So, you see, we do have something to talk about, now, don't we?"

"I don't know what it might be, and I really don't know what you're getting at." She folded her arms across her chest. There was something cruel about his mouth and the way his obsidian eyes narrowed as he talked.

"Don't you? I think you do and that you know you have no claim."

"To what, for heaven's sake!" Olivia reached around the doorjamb and pulled on the cord connected to Tim's apartment. She hoped he wasn't somewhere else at the moment.

"To the jewels my grandfather owns."

Olivia shook her head. "Jewels your grandfather owns? I hate to sound stupid, but you're not making any sense."

"Does this?" The young man pulled a paper from his inside vest pocket. "I just took over his power of attorney this morning when Thomas Gregg retired. It seems my grandfather has been paying the insurance on a tremendous amount of jewelry. On a mint's worth of emeralds, to be exact. Where are they?"

The words were hardly out of his mouth before he was shouldered away from the door as Tim Ryan bumped him back from the sill.

"Them were Miss Cathy's, boy!" Tim shook a gnarled finger in the younger man's surprised face. "I heard you! They ain't no jewels here in the first place, and they ain't yours in the second. Miss Cathy left them to Miss Livvy in her will, ain't that right?" He focused his pale eyes on Olivia for a moment, straightened up and stared at the younger man. "So git!"

Houle stared, open-mouthed. "Git?" He snorted in Olivia's direction, his thin mouth twisting. "Who the hell is this?"

Before she could answer, Tim poked the younger man in the center of his red-striped tie. "Never you mind, you heard right. What I said, git. Before I send for the sheriff!" Tim swallowed, his Adam's apple traveling up and down. "Not that it might do a whole heap of good, but I'll get him anyhow."

"What is this old fossil, a talking guard dog?" Houle demanded. He pulled out a card and thrust it at Olivia. "Call me when you're ready to talk."

"Ain't nothin' to talk about!" Tim declared. "So git!"

Olivia watched in surprise as Houle did an about-face, walked stiff-backed to his red TransAm and slammed its door, but not before he shouted, "I'll be back, Mrs. Hobart. With a search warrant!" His tires spat gravel onto the cement step as he spewed away.

Olivia stared as the car disappeared between the gateposts and shook her head. "Well, Tim, you certainly came on like gangbusters. What's it all about, do you think?"

"Hmpph. About a fortune hunter, you ask me. Seen that kind before. Too darn recently. Good thing you rang for me, Miss Livvy. Can't be too careful."

Olivia stared at the small white rectangle in her hand. Kurt Houle, Attorney at Law. Tyson & Gregg." The same lawyers her parents had done business with. Evidently young Houle had joined the firm. "Tim, do you think he knows what he's talking about?"

"Prob'ly there's insurance through the lawyers. Should'a been, anyways. But those stones were your mother's, I know for a fact. Nobody else's, that's for sure. Fortune hunter, that's all." Tim started to go back to the garage and then turned. "Oh. Just about got the little desk fixed for you now, Miss Livvy. You want it in the big room, or where?"

"Oh...fine, Tim. Anywhere," Olivia said, distracted. What did Kurt Houle have to do with her mother's jewels? And had the lawyer's office taken care of the insurance on the house as well? If so, that must be how the grandson connected her to Dunes House?

It was all certainly confusing, more so all the time. She shook her head and walked to the bluff, where she stood for a few moments letting the soft lapping of the water on the sand below sooth her jumbled mind before she called her daughter in to shore.

That night, long after Pamela was in bed and the light had blinked out in Tim's apartment, Olivia walked the brightly moonlit beach to Heath's cottage, where she knew he waited with the same anticipation she felt.

The air was balmy with early summer though Lake Michigan had warmed very little. Swinging her flipflops, Olivia splashed along the water's edge until her toes were too cold, then moved to the dry sand that still held some sun's warmth. Out on the horizon, a light blinked from an ore ship moving on the shipping lane. A few nighthawks cried above her head, and she looked up to catch a glimpse of one streaking across the full moon's face.

"God's in his heaven and all's right with the world," she said aloud. "At least for this minute."

She stood on one leg, then the other, to slip on her flipflops before walking up the rough rooted path to warm, flickering lamplight and Heath's encircling arms. The guilt she suffered during and after their earlier sexual encounters was harder to muster up now; it was as though in this place, at this time, her other life could be disregarded.

Tonight, anyway, but not tomorrow.

Later, amid rumpled bedcovers, she raised herself on one elbow. "Now, talk to me."

"Lady, I thought we were talking." Heath's deep voice held laughter. "Weren't we?"

"Communicating, for sure, but not talking. Listen to the latest development in the story of Olivia Hobart, heiress."

"Shoot. Want some wine?"

"Sure." She watched his lean body as he threw back the covers and rose to cross the short distance to the kitchen area. His broad shoulders tapered in a vee to his tightly muscled buttocks; she knew his flat belly carried the dark fuzz of his chest hair all the way to his groin. "A fine figure of a fella, you are," she said as he returned with two filled goblets. "I hate to admit it, but you do turn me on."

"Go ahead, admit it." He smiled. "It does these old bones good to hear such randy talk."

"Old bones? I'm the one who should complain about those."

"Experienced, then, not old. Better?" He grinned and handed her the goblet, climbed in beside her, and clinked his glass against hers. "You're something else, you know? Now, shoot."

She told him about the afternoon's visit from Kurt Houle.

He pursed his lips. "The plot thickens. Why would the insurance have been handled by the law firm? What about insurance on the house?"

"I don't know. I hadn't thought about it until today." Olivia shook her head and shrugged her bare shoulders. "There have to be some answers somewhere. And did Tim ever get his back up!"

"Maybe you haven't been looking in the right places, Livvy. Why don't you go to see this Oliver Houle? He's still alive, isn't he?"

"I guess. Probably the farm tenant could tell me where. But

Bert's coming tomorrow…" Her voice trailed off. "And I'm not ready for him."

Heath reached over and took her goblet, setting it beside his on the bedside table. "Just what are you ready for, you sexy vixen?"

On Saturday, Olivia stood on the side step of Dunes House as Bert got out of his rental Buick. She frowned. He looked different, somehow; she couldn't quite put her finger on just what it was.

"Livvy." He stopped, both hands in his suit pockets.

"Hello, Bert."

"That's it? Just 'hello?'" Bert snorted and squinted up at her. Then, looking sheepish, he stared down at his shoes. "Guess I have that coming, though, don't I? After the way I yelled at you over the phone the other day."

Olivia stared. Was he actually apologizing?

"Well?" He shaded his eyes from the afternoon sun.

"Well, what?"

"Aren't you going to invite me into the damn house? Got anything to drink in this godforsaken place?"

"There's some brandy. No mix, though."

"It'll do. Where is it?"

He followed her into the dining room where she poured brandy from the Waterford decanter on the maple sideboard into a small tumbler. She said nothing, letting him take the initiative.

Bert swigged a substantial mouthful and shut his eyes, savoring the flavor for a moment before swallowing. "Well?" he said again, looking around the room. "Ready to go? Packed?"

"Bert..." Olivia hesitated. "Sit down."

"I don't want to sit down, dammit. Are you ready or not!"

"Look. I don't intend to get into a shouting match with you. It's just...I haven't finished here."

"Haven't finished?" He tossed off the last of the brandy, and she winced as he slammed the fragile glass down on the polished maple sideboard. "You just won't understand, will you? You *are* finished here. You're coming back home with me, and that's that! Pour me another shot."

Bert's florid face was even ruddier than usual. He was puffier than she remembered, too, dissipated-looking. She realized with a little shock he must have been drinking regularly while she was gone, more than he should, and, in fact, he was not entirely sober now.

"You don't need more liquor, Bert. You've been leaning pretty heavily on it, haven't you?"

"What do you expect? No wife, no kid—" he broke off and looked around. "Where's she, anyhow?"

"Looking for shells, probably. She's collected quite a few. She'll be back soon."

"Good. I wanted to talk to you without her around." Bert leaned forward, looking over his shoulder toward the garage. "Where's old Tim?"

"Out in the workshop. He's mending my mother's desk."

"Good again. I don't want him around snooping and butting in, either. Listen, Livvy, I've made some wonderful connections with a real estate firm down the shore here, and they've got a buyer for this white elephant. What do you think of that?" He grinned as if this was news she'd want to hear and didn't wait for her answer. "So we can get rid of this place, go home, and get back to living. Now what do you say?" He slapped his thigh as he sucked on his front teeth. "Pretty damn good, huh, all the way from Portland! I did it by phone."

Olivia stared at him. "Bert, I'm not selling. Can't you get that through your head?"

The veins in his neck and along the sides of his forehead bulged. His voice burst out in a strangled shout. "Oh, yes, you are. You're my wife, and you're going to forget this foolishness and come home where you belong!" He slammed his fist on the sideboard, rattling the decanter and glasses.

In spite of her determination to stay calm, take a deep breath to keep from blowing up, Olivia lost the battle. Her voice rose to meet the anger in his. "I'm not! And that's that. In fact, Bert Hobart, I don't think I'm ever coming to Portland again except to get my things."

Bert made a fist and shook it in her face. "You will!"

"I won't!"

Carrying the handful of pretty, fragile shells she had collected, Pamela stopped walking along the path below the open dining room windows. She scowled at the sound of her mother's angry voice, then her father's, and a thump of some kind.

They don't yell at each other like that, not ever!

Their anger rolled out the open window to cover her like a suffocating blanket. She squatted down in the flower bed under the windows, shutting her eyes tight, screwing her face into a mask of frightened uncertainty as she listened.

"I've learned some things, Bert, about my mother."

"So what? She's dead, and who cares now?"

Pamela lifted her head. *Maybe they stopped. Maybe I go in now, see Daddy.*

"Certainly not you! You never really did care, did you?" Hurt came through Olivia's voice to reach the child-woman below the window. "You really don't give a damn!"

Pamela hunched down in the flower bed, shaking her head, tears filling her eyes. She squashed the fragile shells in her chubby fist before spilling them onto bare dirt between blooming marigolds. She wiped her eyes with the backs of her hands and covered her ears with both palms, but she could still hear their loud, heated voices.

Not nice. Not good. Better not listen. Pamela looked out over the calm, blue-grey water. Then she scrambled upright, dusted her hands on the back of her rumpled shorts, and ran awkwardly toward the steps leading to the boathouse. Puffing, she lumbered down the wooden stairs. *Good. Padlock open.*

Pamela flung the door wide and grabbed the short rope on the rowboat's bow, humming loudly to cover the faint but still frightening voices carrying to her on the quiet afternoon air.

With all her strength, she tugged until the small dinghy teetered over the edge of the short dock and dropped with a splash. She hurried into the boathouse, grabbed the oars, threw them into the boat and jumped after them, almost overturning the small craft in her haste.

She fumbled the oars into the oarlocks, nodded in satisfaction, and plopped her heavy bottom onto the middle seat.

Puffing with unaccustomed exertion, she pulled on the oars as hard as she could, sending the small boat scooting over the tranquil water, straight away from shore. "Don't want…to hear! Don't want…to hear!" she chanted. "In the water, out the water." Her mantra kept time with the dip and rise of the oars. Strong from hours of rowing, she propelled the small boat toward the hazy eastern horizon, paying no attention to the dark, roiling thunderclouds billowing ominously before a sudden wind to obscure the western sky.

"Getting cold…cold…" Pamela shivered, shading her eyes to

squint back toward the diminishing shore. "Too far, Pam...too far...Mr. Tim be mad!"

She pulled hard on one oar to turn the boat around, but a sudden squall pushed by the western wind slapped a wave against the side and sent the small craft spinning.

"Too far, Pam..." She nodded, up and down, up and down. "Better go back now."

But there was no going back. The wind whipped around her and pelted her with sudden sheets of driving rain, tossing the little boat this way, that way.

"Mama!" Pamela dropped the oars and clutched the sides of the boat.

"Mama! Come get me!" she shrieked, but her words were sucked away by wind and swallowed by turbulent waters.

13

CATHERINE

There were good years when the weather was fine and everyone prospered; there were droughts and too-wet seasons, there were warm growing rains, gentle winds, and early frosts. Levi's hope for a grandchild near was lost to the many miles between Wisconsin and Oregon.

The first time Olivia brought Pamela home for a visit she was chronologically old enough to have been walking and talking, but was infinitely younger mentally. Pamela smiled and cooed, drooled and burped; that was all.

"It's so hard, isn't it, Chicken?" Levi and Olivia stood at the side of Pamela's makeshift crib in Olivia's old bedroom, looking down at the angelic, empty sleeping face. Levi's steady grey eyes filled with all the old tenderness Olivia had so missed after moving to Oregon with Bert.

She only nodded, choking back tears, and then turned her face into his broad chest. "Oh, Daddy! Is it–is it my fault?"

"No." His arms were a warm haven, remembered and loved.

"But what we did, Bert and I–we shouldn't have…"

"Shhh. You're still so young and have so much to learn," he comforted. Levi took Olivia's cold hand and brought her to sit on her old maple bed beside him. "We all make mistakes, Chicken. God doesn't make us pay for them. We make ourselves."

Her clear hazel eyes clouded. "But there's no other reason."

"There are always reasons for everything. Sometimes we never learn them. Sometimes we are allowed to find them out." He gently turned her face so she had to look at him. "You can have other children."

Olivia shook her head. "No. Bert won't. Unless…he wants me to put Pamela away in an institution." She caught her breath, unable to continue.

Pursing his lips, Levi studied her tormented face. "And will you?"

"No!" Olivia's shoulders straightened. "She's my baby. I'll take care of her."

"Yes. I'm sure you will."

After that, visits from Oregon were not often though letters flew back and forth with regularity. Catherine suspected Olivia's life was busy but not particularly happy, and it was easy to pick up from what was not written that as time passed Olivia and Bert had less and less in common.

"Pamela's talking pretty well now. She's finally into some kind of schooling," Catherine said to Levi. "Listen." She read Olivia's latest letter aloud over breakfast, then, frowning, looked at her husband. "Do you think they'll stay together, Levi?" she asked.

"Livvy and Bert? I hope so."

Catherine sighed. "Because of Pamela, I mean. Bert doesn't seem sympathetic, or even very loving, from the sound of these letters."

Levi was silent for a moment and wearily rubbed his forehead. "She's paying her dues, Catherine. Like we all do, one way or another." He left the room before she could ask him what he meant.

"I'm so sorry, Oliver."

"Are you? Really, Cathy?"

"I only meant—"

"I know..." He held her gloved hands longer than he should have, but there was no one left to see. In spite of the blustering November wind that whipped some early snowflakes across the gravestones surrounding Bonnie Houle's newly-dug resting place, a handful of parishioners had followed the hearse to the cemetery but had left as soon as decency allowed.

Levi had gone to bring his car around, leaving Catherine and Oliver a moment alone in the blustery chill of the small graveyard behind the church. Blind Amery waited in the car with his wife, Lucy, and blond son, Kurt, now a thin, sullen fifteen. Amery had shown no grief during any part of the ceremony.

"It's so odd..." Oliver broke off, staring down at the shiny grey top of Bonnie's casket in the bottom of the yawning grave.

"What?" Catherine squinted up at him against the driving flakes. She hugged her long grey wool coat tighter around her slim body to keep out the raw wind that threatened to snatch her black veiled hat from her head in spite of the pins thrust into her thick braid.

"For years Bonnie knew I wished for freedom. But I never thought she'd just give up. I'm...empty, not glad."

"Of course you're not."

"Cathy. I'll need you more than ever now. You—you could come to the farm, couldn't you? Sometimes?" His eyes pleaded her answer.

"No. Never. You know I couldn't." Levi's words, spoken nearly twenty years ago had burned into her mind and lived there constantly: "I ask that you will never shame me." She put her hand gently on Oliver's arm. "Your life has changed, but mine hasn't," she said, her voice low. "I know you understand."

Oliver made a derisive sound through his lips and turned from the open grave, one hand under Catherine's elbow to steady her over the uneven ground. He led her toward the warmth of Levi's Ford sedan. "Understand? The word haunts me. It seems I've spent most of my life trying to understand one thing or another." He tipped his hat to Levi as he helped Catherine into the car. "Thanks for coming, Levi. I appreciate it."

Levi reached across Catherine to shake Oliver's hand. "Take care of yourself, Oliver." Levi put the car in gear and they bumped away over the ruts in the almost frozen gravel. They had driven almost to the Sommers' farm before Levi broke the awkward silence. "He'll be lonely."

"Yes."

"Even bad company is better than none."

Catherine nodded. "Bonnie wasn't an easy person." That was all she could think of to say.

They turned into their drive and pulled up near the back door. As Catherine gathered up her purse to get out of the car, Levi covered her gloved hand with his and interlocked their fingers. "Catherine."

She looked into his eyes and saw his pain, his fear. "Levi. You don't have to say it. I know what you're thinking."

"Do you?"

"I believe so." Between their palms a warm current began that climbed all the way to her heart. She turned her body to face him fully. "Levi, you must know my life is here with you for as long as we both shall live."

He looked down at their entwined fingers, and when he met her eyes again, the emotion that clouded his was equaled by the mist in hers. "Thank you, my Catherine. I should have known."

She smiled as she blinked back tears. "Yes. You should have."

For some reason she couldn't understand, now that Oliver was free of Bonnie, Catherine felt far guiltier about meeting him. Their few trysts at Dunes House after Bonnie's death were sometimes strained, sexless times, like strangers meeting out of time; others were a passionate coming together denying all else. Twice Catherine found reasons for not going when arrangements had been made.

"What's happening, Cathy? What's happening to us?" Oliver questioned, pacing the smooth buffed floor at Dunes House. "You know I love you more than my life."

"I do know. Oh, Oliver, somehow being together now is just not right."

"It's never been right, but it's all we've had." Oliver's hair, now silvery white, fell over his brow. He impatiently brushed it back.

She fingered the spectacular emeralds around her neck. "I know that, too."

Finally, one early fall morning nearly four years after Bonnie's death, Catherine watched Levi's shoulders slump as he walked slowly away from the depot. Her breath caught as though she'd been struck in the chest. How many times had he brought her here and gone home alone? How many lonely, wondering hours had he spent?

She hesitated only a moment before she jumped to her feet and hurried to collect her few belongings, bumping against other passengers in her haste. She left the train seconds before it pulled away and rushed to a surprised Levi just as he returned to his car.

"Catherine! What is it?"'

She tugged on his coat sleeve, her face flushed. "Oh, Levi, take me home!"

"Are you all right? Don't you feel well?" He, frowned, puzzled.

"I feel…" she caught her breath. "I feel I love you." She stared down at her feet. "And I want…to go home."

He circled her in his still strong arms. "I, too." Levi tipped her face up so she was forced to meet his eyes. "Do you know how long I have waited for just this moment, Catherine?"

"Yes." Her chin quivered, and she dropped her forehead against his solid chest. "Oh, Levi, yes I do."

At Catherine's repeated insistence, there were no more meetings at Dunes House, no more quiet dinners or walks along the wave-smoothed sand beach.

"Please, Cathy," Oliver pleaded in a quick moment after a church service. "It was so wonderful, so much ours. The house waits for us."

She shook her head, her eyes soft, remembering. "It did, and it will again when the time is right. But not yet."

"How long, Cathy? We're–we're old! I'm seventy-two! How many years can we count on? There's so little time left us."

He closed his eyes, waiting for her answer.

"But we've had so much more than we deserved. I am where I must be now, Oliver. Be patient."

His gaze devoured her as she left the church on Levi's arm. As he had so many years ago, he muttered, "Be patient. Wait? For what?"

Less than a month later, Catherine awoke to find Levi's arm a heavy, motionless weight across her chest. "Wake up, Levi, You're crushing me," she mumbled, unwilling to give up sleep.

There was no response. Odd. He seldom slept so deeply in the morning.

"Levi!" She turned and tugged at the covers over them, reeling back as the odor of death overwhelmed her.

Time stopped.

"No!" She swallowed the nausea that filled her throat with bile, her eyes widening with the effort to stanch the rush of tears that burst loose to run unacknowledged down her face. She threw back her head and cried out into the cold morning air, "Oh, no! Levi! No!"

Catherine's long grey hair, loose and tangled from sleep, fanned across his quiet face as she knelt to bring his head against her aging breasts for one last time and smoothed his still strong iron-grey hair back from his brow. "Oh, dear Levi…" she keened, rocking him gently, gently. The old spool four-poster softly creaked with this last, final rhythm of their lives.

"Levi…Levi. You were the one who never faltered." She put her lips to his cold forehead. "Sleep well, my dearest, dearest Levi." Her voice trailed off into a tear-filled whisper, "Oh, sleep well. You have earned it."

The cemetery was green for this burial; the apple trees

surrounding the old church graveyard were in full blossom, sending fresh fragrance to mingle with the early wild violets sprouting along the fence and the deep red roses spread over Levi's mahogany coffin. The cemetery's thin grass was verdant with season's promise; the air was warm though the sunlight was pale. Catherine Sommers was aware of none of it.

Through her black veil, she watched the shining casket descend into the earth. Her blurred vision distended the shape of the coffin and the flowers that lay across it as it sank into the dark hole. The young minister's closing words were properly solemn and religious, yet to her they seemed foolish and ineffectual against the finality of Levi's death.

Catherine closed her eyes. Dearest Levi, whose generous love had given her everything possible——devotion, material possessions, contentment, freedom—and who had accepted Olivia for his own.

He must have known he was not her father. "No questions," he said, choosing Olivia's name. Had he named her because of Oliver? Catherine never knew; she'd never asked. It was Levi's secret to keep, and he had kept it well.

For just a moment, her gaze rose from the grave to see Oliver Houle standing opposite. His spare frame, suited elegantly in expensive grey, tall and ramrod straight, transformed him for an instant to the earnest young poet she had fallen in love with so long ago. *So long ago.*

"Mrs. Sommers?"

She shook her head and frowned her way back to the present.

"You requested," the young minister cleared his throat, "you asked to throw the earth?" He held out the small shovel he had tried to dissuade her from using, telling her the custom was outdated, barbaric.

"Yes, I did." She took the shovel. "I must."

The spring wind tugged a wayward strand loose from her

heavy coronet; she pushed it back under her hat. Closing her eyes for a moment she whispered, "Goodbye, dearest Levi. Goodbye."

The rich black earth hit the casket with a hollow, final sound, one she needed to hear to prove this was real, that their life together was over.

How much of her life had been real?

Who am I? Catherine wondered through mists of memory. The young girl who followed Joel O'Brien to the end of her world and buried her children there? The woman who had lain, spent from passion, on a golden pegged oak floor stained emerald green from sunlight shining through the tiny colored window at Dunes House? She remembered that golden afternoon as clearly as if it were yesterday. Or was she the woman who had given her child and the rest of their lives to the man now gone forever? Who had renewed her adulterous love again and again with stolen hours, stolen days, and been repaid only with devotion and caring? None of it seemed real. Not her life, and certainly not Levi's death.

Her eyes clouded, and the minister took the shovel from her.

"Mother, come away now." Olivia Hobart, her own eyes tear-smeared, touched Catherine's arm.

"Won't they cover it while we're here?" Catherine asked.

"No. They don't do that anymore, Mother. Come now," Olivia urged.

Catherine shook her head. "Let me stay here by myself for just a few moments, will you, Olivia?" Her voice was soft but firm. Her blue eyes, once so clear and brilliant, had faded now, but at 67, though years had taken their toll, she was still beautiful. "Just for a little, please. Then I'll be along."

"Of course, Mother." Olivia took Pamela's hand and walked toward the gate. The other mourners had said their condolences and straggled away to their own blossoming day, a day that held promise for another growing season, another bountiful harvest.

Olivia looked back as she reached her father's car to see

Oliver Houle walk slowly from the other side of the grave toward her mother.

He had always been a background figure in Olivia's life, a stalwart friend and helper to her father, as had many of the local farmers, for Levi Sommers had always been the most respected of them all. Yet there seemed to be a special something about Oliver Houle, something she could have never put a finger on, that marked his friendship and interest in Olivia herself quite different from that of the other neighbors.

"Gramma comin'?" Pamela asked, squinting at Olivia. At 16 chronological years she was still barely beyond pre-school mentality; the long drive from Oregon with her in the car had been aggravating. Bert had refused to come, saying he had business to attend to; Olivia hadn't argued.

"In a minute, Pam." Olivia turned to see Oliver Houle take both her mother's hands in his and lift them to his lips. The words between them were indistinguishable from this distance, but the emotion came across raw. She swallowed hard and turned to help Pamela into the back seat.

Beside the open grave, Catherine turned her head away from Oliver's sympathy.

"Cathy."

"It's done, Oliver. Over. I'll miss him so." Her voice was only a whisper.

He lifted a slightly trembling finger to her cheek to brush away a tear. "My dear, let me hold you, share your loss. Will you let me?" His blue eyes, faded as hers, beseeched. "Just as a friend, no more?"

She shook her head, took a deep breath and raised her chin. "Not now. Not here." She looked down into the grave and then around the churchyard to the blossoming trees, assimilating it all before she raised her eyes to his and said, "It's over, Oliver. All the years…all the good years…he was such a good man."

"Yes." His grip was so tight it hurt her stiffening knuckles. She winced, pulled her hands away and rubbed them together. "I'm sorry," he apologized. "It's just been so long since I touched you. I don't want to let you go."

"But I must." As she turned to walk to the car, he stopped her with a touch on her arm. "Cathy?"

"Yes?" Her slim height, still proudly straight, was silhouetted against the sun.

"Olivia is so much like you. She's a lovely woman. I knew she would be."

"She is. She had all the love in the world."

"From Levi." He couldn't hide the bitterness showing through his voice. "You know I would have given it if I could."

She put a slim hand on his sleeve. "I do know."

"Promise me you'll let her know the truth someday."

"Some day?" She frowned. "How can I?"

"You'll find a way when there is no one left to be hurt." He lifted his arm in farewell. "Cathy. You know my love is still here. Waiting."

"I've always known."

Chin held high, she left him and walked slowly across the soft spring grass. Olivia helped her into the car. Oliver lifted a hand in farewell and watched them drive away.

No one saw Oliver Houle stumble as he reached his own vehicle. No one was there to help him with the hot pain that seared his chest and boiled up into his brain, the pain that crumpled his tall, lean frame onto the churchyard's gravel drive.

The young minister found him an hour later when, his work

finished, he walked toward the parking lot and noticed Oliver's car still standing near the graveyard. Only then did he see the grey-suited figure sprawled on the ground beside it.

"Mr. Houle!"

There was no answer, only pleading for help in the faded eyes and an animal-like sound from the twisted body that had been so tall and straight.

"Room 213."

Catherine nodded her thanks to the nurse and walked down the hall. She hated this place, hated the old people sounds and the disinfectant smells and the cute little seasonal pictures taped to the walls to cheer up the inhabitants.

They called it Crossroads because it was located near the intersection of two highways, but in her mind it was a crossover to oblivion. No one ever came out. Sometimes they lived here, if you could call it living, for years, but they didn't get well. They just were taken care of. Now Oliver was here after spending two weeks in intensive care at Memorial Hospital, no visitors allowed.

Catherine swallowed hard. Room 213 was ahead on the right. As she passed along the hall she looked into sterile, impersonal rooms. A toothless old woman sitting in a wheelchair with a drab afghan over her knees called out, "Help me!"

Catherine stopped, staring. Did the woman mean her?

"Help me! You there!" the woman shouted again.

Uncertain what to do, Catherine saw a nurses' aide coming down the hall.

"Pay no attention," she told Catherine, smiling. "Mary calls to everybody. She's fine. She's just lonesome." The girl went into the room and Catherine heard her chide, "Mary, Mary, you mustn't yell at our visitors. What will they think? Now, what can I do for you?"

Room 213. Catherine shut her eyes and straightened her shoulders. What would she find? She knocked lightly on the open door and walked in, holding her breath.

There were two hospital beds in the room, but one was empty. Oliver lay propped up in the other, his face turned toward the window. He wore a shapeless, colorless hospital gown, the neck gaping to one side. His silver hair straggled over his forehead as it always had, but that was the only similarity to the Oliver Houle she knew.

She approached, hesitating, not wanting to startle him, but needing to absorb this travesty that was Oliver. He had always been slim, but now his body seemed to have no flesh; even his hand lying on the coverlet was nothing but bones covered by translucent parchment. Every vein was visible. A plastic bracelet circled his skeletal wrist. She couldn't tell whether he was awake or not.

She touched his cold hand. "Oliver?"

He turned, and she involuntarily sucked in her breath. His right eye, cheek and the corner of his mouth were out of symmetry; he looked as though his portrait had been wet, stretched, and pulled askew.

He made a sound, but it wasn't intelligible.

She reached over as she had done a thousand times and brushed his hair back from his forehead. Her voice rebelled at speaking and sounded odd when she was finally able to say, "Don't try to talk, Oliver. I will."

There was no way he could communicate verbally, but the faded blue eyes burning into hers were aware. His tears welled up and spilled over; he attempted to lift his left hand to brush them away, but it wouldn't go where he wanted. He grunted in frustration.

"Don't, Oliver. Oh, Oliver, my love." Catherine took her handkerchief from her purse and wiped his tears while hers fell unnoticed on his bed.

She visited him regularly, at first not knowing whether he understood the things she told him. The other bed filled and emptied as patients moved in and out of his room. Oliver's condition did improve, though he was unable to regain full use of his right side, and, like many stroke victims, his speech was often garbled. The words in his mind were not what came out of his mouth. He became more and more susceptible to bronchial disorders.

He was physically able to be up in a wheelchair most days, but not well enough to leave Crossroads. Often Catherine wheeled him onto the sun porch and read aloud the poetry he so loved. Sometimes she read the poems he'd written to her over the years, or poems she'd written to him. At those times, he cried, frustrated at being trapped in his traitorous body. She understood.

Forgetful in streaks, some days he was fine. On others, he seemed so senile it was all she could do to make herself stay with him. Occasionally, they talked of remembered events, but most often memories were lost to results of the stroke.

She filled his hours as often as she could. One particularly lucid day he asked, "Did you...tell...Olivia...yet?"

"Tell her?" She frowned.

"About me? About...us?"

She shook her head. "No."

"But you ...will. Promise!"

He had few visitors other than his Cathy. She learned from his lawyer that the power of attorney over his sizeable fortune would eventually pass to Amery's son Kurt because Amery was blind.

She wondered why Amery or Kurt didn't take Oliver to be near them, but she didn't try to find out; she wanted him near her. For the same reason, she refused Olivia's insistence that she move to Portland. As long as Oliver was here, she would keep living in the small house Levi had made so perfect for them. The big house and land were rented to a couple who ran it as carefully and profitably as though it were their own.

Five years. Seven. Ten. With no one to care how long she stayed, she went to Dunes House alone for days at a time, wandering the rooms, walking the beach and writing her journal for Olivia, the daughter who still did not know who she really was.

Catherine's arthritis became more debilitating until it was difficult even to make the trip to Crossroads to spend time with Oliver. At last, it was time to admit she must make her final journey to Dunes House.

That night she sat for hours at her small wooden desk, writing her last entries for Olivia in her neat, school-teacher script. When she closed the cover on the last of four thick composition books, she sat quietly for just a moment before pulling a clean piece of paper toward her and beginning, "My Dear Olivia, it's time now for me to keep a promise."

The eastern sky was brightening as she sealed the finished note in a plain envelope and wrote "Olivia" across its face. She hesitated for a moment. Where should she leave it for her daughter to find? But Catherine was so tired. She would decide tomorrow. For the time being, she slipped the envelope into the small drawer in the middle of the desk.

"Miss Cathy!" Tim Ryan's Adam's apple bobbed up and down in surprise. "You didn't tell me you were comin,' I'd have picked you up like always."

"I know, Tim, but I found someone to give me a ride." Catherine stood for a long moment looking at the Dunes House on this splendid early spring day. Against the south foundation, red and yellow tulips flourished in a bright patch of color; beyond the building Lake Michigan was as blue as she had ever seen it. It seemed all the world, and especially this particular portion of it that she cared so much about, was readying for another summer.

"You've done a fine job all these years, Tim. Will you stay on?"

He looked surprised. "Planned to. Long as you want me."

"Good."

In the beloved house which still whispered Oliver's presence in every room, she laid her journals on the coffee table and fingered the crystal wine decanter he had brought so proudly to place just where the afternoon sun would reflect brilliant prism rainbows onto the walls. She ran her hand over the hollow in the back of the tall chair where his head had rested when they read or talked. She sat for quiet moments on the lower porch, remembering the simple pleasure of walking the beach together, skipping stones out into the shimmering grey-blue water and watching gulls swoop to catch fish or a big ore ship disappear over the horizon. Finally, she picked up her journals and went upstairs to the blue and green bedroom where she lowered herself stiffly to the burnished floor.

The afternoon sun streamed through the tiny colored glass window, falling on the same spot it had the fateful day so many years ago when she had given herself heart and soul to Oliver Houle. She reached down and loosened one of the short pegged oak boards, revealing a recession between the crosspieces under the floor.

The case was there, as she knew it would be. She opened it and caught her breath once again at the glimmering beauty of diamond-set emeralds warming to the sun. Her arms were stiff and her fingers balked at working the clasps, but she fastened the necklace, then the bracelet.

Rising with difficulty, she walked unsteadily to the long mirror on the closet door. *An old woman, nearly seventy-eight, decorated with jewels. What did it mean now, with no one to share their beauty? No one to look at her with love in his eyes? No one to plan with, dream with?*

She unbuttoned the top of her dress and spread the material away from the necklace, lifting her chin proudly. *I had a love beyond most people's imaginations. Should I have denied it? Made different decisions? Could I have?*

Catherine put her hand to her throat and pressed the necklace against her skin one last time before she took the jewels off and laid them carefully on the grey velvet in the smooth leather box. Through tears, she read once more the note Oliver had included when he gave them to her:

"For my Cathy. One emerald for each year of our daughter's life. My promise to you kept at last today, and someday, for Olivia. With all my love forever, Oliver."

Catherine bit her lip as she slipped the note inside the case, closed it and returned it to the hollow under the floor. Next to the jewel box she placed the composition books, the story of her life at Middle Creek.

She rose slowly, turning her face up to the stained glass window spreading its colors over her pale skin. "Goodbye, Dunes House," she whispered. "Treat Olivia as well as you have treated me."

At the Bayshore station, she alighted with Tim's help from his rattly pickup. The train was boarding. "I won't be back, Tim."

"Won't be back? Oh, Miss Cathy!"

She put a fragile hand on his thin arm. "It's all right. You take care of things as you always have." She smiled up at him and rose on tiptoes to kiss his gaunt cheek. "You've been such a good friend, Tim Ryan. Thank you."

He flushed and swallowed, stuffing his hands into his overall pockets. "Wanted to, y'know. Always hoped Mr. Oliver would come back."

"If only he could." As she stepped up on the train platform, she turned and said, "My daughter will be here soon, Tim."

He nodded solemnly. "Be her friend, too, Miss Cathy. Pleasure."

The next day Catherine spent with Oliver, telling him all about her trip to Dunes House, reliving their happy times there, reminding him of funny, poignant things they had shared, remembering it all for him. He was having a good day, and they laughed together. His speech was more clear than usual and he spoke full sentences as he was often able to when he didn't try too hard. When she left, Catherine held his silver head to her breast and kissed his misshapen mouth with a tenderness that brought all their dreams, all their years together into one sweet moment to last forever.

That night Catherine Sommers died.

14

OLIVIA, 1984

At about the same time Bert Hobart arrived at Dunes House, Tim Ryan received an unexpected visitor.

"You ain't supposed to be here." Tim looked up from where he knelt on the garage floor next to Catherine Sommers' small wooden desk. "I gave you money to get on!"

The younger man pushed greasy, too-long dark hair back from his forehead with a dirty hand and squatted on his haunches next to Tim. "Yeah, Unc, you sure did. But I spent it and I didn't get far, and now I'm back for more." He grinned, showing teeth discolored from overuse of tobacco and underuse of a toothbrush. "So what's new?"

Tim pursed his lips and finished clamping the freshly-glued desk leg before he answered, "What's new is none of your business. Not here, anyways."

"Ah, c'mon. I'm your only living relative, and you treat me like you don't even like me."

"Fact is, I don't, much."

The younger man spat a brown glob onto the dusty cement floor and raised his eyebrows to watch Tim's reaction. "Don't like that much either, do you, Unc?"

Tim eyed him straight. "No."

"So what are you going to do about it?"

Tim picked up a wood scrap and scraped sawdust over the distasteful blot. "Suppose, clean up after you, like I did in the boathouse. Like I've always done." Tim rose, his knees creaking. "Don't never seem to have much personal pride, do you, Rip?"

Rip Stark snorted and stood up. He was slightly built, his head barely reaching Tim's shoulder. "Should I?"

Tim shook his head. "Can't blame anybody but yourself if you don't. What your daddy was ain't got nothin' to do with what you are, 'less you take it on."

"Sure."

"And what your momma was, was a saint. Why don't you take after her side of the family, 'stead of your no-count dad?"

"Come off it! She married a bum and a thief."

"Her mistake, not yours. So you're goin' to be the same as him? Go ahead. I'm through helpin' you."

The younger man's eyes narrowed. "You want another 'accident' to happen around here? Maybe one not quite so slight? Maybe one to *her*, this time." He tipped his head toward Dunes House. "She doesn't scare easy. Not as easy as you, old man."

Tim sucked in his breath and poked a bony finger into Rip's chest. "Listen, boy, and listen good! I gave you money when you first got outta jail, and I let you stay here when I shouldn't of. Miss Livvy wasn't fooled about that loose step. Or about the truck, neither. Both times I gave you money to move on. I 'spose it was you sent that damn note to her in the first place. God's sake, boy, why?"

"Why!" Rip Start spat another blob onto the dust. "Because you've got a real deal here, Unc. An easy way to make a good, comfortable living without knowing too much or working too hard. And you can always come up with a little money when you're scared. If you can't, maybe she can, you hear? Or, maybe..." he paused for effect, "...maybe that dumb, fat broad I've seen waddling around—"

Tim's pale eyes narrowed to slits. "You can go to hell, Rip. My sister would turn over in her grave if she could hear the kid she thought so much of talkin' this way. Can't figure out how to make an honest living so you pull scare tactics to leach off other people's."

Tim pulled himself to his full height and stepped forward, giving Rip another poke in his midsection. "All talk, that's what it is, ain't it? Well, boy, this ain't just talk. One more 'accident' and I'll turn you in. Sheriff around here ain't the best, but he can handle the likes of you."

"One more accident could be your last, ever think of that? Anyhow, you'd need proof."

"Proof!" Tim repeated. He shook his head, then tightened his lips. "Naw. All I have to do is tell him how you broke parole, but for my dead sister's sake, I won't, 'less I have to. Now you git, I don't care where to, and don't show your face around here again. Here's the door. Use it!"

Tim reached over and turned the handle on the small garage door just as the first gust of wind whirled around the building, snatched the door from his hand, and threw the wood with a splintering crack against the side of the building. In a split second, sheets of driving rain followed, obscuring even the short distance to Dunes House.

They stared out into the maelstrom as torn branches tumbled past on the grass between the garage and the house. Pelting hailstones the size of marbles assaulted the figure racing toward the garage.

"Tim! Tim!" Olivia Hobart, gripping a raincoat thrown over her head, called through the wind and hail as she ran toward the garage. "Is Pam with you?"

Rip Stark melted into the shadows in the garage.

"No, Miss Livvy. Ain't she in the house?"

Olivia shook her head and stared at Tim, her eyes wide with

fear. "Tim! You don't think…the …the boat!"

Tim hesitated only a second. "C'mon!"

Together they ran for the bluff, keeping their balance with difficulty against the buffeting wind as they slipped and slid over rolling hailstones down the wet wooden steps to the empty boathouse.

"Oh, Tim, no!" Olivia turned her face into the old man's shoulder, momentarily unaware of the pelting storm that lashed them, unprotected, on the boathouse deck.

"Now, there." He awkwardly patted her back. "Come in here, Miss Livvy." He pulled her into the empty building. "Ain't nothin' we can do till this blows over. She's prob'ly along the shore somewheres, sittin' under a tree." But in his heart he knew his words were empty ones. He'd lived long enough on this changeable lake to know that the little rowboat, riding low with Pam's heavy weight, wouldn't survive the kind of waves this wind churned up.

Olivia hugged her raincoat about her shoulders and shivered, her eyes first searching the grey, heaving waters, and then turning to beg for Tim's reassurance. "Do you really think so?"

Tim shrugged, looking away. "Don't hurt to hope long's you can, Miss Livvy, now does it?" His voice was tired and his shoulders drooped. "That girl's got more sense than you give her credit for most times…oh!"

Olivia followed his gaze to the hooks on the wall where both life jackets still hung side by side. As the enormity of Pam's mistake came at her full force, Olivia sank to her knees on the rough wooden floor and buried her face in her hands. The wind sucked her keening wail out of the boathouse and swirled it away over the storm-tossed water.

Heath found Pamela two days later, where her chilled, death-pale body bobbed gently face down in the now calm shallows near his end of the beach. His earlier efforts, along with those of the county rescue party with their drag hooks and specialized equipment, had yielded nothing as they searched in vain as soon as possible after the storm's wild force. An eddy swirling toward the point had finally brought Pamela's body to shore.

The exhausted and defeated entourage shouldering the canvassed, rope-wrapped bundle up the steep wooden steps to Dunes House was led by Sheriff Knowles.

Olivia and Bert met them at the top of the bluff, where their burden was lowered to the still storm-littered grass.

"Miz Hobart. Mister." The sheriff ducked his head. "Sorrowful thing, here."

Olivia nodded, swallowing hard, her gaze pulled again and again to the too-still bundle. "Do I…I mean, must I?" She took a step forward and then stopped, unable to continue.

The sheriff put a restraining hand on her arm. "No need. Mr. Collins made identification already. Unless you want?"

Olivia met Heath's eyes with gratitude. "Thank you," she whispered.

"Collins." Bert stepped forward. "And everybody, please accept our appreciation."

Wary, Olivia watched him. He'd made no pretense of sorrow during the past waiting hours. If anything, he'd been first angrier than ever, then accusing, then unbelievably harsh.

"Well, how do you feel about your precious Dunes House now, huh? Look what you've done!" he'd accused the evening the rescue squad called off the second day's unfruitful search because of darkness. He poured a full tumbler of brandy and sloshed some around in his mouth before swallowing.

"What *I've* done?" Olivia stared, numbed by guilt and more

than forty-eight hours without sleep.

"You know this is your fault. You brought her here, let her take that damn boat out. You should have known where she was."

Olivia looked at him over the polished maple dining table. "Bert. I almost always did know where she was. And I would have then, if we hadn't been arguing. She must have heard us. You know arguing always upset her. Oh…" She took a deep breath and forced her interlocked hands to stay quiet. "What does it matter now? She's gone."

"Yeah." Bert nodded. "Ever think of all those years we wasted because of her, Livvy? Ever think of the life we could have had without her?"

"Bert! What are you saying?"

He poured himself the last of the brandy from the decanter. "I'm saying that we're finally free. Can't you see, Livvy? This is a stroke of luck. We can live like other people for a change, not with your martyrdom getting in the way of every damn little thing!"

Olivia had stared at him, too tired to even try to comprehend, and left the room.

Now, facing this brilliant storm-washed afternoon with the reality of Pamela's shrouded body and fronted by the people who had worked so hard to find her, Bert put on a remarkable show as the bereaved father. Even his usually self-assured voice cracked at just the right time. A real professional closing the sale, Olivia thought.

"You've been just…just great." With that, Bert put a hand over his eyes and went into the house.

Olivia looked up to see Heath frowning at her husband's back before he gathered her into the circle of his caring arms. "I'm here, Livvy. If you need me."

She nodded. "Thank you. You can see I do."

The funeral was only a few words said in the familiar but

redecorated small country church near the farm where Olivia had grown up. The pastor was a young one who knew nothing of her family, and his platitudes were useless. There were no mourners except Doris Hugh and her stocky husband who had come only from duty to Catherine's memory.

Bert sat stone-faced when he wasn't playing the role he portrayed for anyone he thought mattered, and as soon as the short service and prayers at the grave side were finished he walked off to wait for Olivia in his rented Buick.

She stood in the churchyard for a few silent moments, not hearing the joyous birdsong filling the air, not noticing the beauty of the fencerow's wild daisies, thinking of nothing in particular, just letting her memory touch on the good things about Pamela, the heartbreaking, simple love she had asked and given so freely.

The little graveyard had been opened to admit her daughter into a grave next to Catherine and Levi Sommers. There were two empty plots beyond Pamela's, set aside by Levi at Pamela's birth. Would she someday rest there? Would Bert?

"The Lord giveth, and the Lord taketh away." Olivia whispered, raising her gaze to the clear blue sky and letting healing tears run unheeded down her face. It was God's storm, wasn't it? "Please, God," she whispered, "It wasn't my fault…"

"All right, we've done what we had to, and she's buried now," Bert said. "And I'm leaving." In the lower screen porch, Olivia turned from where she had been looking out over the now peaceful, treacherous water.

Bert stood in the French doors leading into the living room, his shoulders slumped, his suitcase in one hand, his suit coat thrown over his other arm. There were circles under his eyes, and the expression in them was distant and unreadable. His voice sounded mechanical, showing no warmth. "Well? I take it you're not coming?"

"Bert." Her hands clenched at her sides. "I can't."

"Fine." He turned on his heel. "If that's the way it is. I've played your game long enough, and I can make my own life. There are other women who would share it with me."

"I'm sure there are, Bert," she said. "I'm sure there are. And they would probably make you much happier than I ever have." As soon as she said the words she knew with a shock they were true.

He put down his suitcase and walked across the porch to her, both palms up, pleading. "Ah, Livvy. Give me some credit, will you? I'm trying to understand."

"Are you?" She turned back to the lake again and felt his arms around her, his rotund stomach pushing against her back. No answering warmth coursed through her body; it was as though they were strangers playing their parts. She stepped aside to free herself and turned to look into his face. "Bert, did we ever really have anything? Really?"

"What do you mean? We've got a house, some good investments—"

"I don't mean that!"

"Oh." He backed away and pulled at his tie as though it were too tight. "Yeah, we did. A long, long time ago." He reached out and took Olivia's hands. "And we can have it again, now there's just the two of us." He broke off, seeing the pain cross her face. "Don't look like that! Nothing is going to change what's happened." He looked away for a moment, choosing his words. "Okay, I was rotten to say it was your fault, but I was drinking. And..." he looked her full in the face before glancing away, "I wanted to hurt you."

"Well, you certainly accomplished that. Why, Bert?"

"Why? Can you really stand there and ask why?" He shoved his hands in his pockets and strode to the end of the porch, where he turned toward her again, his face distorted. "Why! Because you shut me away. I was always left out, don't you understand? There wasn't any room in your life for me once Pam was there. All you had time for was her. I thought if I waited…" He turned to look out over the water, and his voice lowered to almost a whisper, "…but it never changed."

Olivia shut her eyes, knowing the truth of his words. For a moment that seemed to last forever she heard the gulls screaming as they wheeled above the water, remembering the times she had refused to attend something with Bert because Pamela couldn't be left alone.

"Livvy."

She bit her lip.

"Will you come? Try?" He covered the distance between them with two strides and reached again for her hands. "We can make it work now, I know we can. You can do whatever you want—anything! Please."

Whatever she wanted? For almost twenty-eight years she had subjugated her wants, and to be honest, so had Bert. But was he just acting a part now? She'd seen how convincing he could be. If she went with him, what about Dunes House? Tim could take care of it, as he always had. And what about Heath? Where did he fit in her life now? Or did he fit at all?

She bit her inner lip so hard she winced. How much did she owe this man who had supported her all these years and let her so wrongly protect their daughter at his expense? How much of her life?

"Livvy? Please?"

She almost smiled, he sounded so much like the young Bert Hobart who had wanted her so passionately and swept her off her adolescent feet.

She looked up, hesitating, trying to see beyond his eyes, his voice. Then, slowly, she nodded. "I'll come. I'll try." She sighed with the weight of her decision. "But I won't make any promises."

It rained in Portland, and when it didn't rain it was gloomy. Olivia spent the first week of her return in a cleaning frenzy, removing every speck of dust and litter accumulated during her absence. The second week, she went through Pamela's room with determination and gave away everything, even the stuffed animals, so much a part of her daughter's life. Some other child would love them, too.

Olivia boxed up Pam's clothes and shoes, trying not to remember because remembering was too hard, and there was no use. The really difficult task was going through Pamela's "collection" drawer. The woman-child had treasured the oddest things: a popsicle stick, a picture of a bearded goat, raggedly cut from a National Geographic, an ice cream spoon from Clarissa's Parlor, a tiny ballerina doll from a gum-ball machine. Foolish, worthless things, nothing of value to anyone but Pam. Olivia dumped the whole drawer into the garbage and hauled it to the curb. No one else would have the chance to laugh about those things her daughter had cared enough to save.

Bert was attentive, helpful, willing to take her out to dinner every night of the week if she chose, but she didn't choose. They went to a couple of movies and attended one real estate dinner; she sat in on a meeting of the hospital auxiliary. On the surface, they were putting their lives together.

On the surface.

But underneath was a hollow void. At night when she couldn't sleep, Olivia's thoughts went to Dunes House, to dear old Tim who had loved her mother so and who, Olivia knew, cared almost as deeply about herself…to the surprising journal about her mother's life with Joel O'Brien, and once again to the question of the emeralds. Had they really been Catherine's to give? If so, why had Kurt Houle's grandfather kept insurance papers? Had Kurt come back with the threatened search warrant? And if he had, then what? Surely Tim would have called her from Bayshore; she'd left her number.

And what about Heath Collins? As analytically as she could, Olivia examined their relationship, recognizing it for what it was, an escape, a diversion, a chance to look at her own life from a different perspective. What did it mean to him? Possibly nothing more than a sexual encounter in his otherwise isolated existence?

Yet even the thought of his muscled arms and his sensuous mouth probing hers from within his soft, nuzzly beard was exciting. Now, she was here in this shallow life again, with its committees, dinners with people she didn't care about, and uneventful evenings watching TV with Bert, though she knew he would do anything, take her anywhere she wanted. But what did she want?

Where do you belong, Olivia Hobart? She squirmed in the bed, trying not to wake Bert but unable to find a comfortable position. There were still so many questions, so much she still needed to know.

She lasted a little more than a month. "I've tried, Bert. I've done my best to put our lives back on an even plane as well as I could."

Bert looked up over the morning paper, a cup of steaming coffee in his hand, smiling, lifting his eyebrows. "You've done great. It's like a whole new life."

"Is it?" She sighed. "But now I'm going back to finish what I started."

"For God's sake!" He slammed his cup down so hard coffee sloshed over the saucer and spread a stain on the crisp white tablecloth. "Are we back to that again? Haven't I done every damn thing I could to make our lives what they ought to be? What they ought to have been all along?" He crumpled the newspaper into a heap in his lap. "And this is the thanks I get? Come on, Livvy, what's this nonsense now?"

Olivia rose to get a paper towel and sopped up the coffee before she answered. "I know you don't like it, but I have to go back."

"*Have* to?"

"Yes." Her eyes pleaded his understanding. "I have to know about the emeralds, Bert, and find out what connection Oliver Houle has with my mother's past. Doris Hugh told me at Pam's funeral that he's alive and in a nursing home not far from the farm. It's my past, too, don't you see? And there are so many loose ends, so many questions. Can't you understand?"

"All I know is that you don't want to be here with me. You don't want to build a life together now when we finally have the chance." Bert got up slowly and walked to the kitchen counter where he stood with his back to her, his head bowed, his hands grasping the counter edge on either side. His voice was almost a whisper. "Livvy, in all the years we've been married, even with all the disappointments I've had with our relationship, I've never once, not *once*, looked at another woman." He turned to face her. "Did you know that?"

She stared at him. "I-I guess I never even thought you might, not really."

"Were you so sure of yourself?"

"No. You just didn't seem to be the kind."

He lifted his chin. "There were plenty of opportunities."

"I'm sure there were."

"But I never wanted to. Livvy, I love you. I've always loved you and admired you, even for your devotion to Pam and the way you always did the right thing for my business. Even the way you ran the damn hospital auxiliary with one hand. But it was never just the two of us. Now it is, and you want to leave."

This quiet affirmation of his love was unexpected; Olivia would have been far more comfortable with his anger.

He turned away from her again, his shoulders drooping. "Answer me this, Livvy. Do you ever plan on coming home?"

Home. Where was home? She hesitated. "I don't honestly know. Not right now."

Bert looked at her for a long moment before he met her gaze. "You know, I've been in real estate a long time, Livvy. And there's a point in every transaction where it comes down to a closing date, and either you buy or you don't."

Olivia frowned. "I know that, Bert."

He held up a hand, palm toward her. "Let me finish. I've done what I can for the two of us, and I'll do anything in my power to give you what you need. I know the terms I can live with: You here with me. Not me there with you. You can keep Dunes House and rent it or let it rot for all I care. As you've told me often enough, that's your business."

"I'm not following you."

"It's like this: I'm selling. If you're buying, you'll meet my terms, come home where you belong and we'll work things out from there. Dear God, I'll even go see some damn marriage therapist if you think it will help! Otherwise-well, otherwise, I...I want out." Bert searched her face and waited for her astonished answer.

"Out? You-you want a divorce?" She'd never considered he might be as unsatisfied as she. When had they ever talked like this? Never.

Bert nodded. "Isn't that the only answer? Time is passing us by, Livvy. I want to get on with my life. I'm middle-aged, and I want someone I care about to grow old with. I'd like it to be you. Simple as that."

"Simple? It sounds cold. And dull!"

"Maybe, now." He turned to her, hope coloring his voice. "But we could make it new, exciting. If we both tried. It's not a one-sided deal."

"Bert—"

He went on as though she'd made no sound. "Remember when we first had Pam, and the doctor said she probably wouldn't live very long? I was glad. Glad! Was that so terrible of me? To want a real wife, a real mate? A real life?"

The emotion choking his voice was answered with tears running down her face. Olivia brushed them away. "No. No. But Bert, I have to go back. I *do*."

"Go, then." He straightened his shoulders. "I'll wait, Livvy, because I've always waited, and because whether you know it or not, I love you. But I won't wait forever."

The flight into the inland airport nearest to Bayshore was delayed by foul, foggy weather; the train connection was a two-hour wait, and when Olivia walked from the station to the town's all-purpose grocery and drugstore to contact Morty Morris, Bayshore's "taxi" and general jack of all trades, she was thwarted again by the news he was short-handed due to flu among his three part-timers and couldn't leave the store until one of them showed up.

"Shouldn't oughta be more than about an hour, though, Miz Hobart, care to wait," Morty offered from behind the battered counter where he totaled an order for a heavy-set woman stuffed into a bright blue shorts and halter suit in spite of the unseasonably cool, clammy weather. Her thighs bulged around the edge of her shorts; her knees were barely discernible and her ample calves ran all the way into her high-heeled clogs without narrowing noticeably at the ankles. "That'll be eight dollars and sixty cents, Ma'am."

Tourist season brings out all kinds, Olivia thought as she smiled at the friendly storekeeper. Her long trip had been disturbed by memories of old and new mistakes and guilts warring at cross-purposes in her mind. Bert's unexpected admission of honest caring had rocked her new-found independence. Yet, hadn't he always been there when she'd needed him? It was just so unlike him to open up about anything he truly felt. She found his confession, if she could call it such, as frightening as it was endearing.

She'd thought she could easily walk away from him and her life in Portland, maybe even, as she'd considered in one of her more infatuated moments, to Heath Collins. But not, she knew now, as a permanent arrangement, and she was sure Heath knew that as well. They had simply enjoyed each other at one place at one time.

What drew her back to Dunes House was far more important than a brief sexual encounter, no matter how appealing the younger man. At first it had been the mystery of her mother's life, but now she realized Dunes House itself pulled at her very being. *As though I belong there, as though there I become whole.*

She couldn't explain it, and trying to unravel her mother's story was as frustrating as reading an intriguing novel a few pages at a time, helter-skelter.

Olivia sighed. "I'll wait," she told Morty, turning toward the door. "Thanks."

"Hear you've had a little more trouble out your place?" Morty questioned as he efficiently bagged the amply-endowed customer's purchases.

Olivia stopped short, her eyes widening. "Trouble? I haven't heard anything. What do you mean? Is Tim all right?"

Morty nodded, grinning. "He is now, I hear. 'Bout got his head shot off by the sheriff, though, just the other day. Least that's what I heard."

"Really? Tim?" Olivia clutched her purse so tightly the metal clasp dug into her palm. "What happened?"

Without missing a beat in his conversation with Olivia, Morty leaned over the countertop to ask a red-headed tyke, "What can I get for you today, Billy?" Eyes on the boy, he continued, "Seems some young punk tried to run Tim down with his own old pickup, what I heard. Two pieces of red licorice, Billy? Four pennies." A pudgy little hand opened and the coins rolled onto the counter. "Thank you, young fella." Morty grinned. "See you tomorrow."

The little boy grinned back, one of the sticky red ropes already protruding from his gap-toothed mouth.

"Morty, for heaven's sake, tell me!"

"That's the gossip. Don't really know all the particulars. Maybe you better let Tim tell you the rest."

"The young 'punk,' though—do you know who he was?" Could it have been Kurt Houle? Somehow running over an old man with a banged-up truck didn't seem his tie-and-suited style. Who, then? Olivia shivered in spite of the day's warmth. Perhaps the odd 'accidents' at Dunes House would be explained at last.

Morty shrugged. "I didn't hear. Sheriff Knowles was there for another reason, with some lawyer."

That would have been Kurt Houle. With the sheriff and his

search warrant! His threat had evidently not been idle. Had they found the emeralds? Had they taken them? Why hadn't Tim called?

"Please, Morty, can we hurry? I've got to get out to Dunes House."

"I know, I know." He motioned toward a tall teenage girl coming in the door. "Here's my helper now. Sit down on the bench out there, and I'll be with you in a minute."

Olivia pushed open the screen door and sank down on the wooden park bench which served as a popular spot to watch whatever might be happening up or down Main Street. Tourist season was in full swing; the ice cream shop kitty-corner from the grocery was doing a rousing business, as were the two small gift and souvenir shops on either side of Morty's store. She was aware of none of it.

Dear old Tim hurt? Almost run down and shot at by Sheriff Knowles? It all seemed so far-fetched as to be unbelievable. The lawyer had to be Kurt Houle, but who was the "young punk?"

At Dunes House, Tim, limping, hurried to Morty's car. "Miss Livvy! Glad to see you." Tim lifted her suitcase from the back seat. "Tried to call your place from town this morning but there wasn't no answer."

"Thanks, Morty." Olivia reached into the window and handed the grocer a ten-dollar bill. "I appreciate your taking the trouble."

"No trouble. You okay, Tim?"

"Better'n ever, Morty. Little stiff is all."

"Glad to hear." Morty waited for a moment before putting

the car in gear, obviously hoping for more enlightening information, but was disappointed as Olivia turned to follow Tim toward the house with Olivia's bag.

Morty sighed and started the car.

As soon as they were inside the kitchen and Tim had set down her suitcase, Olivia grasped both his thin arms and searched his face. "What in the world has been happening here, Tim? Morty said you'd been run down and almost shot!"

"Correct on both counts. How 'bout a cup of coffee while we talk? Made it this morning but it will only take a minute to warm up." He looked hopefully at Olivia whose empty stomach would surely rebel at Tim's potent brew. It was bad enough fresh, let alone warmed up.

"Sure. But talk while you're fussing with it."

"Fussing! Women fuss, not men. Huh! Well, things been interestin' since you left and that's God's truth. Set down there." He gestured toward the kitchen table with the old enameled coffee pot. "You remember that note you got way back when you first come here?" Stooping, he lit the gas burner under the pot.

"Do I!"

"And the mess in the boathouse?"

Olivia nodded. "And I remember a loose step in the basement and your truck mysteriously falling over on you, too."

Tim swallowed, his Adam's apple bobbing furiously. "Thought you would. And you remember I told you I had a nephew somewhere?" He moved slowly to the cupboard and got down two crockery mugs.

This was beginning to sound like a quiz game. "Tim, go on!"

"Well, it's a long story and I'm halfway ashamed of it. If I'd just turned him in at the beginnin,' things would'a been fine." He stared out the window for a moment, lost in thought.

"Who? Your nephew, you mean?"

"Yes. Anyways, Rip Stark, that's the one, my sweet dead

sister's rotten boy, broke parole and came here askin' for money. Just before you first came, that was." He shook the coffee pot vigorously to stir up the mixture.

"And you gave him some?"

"Not at first. No, sir, I refused."

Comprehension dawned in Olivia's mind. "And then I got the note. And the stair was loosened."

"And I still refused. Wasn't about to be blackmailed, not Uncle Tim." He stared at Olivia, anger sparking his pale eyes. "I loved my sister mor'n anybody, Miss Livvy, and I didn't want to turn him in. I thought if he could just get him a start somewhere…"

"But then he tipped the truck and nearly killed you."

Tim nodded. "And I gave in. Gave him enough to get him clear to California. Been savin' for years, you know, nowhere to spend it anyways 'cept once in a while on a movie."

"And it still wasn't enough."

"Not for him." Tim poured two cups of the blackest, murkiest coffee Olivia had ever witnessed. It was almost too thick to pour. "Milk?" he asked, as though she could have drunk it without.

"Please! Go on."

"The day Miss Pam drowned. He was here then, demandin' more. And I said nothin' doing, told him if I heard any more from him I'd turn him in for busting parole. He was mad. Not hot mad, real cold mad, but he went away."

Olivia took a sip of the brew in her cup and almost choked. "Hot," she said, an excuse to get up for water. "But tell me what happened the other day."

"Comin' to it. Rip came back again the next mornin,' demandin,' would you believe it, five thousand dollars! He said I'd never see nor hear from him again. It was temptin,' let me tell you, but I knew he'd never quit, so I told him to go to hell—sorry,

Miss Livvy—and he stalked off, madder'n a wet hen. Always did get terrible mad. Went off like a firecracker…" Tim's voice trailed away.

"Tim! Then what?" Olivia sat down again, put her elbows on the table, and leaned forward.

"He'd interrupted me mowin' on the far end of the big side yard, and I went back to it. You know how noisy that hand mower is, can't hear a blessed thing when it's runnin.' My truck was parked by the garage, keys it in, o'course, 'cause I just come back from buyin' gas for the mower. And that damn kid jumped in it and tried to run me down!"

"Tim! That's terrible!"

"But that ain't all. I headed away from the truck so's he wouldn't hit me, and just as I was high-tailin' it to get inside the house, the sheriff pulls in, screechin' to a halt. He's got the young lawyer with his search warrant with him. He sees what's happenin' and rolls down his window like he was goin' to bag a rabbit and starts firing away at my truck tires, I guess to stop Rip. Hit two of 'em, too, but that didn't slow Rip down much."

Olivia put her hand on Tim's arm. "But Morty said he almost shot you."

"Yeah. Well, the crazy kid musta figured the sheriff found out Rip had skipped parole and was after him, so he pulls out a pistol, too, and starts shootin' back. Anyhow, the truck is runnin' crazy all over the grass with two flat tires, and the Sheriff's chasing it in his patrol car, both of them diggin' up the whole yard with fast turns and shootin' at each other. Wait'll you get a look at that yard! All tore up, and I'm runnin' around like a chicken with its head cut off tryin' to get out of the way. Altogether musta' looked like some dang Three Stooges movie," Tim said, disgust coloring his face.

Olivia couldn't help smiling at the picture Tim painted.

"Then Rip stopped the truck and jumped out beside it, still

shooting at the sheriff, forgettin' all about me. So I tippy-toed up behind him and grabbed him just as a damn bullet went right through my hat." He pointed to the chair beside him at his battered high-domed cowboy hat sporting a hole in one side and out the other.

"So I wrestled him down and sat on him while the Sheriff handcuffed him." Tim dusted his hands against each other. "Damn fool kid. Always had a temper."

"What a story!" Olivia attempted another swallow of Tim's coffee and added more milk. "I'm just glad you're all right. Is he back in jail now?"

"For a long, long time. Seems like the sheriff really was lookin' for him, 'cause he robbed a couple liquor stores up beyond Bayshore when I didn't give him money the last time he was here. Armed robbery." Tim's pale eyes narrowed. "He was threatenin' you, Miss Livvy. I couldn't give in to that."

His loyalty was touching, and she smiled at him, then sobered. "What about the lawyer? Did the sheriff bring the search warrant, or what?"

Tim hung his head. "I couldn't do anythin' about it, Miss Livvy, it was all legal as can be. They turned everything pretty well upside down in the house, looking, but I stayed with them every minute, and they didn't find a thing. Not a thing. And I put everything back right."

"Thank you, Tim." Olivia was quiet for a moment, sipping the potent coffee. "But his grandson said Oliver Houle was paying the insurance. Do you know why?"

Tim pursed his lips. "Miss Cathy didn't give me leave to tell much why, y'know. Things just was the way they was. You just keep lookin', Miss Livvy, and it will all come right." He drained his cup.

Olivia bit her lip. "Tim, do you think I ought to go see my mother's old friend?"

"Who?"

"Oliver Houle. He paid the insurances. He must know something."

Tim was silent for a long moment, not meeting her eyes. "Maybe, Miss Livvy. But you might find out more'n you want to know."

"What do you mean?"

"Nothin.' Just ramblin.'" From the set of his lips as the old man went to the door, Olivia knew the subject was closed. "I got the last piece glued on the desk now," he said. "Needs to dry overnight, and then I'll bring it in."

"Thanks, Tim." The screen latched quietly behind him, and Olivia sat at the table for a few minutes after he went out. The sandy beach beckoned her to walk, and she knew she would be welcome at Heath's cabin, even in his bed. But she didn't need to be there, not tonight. There was so much to sort out. The "danger" was over, thank God, but the more important mystery remained.

Lost in thought, she moved through the rooms to the lower porch. Oliver Houle might have some answers if he were able to speak. Doris Hugh had told her where he was. Somehow, even without considering Tim's mysterious comment, she knew seeing Houle could change things for her forever, yet she had no idea how. She shivered, though the day's clammy chill had drifted into a warm, balmy evening.

She pressed her forehead against the window screen, listening to the coming night and staring east as dusk obscured the horizon and an almost-full moon rose across Lake Michigan to create a golden ribbon on the now serene waters which had so changed her life.

"Room 213, last door on your right. He's alone." The nurse at Crossroads was cheerful. "I'm glad you've come. It will be so good for him to have some company."

Olivia nodded and walked apprehensively down the corridor, moving to the wall as she passed a drooling man pushing a walker. She stopped momentarily when a raspy, shrill voice called "Help me! You, there!" She stopped at the open door to stare at the ancient, angry woman strapped into a wheelchair.

"Don't you bother. It's just Mary," said another old woman shuffling along the hall on paper slippers, her wrongly-buttoned robe hanging crooked on her gaunt frame. "Be quiet, Mary!" she shouted, sticking her pink-curlered head into the room. "Always bothers everybody," she explained to Olivia, nodding. "She's about deaf, too. Just go about your business, dearie."

Relieved, Olivia continued slowly toward the end of the hall. Toward Oliver Houle. Would he be able to talk? Perhaps, if it was one of his "good days."

"He's not in his right mind some of the time, they say," Doris Hugh had told her.

"You mean he's...insane?"

"Oh, no. Just forgetful. Senile, like. Confused. Your mother used to visit him a lot. Some days he was fine, and some days he could only remember things way past, she said. They were real good friends."

Real good friends. How good? Enough to insure Catherine's house and probably thousands of dollars worth of emeralds without her husband's knowledge?

Oliver Houle sat in a wheelchair facing the window. From where she stood at the open door, all Olivia could see was the back of his silver head. It was bowed, as though he were praying, or asleep sitting up, so she tiptoed quietly around the foot of the hospital bed to look into his face.

She knew he'd suffered a debilitating stroke, but in repose he didn't look much different than she remembered him, though she hadn't seen him for years. He'd always been tall and slender; now his physique was skeletal. A wayward forelock from his still full head of hair fell loosely across his forehead, almost covering his eyes, and without thinking Olivia reached out and brushed it back, unaware that the tender gesture was the same one her mother had so often made.

Her touch awakened him, and she stepped back, sorry, hoping she hadn't startled the fragile old man.

He frowned, orienting himself as his eyes slowly focused, and he stared up at Olivia for a second before awareness shone through his misshapen features, and he opened his mouth with a sharp intake of breath.

"Cath-y!" His whole countenance shone with joy as his thin bloodless lips worked hard to form the words that were barely more than a whisper as he struggled to reach out with a trembling arm. "Oh, my...Cathy-y...you've come...back!"

Startled, she realized that in his awakening confusion she had become her mother. Tim said she was the image of Catherine at her age. Tentative, Olivia smiled and pulled a chair close to his.

The old man shook, rocking, his mouth working as he tried to speak. It was obvious her being there agitated him, but he didn't seem upset as much as simply excited. She looked toward the door—should she call a nurse?

He reached his unsteady parchment-like hand out to her. "My...love . Take my...hand."

Cathy? My love? Olivia's brows knit with confusion. "Hello, Mr. Houle." His fingers were ice cold.

He laughed, a pitiful intake of breath. "Mr...Houle," he repeated. "Funny...so...formal." With an obvious effort he straightened his neck to look more fully into her face. "I've been...waiting...so long."

Olivia swallowed. She could see into his eyes, see the soul, alive but imprisoned there, confused, perhaps, trapped and wanting to communicate. Did this man hold the key to her mother's mystery? And if he did, could she find the way to unlock it? He thought she was Catherine Sommers. Perhaps it would be best to go along with his illusion.

His face twisted, a grotesque imitation of a smile. "You…prom-ised…re…mem…ber?" His thin fingers gripped hers with surprising strength. "You said…you'd give…did you?"

Her mother had promised him something. "Did I what?" She spoke slowly, haltingly, knowing she intruded on his memories, yet—

"Did you…give the…letter?" His whole body contorted with the effort to make his meaning clear. "To Oliv…ia."

She caught her breath. His faded eyes held hers in a mesmerizing stare, even though his whole face was agonized as he tried to speak.

She swallowed and took a deep breath, closing her eyes, willing a lucid answer from him. "The letter? To Olivia?"

He attempted a laugh again, then sobered. "You…tease. You know." He spoke clearly now, sounding almost angry, sure of his words, as though he had practiced them many times. "The letter…about me."

"Oh." Her mother was dead, surely he knew that, yet his mind had retreated to a distant time, another place. "Not…not yet…" she faltered, hoping that was the right thing to say.

"Did you…give her the…emeralds?" Now his eyes were piercing, searching.

"Yes." Olivia nodded. That was not a lie. She just hadn't found them yet.

The old man nodded his silver head in satisfaction. "Good." There was a quiet moment when neither of them spoke. Then his voice, almost a whisper, reached her. "I wish I…could have…told her…my…self."

Olivia sucked in her breath. "Told her what, Oliver?"

He leaned his head back against the chair and closed his eyes, his fading voice making barely any sound. Olivia leaned within an inch of his mouth to hear.

"You know! That she's…my…daughter …"

His voice trailed into nothing. He was asleep, as though the effort to communicate had tired him beyond his abilities.

Olivia reeled back, nearly upsetting her chair, and stood, shock and disbelief coursing through her. Could what he said be true? Or was it only the fabrication of a mind riddled with scars, a wishful dream of an old man who might have coveted his neighbor's wife for years?

She stared down at Oliver Houle's peaceful face. She had come to him for answers, and she had only found more questions.

Olivia hurried past the nurses' station in a daze, not even answering the friendly desk nurse who called after her, "Thanks so much for coming. Do come back."

Pushing out the door into the brilliant morning sun, gasping from shock, Olivia made herself breathe deeply for a few moments as she attempted to regain self-control before walking unsteadily around the low brick building to the parking lot where Tim waited for her in his battered pickup.

She climbed in and sat beside him, silent, staring straight ahead, her mind a tumble of questions, her confusion plain across her face.

She knew Tim watched her obvious effort to compose herself.

Finally she turned to him. Only the rapid bobbing of his Adam's apple showed his appreciation of her inner turmoil.

"Did you know?"

"Know what, Miss Livvy?"

"Don't look so innocent! That man, Oliver Houle, says he's my-my father!"

Tim nodded, not meeting her eyes. "Figured he would."

"Well, is he?" Olivia's eyes filled with tears. She grabbed Tim's arm and forced him to look at her. "Is he, Tim?"

"Far's I know," he said reluctantly.

"Why didn't you tell me?"

Tim sighed. "Wasn't my story to tell."

That damn loyalty to her mother again! Olivia bit her lip. "All these years! All these years I thought…" She looked at Tim, annoyed at the tears that spilled over, swiping at them with the pads of her fingers, pleading. "It can't be true, Tim. My father—Levi Sommers was my father. Did you know him?"

"Never saw him. Never even heard the name, 'til now. Was always just Mr. Oliver here."

"Oh," Olivia said, misery covering her like a blanket. "Let's go home, Tim, please."

"Sure thing, Miss Livvy." Tim pumped the gas pedal and the old truck roared into service. Olivia was quiet though her hands were clasped together so tightly her fingers were numb. He respected her silence as they bumped along toward Dunes House.

Finally Olivia asked in a small voice, "When she was here, was it always with him?"

"Mr. Oliver." He nodded, and she was sure he hadn't missed the disdainful note in her voice. "Until he took sick."

"Only with him?"

"Just him. And you, when you were just a little thing. And then alone."

So this was where her mother had come to "renew" herself. A lover's tryst. A clandestine romance. Dunes House was where "Cathy" had come to cuckold her loving husband, Levi Sommers. Over and over again. And with a neighbor, a friend of Levi's! Anger rose up and boiled out. She turned to face Tim. "Did you know they weren't married?" she demanded.

Tim smiled a little. "Figured they weren't."

"But—"

"Now, Miss Livvy. Don't you go gettin' all riled up." He turned in between the Dunes House gateposts, talking all the while. "They might not have been married by no minister, but they were married in their hearts. I never saw love so deep between two people, never. It was like you could see it hoverin' around them. And around you, too, when they brought you, so little. You think you're mad about it, don't you?" He accused, his pale eyes assessing her. "Well, just you should be so lucky as to have a love like that in your life." Tim spun the wheel and brought the truck to a rocking stop at the side door of the house. "Don't you go makin' judgments, that's all!"

Olivia stared at him for a moment before opening the door. Tim was angry at *her*. It was all too much to think about. Oliver Houle her father? Tim part of the whole picture? And Levi Sommers, whom she had known as her father—where did he fit in all this?

"Tim…please…I don't want to judge." Her voice caught and she brushed tears from her eyes. "I just want to understand."

Tim Ryan fixed his pale stare on her with a scowl. Then his expression softened. "Some things are beyond understandin,' Miss Livvy. Some things just got to be accepted."

Accepted. Olivia turned everything she'd learned over and over in her mind as she poured herself a cup of Tim's leftover coffee and sat at the little maple kitchen table to think. Could she accept the fact that her mother was pregnant when Levi Sommers married her, but not by his seed? That she was an adulteress and continued to be, for years and years? That loving, steady Levi Sommers knew? How could he not have known? And if he knew, did he "accept"?

With a burst of shock that caused her to gasp out loud, Olivia realized for the first time that her name was the female form of Oliver. Of course! How had Levi allowed such a slap in the face?

"But he loved my mother!" Olivia cried out in the empty kitchen. "I know he loved her more than life itself. And he loved me."

She slammed down her empty cup and got up. Evidently Tim felt she needed some time to herself to wrestle with this new knowledge of her heritage; he had disappeared as soon as they got back to Dunes House. She wanted to think this whole crazy declaration of paternity might have been only a fabrication in Oliver Houle's addled mind, but Tim had not been at all surprised. No, dear, loyal Tim had been part of it all.

It was so confusing. And so wrong!

Olivia started through the living room to the lower porch which seemed to be where she did her best thinking. She stopped with surprise at the sight of her mother's little wooden desk, finally repaired to Tim's satisfaction. For a moment Olivia looked at the offending piece of furniture as though it had been contaminated by the new vision she held of Catherine Sommers, but the desk and its secrets beckoned to her as surely as if they spoke her name.

"All right, then," she said aloud, squaring her shoulders. She pulled one of the dining room chairs in front of the desk and sat, hesitating before she pulled open the simple drop front. Whatever was in here—and there might be nothing at all—could certainly be no worse, no more upsetting, than what she had already learned this morning.

The desk's left cubbyholes yielded nothing but some old paid bills and unused note papers and envelopes. The right side contained miscellaneous letters, some from herself in Portland, one from a distant cousin in Arizona, now dead, a notice from the church about a raise in pew rent to cover some redecoration, and a religious birthday card signed "Yours in Christ, Myrtle."

Myrtle who? Olivia had no idea. Surely Myrtle didn't know the truth about Catherine Sommers, or she wouldn't have signed the card that way.

The middle cubbyhole held a metal box filled with paper clips, pens, a small stapler. Olivia sighed. It was all so predictable.

Then she pulled open the tiny drawer under the middle section and caught her breath. A small blue envelope was plainly marked "Olivia" in her mother's hand, but it wasn't written in the sure script Olivia was accustomed to; this was quavery, scrawled as though the writer had been exhausted by the effort.

Olivia shut her eyes for a moment, gripping the sides of the desk drop. Was this the letter Oliver Houle asked about?

With shaking fingers, she ripped open the envelope and pulled out the short message:

Olivia, my dearest daughter. It's time, now, for you to know the truth, all of it. Upstairs at Dunes House, under the pegged floor where my beautiful little window shines green and gold on early summer afternoons, you'll find your jewels. And my journals. They were written for you.

I do not ask forgiveness. I only pray you accept me as I am, not as you thought I was, and that you'll know without a doubt I've loved you always.

Mother

Her heart pounding, Olivia clutched the note to her breast and closed her eyes. "Some things got to be accepted," Tim had said. But could she?

The secret was here, upstairs, waiting for her. All of it.

In a daze, Olivia looked around the familiar living room, her mind almost unwilling to continue, to find out more, but her body rose from the chair and her feet carried her up the stairs of their own accord. Slowly, moving as though in a dream, Olivia entered the blue and green bedroom, brilliantly lit by the southern sun that streamed through the windows, illuminating the whole room.

She rounded the bed and stared first up at the tiny stained

glass window set between the two large, ordinary sashes. "Your mother loved that window," Tim had said the first day they'd come to Dunes House. Olivia let her gaze drift down to the familiar honey oak floor where sun-spread patches of blue, gold, and green lay across the ripe wood. There must be something special about it all, something special to her mother from years ago, thought Olivia. *But what?*

The blue and green patterned window curtains lifted gently against the sills, and the sea gulls' mewling wafted in through the upper porch on the afternoon breeze, but Olivia was unaware of anything except her purpose. She knelt, her whole body trembling, and felt along the boards with trembling fingers to find which loose wooden pegs would release the mystery of her mother's life. Olivia had never noticed any board that wasn't secure, but there had been no reason to look for one.

She caught her breath. There! That peg was loose. So were the others on that board. Biting her lip, she tried to lift the peg with her fingernail. It wasn't possible, and with a muttered, heartfelt "Damn!" she scrambled to her feet, hurried to the dresser for a nail file, a bobby pin, anything to help. She realized she was shaking as she scrabbled through the top drawer, and mentally forced herself to relax, take deep breaths, and release them slowly.

Returning with a slim file, Olivia pried the four pegs loose, then lifted the board and stared into the dim recess under the floor. "Oh." Her breath released; her knees seemed to dissolve beneath her and she sank back, staring at the long, slim leather box and the composition books lying in wait for her.

Hardly breathing, she gathered them up with trembling hands and held them against her chest.

Suddenly an unexpected, insistent knock on the kitchen door startled her. Tim wouldn't knock like that. It had to be someone else. An intruder, for that was how she thought of anyone who infringed on her privacy at Dunes House, especially now when the answers to her mother's life were literally within her grasp. Surely Tim would take care of whoever it was.

Perhaps it's Kurt Houle! She cringed against the side of the bed, clutching the journals and the jewel box.

The knock came again, more insistent this time, accompanied by a deep male voice. "Livvy! Are you home?"

She swallowed in relief. Heath Collins. He was not an intruder. Right now she couldn't think of anyone she would rather see.

Shaking her head to clear it, she scrambled to her feet and laid her precious booty on the colorful blue and green bedspread. "Coming!" she called and hurried down the open stair, through the living room to the kitchen door.

"Ah, you are here. I was about to give up," Heath said as she threw open the inner door and screen. "Tim's truck is gone, and I thought you might be, too." His healthy, tanned body, comfortable in cutoff jeans and baggy T-shirt, filled the door frame. "Busy?"

She shook her head. She'd been so engrossed she hadn't heard Tim leave.

"Hey! You look a little dazed. Something the matter?"

She shook her head again.

"Well, then, invite me in? Cat got your tongue?"

"Sorry." She found her voice. "I am in a kind of daze, I guess. Sure, come in."

He studied her for a moment, leaning against the jamb. "I repeat, something the matter? You look like I always thought somebody might look when they'd seen the proverbial ghost."

Olivia smiled shakily, gesturing him inside. "Not just seen. Found."

He grinned engagingly. "Super. Perfect afternoon for ghosts, don't you think? Dark and dreary and all that?" He waved one arm at the brilliant, breezy afternoon behind him and she laughed, brought back to reality.

"Come in, Heath. I've found the answers to all my questions, I think. I'll show you." She took his hand and pulled him through the kitchen. "How did you know I was back here?"

"Village gossip. Morty told me when I went in for groceries this morning. I took a chance you'd be home."

Olivia sobered. "Oh, I'm here all right. Olivia Houle Hobart is in residence."

Heath stopped short. "What? Did I hear right? Olivia Houle Hobart?"

"You did. I don't believe it myself, not yet, anyhow. It's all crazy, and I really need to talk about it to someone beside Tim, who won't answer anything. Sit down and I'll get us something to drink. Then I'll tell you about my visit to Crossroads this morning."

Twenty minutes later, Heath leaned back and said softly, "Wow!"

"For sure, wow," Olivia repeated. "But then I came home and looked through my mother's desk, one Tim's been repairing. It hasn't been in the house until now."

Heath leaned forward. "And you found your emeralds?"

"Not quite. But I found a letter telling me where to look. Come." She led him up to the bedroom and pointed to the open recess under the floor.

Heath let a low whistle through his lips. "There all the time?"

"I guess. Probably where she always kept them. If the house burned down they'd have gone with it. I really don't think Tim knew about this hiding place, not from the way he talked." Olivia gestured at the items on the bed. "Here they are, I think." She paused. "Maybe the case is empty. Wouldn't that be a joke? I haven't looked in it yet. Want to be my witness?"

"Trust me? I might hit you over the head for them if they're as great as Tim said."

Startled, Olivia looked up to see the twinkle in his light blue eyes. "Now, that would surprise me, a big teddy bear like you."

"Oh, shoot. My boy scout image always ruins my sinister plans," Heath complained, then grinned. "For heaven's sake, woman, open the box!"

They sat together on the bed, and with trembling hands Olivia slid back the silver clasp on the leather box and lifted the lid.

A piece of note paper lay across the contents, but she put it aside, gasping as sunlight caught on the myriad facets of the brilliant emeralds and diamonds filling the case. "Ohhhh! They're…they're exquisite!"

"My God!" breathed Heath. "What an understatement! Them's jewels, for sure."

"No wonder there was so much insurance," Olivia said, looking up at Heath. "They're unbelievable."

"And all yours."

She made a face. "Not if Kurt Houle has anything to say about it. I have to have some proof they were actually given to my mother by," her voice broke, "my…by Oliver Houle."

"Your father."

Reluctantly, Olivia nodded.

"Well, here's your proof." Heath picked up the note paper she'd set aside and read aloud, "For my Cathy. One emerald for each year of our daughter's life. My promise to you kept at last today, and someday, for Olivia. With all my love forever, Oliver."

Olivia looked at Heath for a long moment and then burst into tears.

He pulled her to him and held her gently until the storm passed. "Better now?"

She sniffed and swallowed. "Sorry. It's just all too much."

He got up and walked to the window, his hands in his back

pockets. "Poor little rich girl? I'll bet you'll survive the shock." There was just a trace of envy in his voice before he turned and smiled at her. "But you still don't know her story."

"It's all here. Four journals' worth." She pointed to the thick composition books beside her on the bed.

"Think you can handle what's in them, or do you want me to stay while you read?"

She thought for a moment, then shook her head. "Thanks for offering. You're very kind, as usual. But no. Right now I guess…well, it's a private thing between my mother and me."

"I understand. I'll go, then." Heath pulled her to her feet. "Come see me later? When you've sorted everything out?"

Clutching the gem case and the notebooks, she nodded. "I'll walk you down."

He looked around the attractive bedroom and made a face of resignation. "Great. I'm finally invited up to the beautiful lady's boudoir, and she shows me a hole in the floor and then primly walks me down. Story of my life…" He let the sentence trail off sorrowfully.

"Clown!" She laughed at his lugubrious expression.

"Who's clowning? All right, all right, I'm going. Don't push!"

At the kitchen door he pointed to the jewel case and cautioned, "I'd hide those again if I were you. I certainly wouldn't let anyone know I'd found them. Even old Tim."

"But they're mine. The note proves it."

"Sure, as long as you have it. And them."

She studied his face. "You're serious."

"Damn right. That kind of jewelry is worth killing for."

As Olivia closed the screen door behind him, a shiver ran through her body in spite of the warm and sunny late summer afternoon. She took his advice and replaced the jewel box under the bedroom floor.

"Feelin' better?"

"Oh!" Olivia jumped at the voice and the figure looming at her through the lower porch screen an hour later. She closed the composition book with a slap. "Tim! You scared me right out of my skin."

"Sorry, Miss Livvy. Didn't you hear me come home?"

How did I miss his rattly machine? "No, I didn't. I was reading."

"Must be a dang good book." He pulled off his old domed hat to scratch his head and examined the bullet holes in it before he said, "I been to see about some grass seed, fix those tore up places in the side yard."

"Oh. Good idea."

"Want me to do anything 'fore I go back inta town?"

"Movie night?" she guessed.

"Yep."

You and Emilie Harris?" Olivia smiled.

"How'd you guess?"

"And what kind of pie has she made today?"

"Crumb cake, she said. Want me to bring you a piece?"

"Sounds great. No, I don't have anything for you to do, Tim. Just go and have a good time."

"See you later, then." With a choppy wave he was gone, and Olivia was again left to bury herself in her mother's journals. Tim's truck revved up and bounced out of the drive, but Olivia scarcely heard it. The afternoon wore on into dusk, dusk into dark; she didn't notice except to switch on a reading light.

Five hours later, she wearily rubbed her eyes and leaned her head against the back of the chair for a long moment before she re-read the last page of her mother's journal, dated the day before her death:

My dear child. You have found the emeralds. They were always meant to be yours, from the father who loved you beyond words and was never able to claim you. And you have, with reading these lines, at last found me.

Forgive if you can. Understand, if you are able. Judge if you must. But know I open myself to you hoping you see beyond the facts and that what you see may cause you to examine your own life.

Are you happy? It is not always good to do the "right" thing, not always right to be bound to convention— as I and your father Oliver and dear Levi were.

Olivia, my child born of two hearts so much in tune; no miles, no years, could change their feelings. Never think I did not love Levi Sommers, for I did, deeply. And I made his life a joy in every way I could. But by my choice, my enduring passion was only a small bit of my life.

It should have been all.

Olivia closed the book before her tears could overflow onto the spidery lines. How different all their lives would have been, had Oliver Houle been morally able to divorce his crippled wife. Olivia would never have known the solid caring of Levi Sommers, who loved her mother so much he could understand her passion and willingly give her the freedom of hours she desperately needed. Surely his was the greatest love, far deeper than theirs, far more giving.

"We'll be all right, Chicken. She'll be back soon." Levi's strong, deep voice came through her mind as clearly as though he spoke beside her chair. If he could forgive Catherine Sommers, what right did her daughter have to judge?

And was she any better herself? Her relationship with Heath

Collins was certainly not above reproach. She wasn't even sure she wanted to be with him tonight, especially sexually, which was certainly what everything she'd done so far had led him to expect. Or did he want more? A continued relationship? Maybe even marriage? He knew her own was not, at least at this point, anything near satisfactory. She put the journals aside and rose.

Olivia walked barefoot on the solid, wave-packed sand along the shore to Heath's cottage. Though it was very late, a flickering kerosene lantern in his window beckoned her; she knew he would be waiting, perhaps in bed, even asleep, but waiting nevertheless.

At the soft click of his screen door, Heath's voice came from the dark bedroom behind the fireplace. "Livvy?"

"You're expecting someone else?"

A low chuckle. "Minx. It might have been Rastus, and then I'd have been in big trouble."

"Rastus? Oh, the raccoon!" Olivia hesitated at the side of the fireplace dividing Heath's bedroom from the rest of the cottage, not really wanting to commit herself, not really wanting not to.

"Come here." His voice was husky.

She perched gingerly on the edge of his bed. His large body was lightly covered with a sheet, but it was obvious even in the dim light from the lantern in the other room that he was nude beneath the cover.

"Join me?"

"Just like that?"

"You want music and candles?"

"That might help."

He reached up for her. She resisted for a moment, then let him pull her head to his chest. He stroked her hair gently. "It's been a tough day for you, hasn't it?"

She nodded, wrinkling her nose as his curly chest hair tickled her face.

"You're tight as a bowstring." He rubbed her shoulder

muscles. "Feel like talking? Or something better."

"Just hold me, please. Then talk."

"Excellent idea. First things first, as they say."

She didn't stop him as his fingers moved down from her shoulders to loosen the buttons on her shirt and tenderly caress her breasts, teasing them into wanting his sensuous mouth. He pushed the material off her shoulders. "You're still too dressed," he chided. "Want some help?"

She surrendered, standing up to slip out of her jeans and bikini as he threw back the sheet, and she slid into his bed beside his warm, welcoming body.

"Nice," he approved, running his palm slowly over the curve of her hip.

Olivia closed her eyes and let herself forget everything but where she was at this moment in time. She nodded against his chest. "Nice."

An hour later, Heath propped himself up on pillows against his hand-hewn headboard, pulled her against his shoulder, and said, "Now, tell me about the journals."

"I thought you'd never ask. What an unbelievable story!" Olivia snuggled comfortably against him. "Listen, I'll give you a capsule version."

When she finished, he agreed. "You're right, unbelievable. Makes you think, doesn't it?"

"About what? Love?"

"Yes. Hers and Oliver's—the passionate kind. And Levi Sommers.'"

"The giving kind." Olivia nodded. "So different, yet for the same woman. And hers so different for each of them. I admire the man I thought was my father for everything he was, for everything he did. That man who is my father is an enigma, someone I never knew except as a neighbor and friend of my family."

"And, so, what now?"

"What do you mean?"

"They're all dead, except Oliver. And he might as well be. So what about you?" Heath hesitated, then asked, "Are you staying? Or going? Now that you have your inheritance jewels and you're independently wealthy, what are your plans?"

There was an undercurrent in his voice Olivia couldn't put a label on. Puzzled, she studied his face as best she could in the dim light. "That's not really what you're asking, is it?"

He hesitated again. "No."

"What, then?"

He was quiet for a long moment before he said, "You don't love me, really, do you, Olivia Houle Hobart?"

She reached over and put her hand on his furred chest. *Do I?* "Love as in unending passion? Love as in friendship? Love as what?" she asked. With one finger she traced a line toward his belly button and enjoyed the answering shiver through his large frame. "Love as how defined?"

"I don't know. I'm a diversion, a sounding board, physically able to please you. But you don't love me, do you? Really."

Olivia lay back on the pillows, confronting the issue, and met it head on. "No," she answered, shaking her head. "Not a forever, death do us part Catherine and Oliver kind of love, if that's what you mean."

"Good!" He leapt nude from the bed and, taking three long strides, picked up a wine bottle and two of his heavy, hand-crafted goblets from the kitchen counter. "You had me worried for a minute or two, there," he said, grinning. "A toast."

Ignoring her open mouth and startled expression, he handed her a goblet and filled it to the brim, then did the same with his before slipping in between the sheets beside her. He lifted his glass to touch its edge to hers and said soberly, "To friendship." His light blue eyes were shadowed in the darkened room; only flickering lamplight from around the corner illuminated their figures.

Startled at first, verging on anger, Olivia frowned. Then with a flash of comprehension, she understood. Heath was releasing her—and himself—from whatever obligation she might have felt, whatever hurt she might have thought their relationship would bring either of them.

And, sure now what they shared was no more, but certainly no less, than two needing, caring people at a given moment in time, she grinned back at him, lifting her glass. "To friendship," she repeated. "It was never better."

Heath walked Olivia back to Dunes House through early morning first light. The grey lake, its horizon indistinguishable from the pale Eastern sky, seemed to go on forever, into infinity. Quiet water barely moved against the hard-packed sand underfoot. Out over the lake, a single early gull mewled, its cry softened by mist rising from the water's surface.

Her tied-together deck shoes dangling from one hand, Olivia stopped walking to breathe deeply of the lake air, to watch an enterprising gull swoop down from the mist to snatch up an unsuspecting tidbit for breakfast.

So much had happened since the first time she'd looked out over this lake. Her life, and Bert's, had changed forever, Pamela's had ended. Yet these waters, imperturbable, lapped as softly at the shore today as they had when her mother walked here with Oliver Houle, as they would for generations to come.

Heath watched her silent contemplation for a moment before he spoke, his voice hardly louder than the soft slap of water on sand. "Wonderfully beautiful, isn't it? Even without the color that comes later with the sun. At this hour, the whole world belongs to anyone lucky enough to be up to witness its waking."

Olivia nodded, then shrugged. "The whole world…but what to do with it? That's the question." She began to walk again, slowly, digging her bare toes into the beach, absorbing the experience of each step, the abrasive sand beneath her feet, the soft, moist air against her face.

He fell into step beside her. "For you, right now, I suppose that is the question. What now, Miz Olivia Houle Hobart? Now that you've solved your mystery and found your jewels, where do you go from here? Are you off to Portland for a while? For good, back to Bert?"

"Off to Portland, yes, for a while. But not back to Bert and not for good." Olivia stopped again to look ahead at Dunes House on the bluff above the beach. "This is where I belong, Heath. That house holds my past, though I didn't know it when I came here. I'm going to make it hold my future."

"And do what? Read novels and eat bonbons? You won't find any hospital auxiliary to run here, or book clubs. For any social life, if you could call it that, you'd have to go into Bayshore."

"I know, but those aren't the things I want now. I never really did, but I guess I didn't know that until I had a taste of freedom from them." Olivia's voice trailed off as Pamela's face surfaced in her mind. Maybe Pamela was free, now, too. Who knew what lay beyond this life? Perhaps a different and, perhaps for Pamela, a better one?

"You didn't answer my question. What will you do here?"

Olivia pursed her lips. "Well, after I get things settled with Bert—I think he wants out as badly as I do, though I know he'd stay forever if I'd just come home and be the kind of wife he wants—I'm coming back to Dunes House. And, laugh if you want, but I'm going to do something I've always wanted to and never had time for."

"Hey, don't look so belligerent. Am I laughing?" Heath protested. He skipped a pebble onto the quiet water. "What is it you've always wanted to do?"

"Write." She thrust her chin up as she spoke.

Heath grinned. "You expecting an argument, or what? Put your chin down and get that chip off your shoulder. I should think you'd be good at anything you set your mind to. Write what?"

They'd reached the boathouse steps. "I have an idea, but it's not ready yet. Thanks for walking me home, Heath."

He took both her hands in his and kissed her lightly on the lips. "Don't be a stranger, Livvy. You're important to my life, at any level."

"And you to mine. I'll be back soon." She looked up into his blue eyes, now catching the first rays of sunshine. "Thank you, dear Heath…for everything."

She stayed at the bottom of the steps to watch his stalwart figure stride down the beach before she turned and began the steep climb to the top of the bluff.

Two seasons passed before Olivia returned to set up residence. The whole time had seemed nothing more than a stopgap to living as she did the things she must to clear the way for the future she'd chosen.

"It's just great havin' you back, Miss Livvy," Tim Ryan said through the screen of the downstairs porch on her first evening home. "Wasn't the same around here without you."

She raised her eyes from the pad of paper on her lapboard. "Thanks, Tim. Are you off to town?"

"Yep. Me'n Emilie are goin' to the movie." He paused. "You'd be welcome."

"Thanks again, but no. What did she bake today?"

"Cherry pie." Tim grinned. "You've been workin' awful hard at somethin' all day. Mind if I ask what?"

"A story, Tim. A wonderful story, if I can do it justice."

"Well, if anybody can, you can. See you later." Tim disappeared into the evening dusk.

Olivia lifted her head to gaze out over the now tranquil grey-blue water, reveling in the knowledge that now, at last, she was home where she belonged.

A late seagull cried distantly over the water as Olivia bent again to her pen and paper. She reread her opening line:

"I begin this journal with a heavy heart, for I am forced to stay…"

Olivia smiled. *The House on the Dunes* was a wonderful story.

And it was hers to tell.

About the Author

Nancy Sweetland has been writing professionally since selling her first essay to *Family Digest Magazine* in 1962. Since then she's sold over 350 feature articles, 100-plus adult short stories; poems to both adult and juvenile magazines, 65-plus children's magazine stories and seven picture books. She's been awarded regional and national awards in adult and juvenile fiction and poetry, essays, commercial copy writing and outdoor writing. Her published titles include, *The Door to Love*, *Wannabe*, *The Virgin Murders* and *The Spa Murders*, amongst others. Writing colors her life and the way she looks at the world around her.

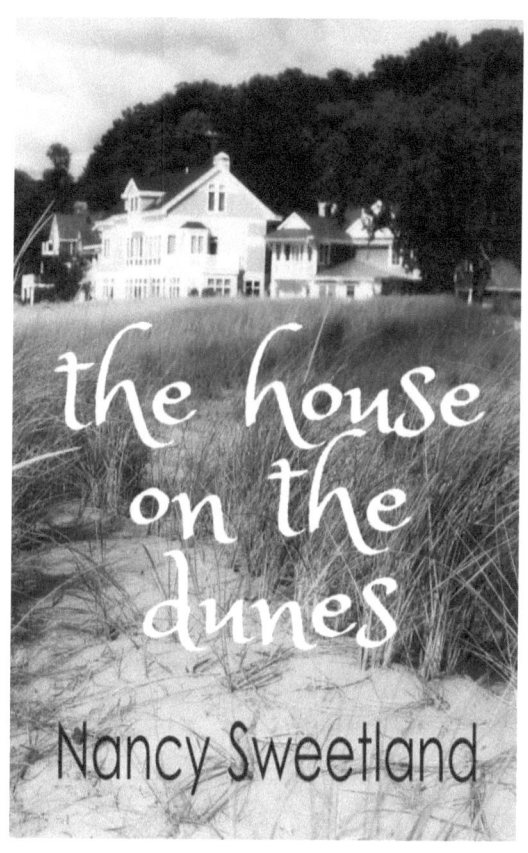

VISIT WWW.DIVINEGARDENPRESS.COM
FOR OTHER EXCITING TITLES!